Highland Rogue

TESS MALLORY

BERKLEY SENSATION, NEW YORK

THE BERKLEY PUBLISHING GROUP
Published by the Penguin Group
Penguin Group (USA) Inc.
375 Hudson Street, New York, New York 10014, USA

Penguin Group (Canada), 90 Eglinton Avenue East, Suite 700, Toronto, Ontario M4P 2Y3, Canada
(a division of Pearson Penguin Canada Inc.)
Penguin Books Ltd., 80 Strand, London WC2R 0RL, England
Penguin Group Ireland, 25 St. Stephen's Green, Dublin 2, Ireland (a division of Penguin Books Ltd.)
Penguin Group (Australia), 250 Camberwell Road, Camberwell, Victoria 3124, Australia
(a division of Pearson Australia Group Pty. Ltd.)
Penguin Books India Pvt. Ltd., 11 Community Centre, Panchsheel Park, New Delhi—110 017, India
Penguin Group (NZ), 67 Apollo Drive, Rosedale, North Shore 0632, New Zealand
(a division of Pearson New Zealand Ltd.)
Penguin Books (South Africa) (Pty.) Ltd., 24 Sturdee Avenue, Rosebank, Johannesburg 2196,
South Africa

Penguin Books Ltd., Registered Offices: 80 Strand, London WC2R 0RL, England

This is a work of fiction. Names, characters, places, and incidents either are the product of the author's imagination or are used fictitiously, and any resemblance to actual persons, living or dead, business establishments, events, or locales is entirely coincidental. The publisher does not have any control over and does not assume any responsibility for author or third-party websites or their content.

HIGHLAND ROGUE

A Berkley Sensation Book / published by arrangement with the author

PRINTING HISTORY
Berkley Sensation mass-market edition / May 2008

Copyright © 2008 by Tess Mallory.
Cover design by George Long.
Hand lettering by Ronn Zinn.
Interior text design by Laura K. Corless.

ISBN: 978-0-425-22042-9

BERKLEY® SENSATION
Berkley Sensation Books are published by The Berkley Publishing Group,
a division of Penguin Group (USA) Inc.,
375 Hudson Street, New York, New York 10014.
BERKLEY SENSATION and the "B" design are trademarks of Penguin Group (USA) Inc.

PRINTED IN THE UNITED STATES OF AMERICA

10 9 8 7 6 5 4 3 2 1

This book is lovingly dedicated to:

My husband, Bill, for his love, his patience, his crazy humor, and for saying every day, "I'm proud of you, Moonbeam."

My daughter Erin Burns for her extraordinary editing skills, amazing butt-kicking abilities, and for saying, "It's good, Mama," when I really need to hear it.

My daughter Heather for giving me the best hair in Texas, for sharing her faith, and for always telling me, "You look beautiful!"

My son, Jordan, for cheering me up with Mystery Science Theater, *and taking the dog out even when it's cold, but most of all for saying, "I love you, Momarr," with amazing frequency.*

And darling Mackenzie for bringing light and joy to my heart every time I see her precious face.

I love you all so very much.

Acknowledgments

This book has been quite a journey. To those of you who traveled along with me, offering your support and encouragement, you have my heartfelt love and thanks. Those stalwart companions especially include my extended family and the Usual Suspects. I hope you all know how much I love and appreciate each of you.

Special thanks to:

The Tuesday Afternoon Group, for listening to me babble. I love you all.

Piper Mark MacIntire of Sisters, Oregon, for sharing his knowledge of all things piper and MacIntire, which helped to make this a better book.

Charles Buchanan of Birmingham, Alabama, for sharing his website on the Buchanan House in Scotland and for sending me a picture of the duke's eighteenth-century domicile.

Jdeancorp.com for producing an awesome website for me! (Thanks, Jason!)

My agent, Roberta, and my editor, Kate—for being so amazing.

prologue

Quinn MacIntyre fixed his gaze upon the distant purple hills and watched as the moon, a round copper disk perched between earth and sky, ruined his plans.

The brisk Highland wind howled like a banshee across the rough mountainside where he waited, his hair dancing in the gale as if some vile enchantment had given the dark strands a life of their own. Ignoring the fanciful thought, Quinn shifted his attention back to the narrow road below and began to plan anew. His horse nickered softly in the stillness, the sound echoing against the Scottish night.

"Easy, Saint," he said. "Where the bloody hell are they?"

"Aye, where indeed?" Ian MacGregor whispered beside him, astride his own black pony. "Ah, well, 'tis the luck of the draw."

Quinn smiled at the unconcerned tone of his friend's voice. Never mind that they were about to risk their lives once again for ill-gotten gain. No matter that the expected carriage filled with aristocrats dripping with jewelry and velvets had not arrived as scheduled. Never mind that if the moon got much higher, they could be recognized in the bright moonlight.

No, Ian was as boneless as a kitten about such things. If it didn't concern a woman, it was no serious matter. In all the years Quinn had known him, he'd yet to see Ian lose his temper. He wished he could say the same for himself.

"Something isna right," he murmured. A tiny muscle in Quinn's jaw began to twitch.

Ian shrugged. "Either they will come or not."

"'Tis bright enough on a summer's night already," Quinn said in irritation, "and once the moon rises completely, we could be recognized. I've no desire to see a badly drawn sketch of my face posted on the kirk door, nor to feel the steel of the duke's iron shackles around my wrists."

Ian looked over at him with a frown. "This should be a rich haul tonight. Surely ye willna let a little thing like the moon keep ye from it?"

"'Tis hard to spend riches when ye're dead," Quinn said.

Ian laughed and leaned back in his saddle. "Aye, but I'd rather take the risk than plod behind the rump end of a cow the rest of my life."

Leave it to Ian to put things in perspective. Quinn's black mood lifted, and he grinned. "Aye," he said. "Though Rob Roy wouldna agree. He thinks me a villain for ever getting ye involved in this." His smile faded at the thought.

Ian reached up and pulled the black scarf he wore from his head, releasing a wealth of white blond hair tucked beneath. The two men wore the same black clothing, from boots and breeches to shirts and the gloves on their hands, down to the black cloaks around their shoulders. His friend's blue eyes gleamed boyishly from the two eyeholes in his black mask. Quinn had not yet donned his own mask, but when he did, the two would look like twins, except for his own green eyes.

"Och, Rob Roy was just angry to have lost two of his best drovers, ye know that," Ian went on. "He admires what we're doing."

"He thinks I'm daft, and ye as well."

"Aye," he agreed, "but he still considers ye family."

Quinn let the tension in his shoulders relax a little. "Although I am not," he reminded him.

Ian turned to him, his gaze serious for once. "Ye know that isn't true."

"I'm no MacGregor, laddie." He kept his voice casual, even as his grip tightened on the horse's reins.

Ian frowned at him. "Ye came to Rob after Montrose hanged yer father and brother for reiving his cattle. Ye asked his protection and he granted it. That makes ye a MacGregor." He paused, one hand stroking the tuft of beard at his chin. "Though whether that's a good thing or no at present remains to be seen."

Quinn shook his head and smiled without humor. "I'm a MacIntyre, and proud to be one, though my clan has all but disowned me for my father's crimes."

A rumble behind them made Quinn glance over his shoulder. Dark gray storm clouds brewed in the distance. Saint shifted nervously beneath him once more.

"If yon thunderheads will cooperate and arrive with the carriage, darkness will be ours," Quinn mused. "Then we can still keep to our plan this night."

As if to give lie to his words, the moon rose above the treetops, leaving the clouds behind. The full force of the light struck Ian's blond hair and chiseled features, bathing them in stark relief. A year younger than Quinn at twenty-five, Ian was almost foppishly handsome, with a smile that made every lass in the Highlands sigh.

"Cover that hair. The glare fair blinds me."

Ian tied his hair back with a strip of cloth, and then retied the black scarf over his head, tucking wayward strands of blond hair under the makeshift cap, while Quinn tied his own mask in place.

Quinn had always been the leader of the two, ever since they first met at the MacCrimmons School of Piping as lads. He'd once been fool enough to think that he could be a piper to a clan. That was before he had his illusions shattered and his dreams ground into pulp. He should never have asked Ian to join him after his father's death forced him to leave MacCrimmons, but his friend had insisted. As a result, Ian's own father had disinherited him, and now Quinn lived with that guilt as well.

So far they had played the game well and their wits and skill had kept them from being caught or recognized. But he knew, as in every game, it was always possible to lose. He pushed the thought away. They weren't going to lose.

"I keep thinking the duke will send his guards one night," Quinn said.

"Montrose is too cheap," Ian said. "But t'would seem the guests are as tight-fisted as the duke, for few come with guards."

"Whist!" Quinn's fingers tensed against Saint's mane. The sound of horses and carriage wheels traveling over the rough Highland road echoed in the distance. He glanced up at the sky and grinned. "Luck is with us, lad. Look."

The storm had picked up speed and moved across the horizon. As the two men watched, the clouds swaddled the moon and shadowed the land.

"Make ready," Quinn said. The familiar surge of excitement coursed suddenly through his veins. He might have become more cautious, but he still felt the intense thrill that came with taking a chance.

"Do ye have the pipes?" Ian whispered.

"Aye." Quinn patted a bag tied to his saddle horn. "Safe from the rain to come."

"I still think ye should just play a few notes first," Ian said. "That alone would send those in the carriage to their knees."

"And who was it burst our first teacher's eardrum with his ill-played skirl?" Quinn demanded with a grin. "Off with ye now, while the storm is with us." He kicked Saint into action, and plunged into the darkness below.

Thirty minutes later, the storm and the highwaymen had swept through the glen below, leaving a group of wet aristocrats, drivers, and guards tied and gagged and shoved into the bottom of the carriage. From the top of a nearby hillside, the two drenched highwaymen sat on their mounts, as the haunting strains of a bagpipe danced upon the now still night air.

Quinn let the end of the blowpipe slip from his mouth, feeling strangely somber as he rested the pipes against his saddle horn. For once Ian did not have a joke or a quip, but sat in respectful silence as the last notes echoed down the glen.

"That is your own composition, aye? 'MacIntyre's Revenge.'" Ian smiled respectfully. "'Tis a bonny tune."

Quinn straightened his shoulders beneath the sodden cloak he wore. "The driver said they got a late start because of a broken wheel," he said thoughtfully. "So Montrose still doesna care that his guests are being robbed."

Ian nodded and glanced over at him. "Aye. What are ye thinking?"

Quinn lifted his face to the calming sky and watched the last of the storm clouds drift across the setting moon.

"I am thinking," he said, "that perhaps it is time we made him care."

one

Austin, Texas, Present Day

"Do we have to listen to that Scottish garbage again?"

Maggie Graham stuck her tongue out at her best friend, Rachel, and turned up the volume on the ancient CD player, smiling as the first song on the sound track from her favorite movie filled the interior of the VW Bug.

"You know you love it," Maggie said.

"I don't love it. I hate it. I hated the movie and I hate the sound track." Rachel reached up to tighten her white and blue streaked ponytail and scowled as her turquoise glasses slid halfway down her nose. "Plus, if I have to swelter in this heap you call a car, I should at least get to listen to some decent music." She pushed her glasses back in place and folded her arms across her chest.

The little car's ever-faltering air conditioner had finally died earlier that week, and the July heat settled around the two women like a heavy blanket. A breeze devoid of coolness billowed through the open car windows and a strand of Maggie's auburn hair escaped from her French braid. She pushed it behind her ear and smiled at her friend.

"It's my birthday," she said good-naturedly. "Suck it up. And please tell me how a drama teacher could possibly hate the movie *Rob Roy*?"

Rachel tapped her chin. "Um, lemme see—accents you can't understand, Liam Neeson in a dress, Scottish history—did I leave anything out?"

"It was a kilt."

Rachel reached over to pat Maggie's hand resting on top of the gearshift knob. "I love you, kid, but you gotta get over this fixation with men who don't exist."

Maggie frowned as the sound of "Home from the Hills" swept over her. Her obsession with Scottish history—and Scottish heroes—had long been a source of amusement to her sisters and her best friend.

"Liam Neeson exists."

Rachel shook her head. "But you aren't in love with the actors—that would be understandable. You're in love with the characters. And honey, they've all been dead for a thousand years!"

Maggie shifted into third gear. "Two hundred and seventy-three."

"What?"

"Rob Roy MacGregor has been dead for about two hundred and seventy-three years."

Rachel shook her head. "You are hopeless. Is it any wonder that you haven't had a real boyfriend in the last ten years?"

The light ahead turned red and Maggie slammed on the brakes and then glanced into the rearview mirror to make sure she wasn't about to get rear-ended. As she thought about Rachel's question, she met her own gaze in the mirror.

It was the same heart-shaped face she met every morning in the mirror, pale, a few freckles scattered across her nose, framed by waving tendrils of bright red hair with golden highlights. Her sky blue eyes tilted at the corners and used to sparkle with life, but now there were shadows beneath them, and they held a sadness she doubted would ever go away completely.

"Been a little busy, Rach," she muttered, "what with raising Allie and Ellie and keeping food on the table."

Rachel drummed her short nails on the glove box in front of her. "Maggie, your sisters are both twenty-one years old and you still act like they're eleven! When are you going to stop using them as an excuse for not getting on with your life?"

Maggie bit back a sharp retort. Rachel was right. The twins were officially independent, and after taking care of them for the last ten years, she could finally have her own life again. She just wasn't sure she knew what that meant anymore.

Ten years before, Maggie had graduated from college intent on pursuing her dream of becoming an archaeologist. She would travel the world, going from dig to dig, learning what she could, taking classes one semester, going on digs the next, hopefully gaining graduate credits as she did.

Then everything changed in a heartbeat, or rather, the lack of two. Her parents were killed in a car crash, leaving Maggie to finish raising her eleven-year-old twin sisters. She adored Allie and Ellie and was determined not to let her sisters down.

As soon as her parents' funeral was over, she took a job teaching history in a local high school, doing private tutoring on Saturdays to keep the bills paid. All that had mattered was keeping the family together. So what if her dreams had to be put on hold? If life had taught her anything, it was that it could change in a matter of moments.

"There is nothing wrong with my life."

"Oh, puh-leeze." Rachel rolled her eyes and turned down the CD player. "You work, you go home, you grade papers, and you spend Saturday mornings tutoring. In between, you buy groceries and cook supper for your sisters. That is not a life."

"I won't be cooking supper for the twins anymore," Maggie pointed out. "They moved into their apartment last week."

"And do not tell me that you're going to allow yourself to sink into some kind of empty-nest depression," Rachel said.

Maggie looked at her in surprise. "I'm not depressed."

Her friend snorted. "Right. Just look at yourself."

She looked back into the mirror. Her slight attempt at makeup had long ago dripped down her face, and her long French braid was gradually coming undone. She'd gotten up late that morning, thrown on a pair of worn jeans and a T-shirt, and rushed into Austin to teach her usual Saturday classes, forgetting she had to leave directly from there to pick up Rachel and meet her sisters.

Rachel didn't look a whole lot better, thanks to the heat, but her vintage fifties' skirt in turquoise and white checks and the cute, short-sleeved white blouse she wore gave her the edge over Maggie's unintended grunge look. The light turned green and she pulled her gaze from the mirror and back to South Congress as she shifted into first gear.

"I always look like this."

"My point exactly." Rachel's voice softened. "Look, Maggie, when your folks died you had to become the parent, and I get that, but now it's time for you to start taking care of yourself."

Maggie pushed back sweaty tendrils of hair from her face. The light ahead turned red and she eased to a stop. "We are never going to get there at this rate. What time is it?"

Rachel glanced down at her Mickey Mouse watch. "Six o'clock. Did you hear what I said?"

"Fine. I need to take care of myself. What would you suggest? A facial? A weekend at a spa? Not in the budget."

"No, I was thinking more along the lines of something like . . . that."

Maggie turned to see what she was talking about, and her mouth dropped open.

A man sat beside them, one tanned arm dusted in gold and draped over the open window of his sleek black Ferrari convertible. His aquiline nose, carved lips, strong jaw, and chiseled chin created a profile that Maggie had only seen in stone sculptures of ancient gods. But this guy was real. Real and hot. He turned slightly and glanced in their direction, then his dark brown eyes narrowed and focused on Maggie.

She gulped as his smoldering gaze raked over her face and paused at her lips. Of its own volition, her tongue suddenly refused to stay in her mouth, and instead darted out to caress her bottom lip. One corner of the man's sensual lips curved up in what could only be described as a sardonic smile, and Maggie blushed, quickly putting her tongue back where it belonged.

The Ferrari Man closed his eyes and lifted his face to the hot Texas wind, allowing it to toss his sun-bleached brown hair, and she sighed. He was arrogance personified. A smorgasbord of sexy features all rolled up into one beautiful, rugged, manly man package.

Maggie and Rachel heaved a collective sigh.

Then he turned and looked at the two women watching again.

You want me, his smile telegraphed. *All women want me.*

Maggie swallowed hard. He winked, gunned his motor, and sent his insanely sexy sports car speeding forward. She stared after the disappearing convertible and blinked.

"HEY LADY, WILL YOU MOVE IT?!"

The sound of an angry voice and a horn blaring from

behind tumbled Maggie back into the real world. Right, right, the light had changed. It was green. Green meant go, right? She took a deep, cleansing breath and released it slowly, then shoved the little car into first gear and sent it chugging through the light.

It was a few minutes before Rachel broke the silence.

"Now *that* is exactly what you need."

Maggie laughed, surprised at how shaky she sounded. "No way. Okay, I admit it's been a long time since I—uh—since I was in a relationship, but ugh and double ugh! I'd never fall for a guy like that."

"Ha. I had to wipe your drool off the gearshift knob. You thought he was hot, so don't even try to say you didn't."

Maggie shrugged. "He was hot, and any woman would respond to that kind of primal animal magnetism, but that's not the kind of guy I want to settle down with."

"Who said anything about settling down?" Rachel asked. "You aren't ready to settle down. You need to have some fun first. Go out and sow a few wild oats."

"Guys sow oats. Women get plowed and they get hurt."

Rachel grinned at her. "Well put, but c'mon, Mags, you've been tied down by responsibility for the last ten years. You're thirty-two years old today—don't you want to live a little?"

"Sure, but not with someone like him. Like I need that kind of drama in my life." She shook her head. "That whole 'bad boy' thing. Definitely not for me."

"He was perfect."

"Oh, please. He was not perfect."

"Because he wasn't Scottish?"

Maggie shot her a startled look, and Rachel smiled and nodded. "Oh, yeah, I know your secret fantasy. You don't just want a guy who lived a billion years ago, you want a Scotsman who lived a billion years ago. Guess what? They don't grow them around here. And you do like bad boys."

"Do not."

"Colin Farrell and Russell Crowe. Antonio Banderas. Vin Diesel. Shall I go on?"

Maggie blushed. "Sure I love the bad boys in the movies, and in *theory* that fantasy is definitely *hot*; but I know myself, Rach, and the reality wouldn't be what I'm looking for."

"So what are you looking for?"

She frowned, tightening her hands on the steering wheel as she passed a slow-moving van. "I want a nice man, a man who's a teddy bear at heart. A bring-you-breakfast-in-bed kind of guy." She considered again. "A guy who's loyal, honest, and brave."

"Sounds like a Boy Scout," Rachel said.

"So what's wrong with that?" Maggie demanded. "A Boy Scout, but more manly of course." She shook her head. "That selfish rogue fantasy doesn't fit into my plans for the rest of my life."

"So you want to be bored for the rest of your life."

Maggie stuck out her tongue, even as she considered her friend's statement. Was that the choice? A selfish bad boy or a loving boring guy? She turned the volume back up on the CD player and was hit with a fresh wave of Scottish music.

"I know my ultimate dream guy doesn't exist, so if I have to choose between boring and bad, I'll take boring, hands down." She sighed. "They just don't make heroes anymore."

"You're pitiful, kid."

"I don't even want a guy in my life right now."

"Sure you don't."

Maggie saw the sign for Fado's Irish Pub and made a hard right, then managed to snag a parking spot.

"Look," Rachel said, "I'm sorry I said all of that. I just worry about you. I want you to be happy."

Maggie forced a smile. "I'm happy, Rach. I've just got to figure out my future a little at a time, okay?"

"Okay." She hesitated. "Happy birthday, kiddo."

"Thanks."

It was fashionably dark inside Fado's, with muted lighting that gave the place the authentic look of an Irish pub. An Irish band played on a small stage in a far corner of the room and already Maggie felt cheered.

The hostess led them farther into the dimly lit interior, to a table where Allie and Ellie sat across from each other, their heads almost touching as they held an intense, whispered conversation.

"Slainte!" the hostess said as she walked away, but Maggie's attention was on her sisters, who had stopped talking when they saw her. They were up to something. Their faces lit up as they jumped up and moved to throw their arms around her.

"Maggie!" they cried.

As Maggie felt the familiar warmth of their love encompass her, she knew she'd been telling Rachel the truth. Her life really was just fine.

"So, where's the stripper?" Rachel asked as she sat down in one of the mismatched chairs that was part of the pub's ambiance.

Ellie laughed and sat down beside her. "Right."

"Like we want to watch Maggie dissolve into a pool of embarrassment in public," Allie added as she took the chair opposite Rachel.

Maggie looked at her sister fondly. Allie was thin and naturally blonde and wore a trendy skirt and blouse and a pair of designer heels, a Louis Vuitton handbag at her side.

"Yeah, I mean, it *is* her birthday," Ellie said. "Hey, we ordered drinks for you guys."

Ellie was curvy and presently black-haired, and her blue eyes, identical to Allie's except for being outlined in black, were hesitant as she glanced at Maggie. Maggie frowned. Ellie was never hesitant. She met life head-on, without fear.

There were three tall glasses on the table and one short, squat one. Rachel picked up the tall glass in front of her and took a sip. "Yum, an appletini."

Maggie plopped down across from Ellie. "Where's my drink?" she asked. Allie pushed the short glass in front of her. She frowned. "Why don't I get an appletini?"

"We thought you needed something stronger," Allie said, her eyes sliding away from connecting with Maggie's. "It's whiskey. You love whiskey. It's Scottish."

"Whiskey?" She frowned more. Whiskey was her drink of choice, but she rarely indulged, and then usually only on New Year's Eve. "I'm driving."

"We'll call you a cab. No one will bother your Bug. That way you can, er, relax, you know, drink as much as you want."

"Awesome," Rachel said, lifting her drink to her lips.

Maggie leaned back against her chair as a wave of apprehension swept over her. "You two know I never drink more than one whiskey."

The twins exchanged glances.

"Well, that might change tonight," Allie muttered.

Maggie closed her eyes briefly. "Okay, let's have it. What's wrong?"

"Wrong? Nothing's wrong," Ellie said, her gaze darting over to Allie. "But we do have something to tell you." She hesitated. "You tell her, Allie."

Allie widened her eyes and tilted her head slightly. "*El*, I thought we agreed that *you* were going to tell her."

"You said—" Ellie broke off and glared at her sister. "Fine." She reached across the table and took Maggie's hand in hers. "Mags, I have something important to tell you." She paused again and sighed heavily before her next words came out in a rush. "Allie is pregnant."

"What?!" Maggie's voice came out as half shriek, half

squeal as she stared first at Ellie and then at Allie. Somehow she found the whiskey glass and drained it, oblivious to the burn as it traveled down her throat, gasping a little as she set the glass down. Then she reached over and took Allie's drink out of her hand. "Are you crazy?" she hissed. "You shouldn't be drinking!"

"Ellie!" Allie glanced around the pub, her face scarlet. "Do you have to say that so loud?" She turned back to Maggie and patted her arm. "She's kidding, I'm not pregnant." She turned innocent blue eyes back to her twin. "*She's* pregnant."

"Allie!" Ellie mocked, rolling her eyes. "Takes a preggie to know a preggie."

Maggie's mouth fell open as she jerked Ellie's drink from her hand, slamming it down on the table. "Dear Lord, you're both pregnant!" she said. A waiter walked by, and without tearing her gaze from her sisters, Maggie thrust her empty glass in front of him. "Whiskey," she choked out. "A double!"

As her sisters continued to smile at her complacently, Maggie leaned both elbows on the scarred wooden tabletop, closed her eyes, and covered her face with her hands. Visions of the next ten years of her life spent raising Allie's and Ellie's kids danced through her head like evil and demented sugarplums, and for a minute she couldn't breathe. Then the sound of a giggle made her open her eyes, lower her hands, and inhale hopefully. Rachel sat with a big grin on her face as the twins dissolved into hysterical laughter.

"Good grief, Maggie," Ellie said, her dark red lips twisted in a rueful grin, "after all these years, you're still so gullible!"

Maggie drew in a ragged breath and unclenched her fingers. "You mean, you aren't pregnant? Either one of you?"

It was Allie's turn to roll her eyes, looking the spitting image of Ellie in spite of her blonde, Barbie-doll beauty.

"Of course not," she said with a sigh. "Come on, Maggie, you know better than that! No kids till the careers are solid and the men of our dreams come along."

"You only drilled it into us our whole lives," Ellie said. "We got it, okay?" She nodded at Rachel. "I owe you twenty. I really didn't think she'd fall for it."

Rachel raised both brows. "Told ya," she said.

The waiter returned with her whiskey, and Maggie picked up the short glass and then set it down again. She glared at the three of them. "You know," she said, "one of these days I'm going to drop dead from a heart attack after one of your 'practical jokes' and you guys won't think it's so damned funny."

"Oh, come on, Maggie," Ellie said, "you're too uptight."

"You always think the worst is going to happen," Allie added.

"When ma-a-ybe the best is just around the corner," Rachel drawled.

Maggie glanced from grin to grin, her senses once more on alert. "Okay, you guys are really freaking me out now. No more jokes. What's going on?" She glanced over her shoulder. "Is there a stripper? I swear if there really is a stripper, you are all *toast*!"

"Relax," Allie said. She reached beside her and lifted a large, shimmering silver gift bag from the floor, plopping it in the middle of the table. "First present."

"Open it," Ellie said, bouncing a little on the bench.

"It's from all of us," Rachel added.

The bag was so big Maggie had to stand to open it. First she removed the tissue paper sticking out of the top and then she reached inside, pulling out something large and made of leather. "A backpack?" she frowned. She didn't hike, didn't camp, and didn't go to college. "Uh, gee, thanks, guys. It's great."

"Open it," Ellie said again.

"Oh-kay." Maggie unzipped the pack and reached inside. Her fingers closed around something furry and her eyes widened as she pulled out a stuffed animal. It was green and looked like a brontosaurus, but wore a T-shirt that said, "I Love Nessie."

"Nessie? As in the Loch Ness Monster?"

Allie gave her an evil grin. "Push the button on the bottom."

Maggie turned the toy over and pushed the button. Instantly a loud, raucous rendition of a hundred bagpipes playing "Scotland the Brave" poured from the small animal and filled the pub. Knowing her face was as red as a beet, Maggie punched the button until the noise finally shut off. Everyone in the crowded room immediately burst into applause.

"Sorry," she said, waving her hand and feeling like an idiot. She glared at Allie. "Very funny."

"Keep going," Rachel urged. "There's lots more stuff in there."

"Fine," Maggie said, "but I'm not punching any more buttons." She began digging around in the pack and pulled out a flashlight, a box of Band Aids, a roll of gauze, adhesive tape, hair barrettes, rubber bands, safety pins, antibiotic ointment, matches, a lighter, a pair of tiny scissors, a huge package of bubble gum, and four chocolate bars.

"Wow," she said. "I—uh—don't know what to say."

"Wait, you missed something," Rachel said. "Dig around in the bottom, under the envelope."

"Envelope?" Maggie reached in again and pulled out a large brown envelope. "What's this?"

"Wait, wait," Allie said, "first the rest of this present."

Maggie obediently went back to digging and her hand closed around something long and flat and crinkly. It wasn't until she had dragged the three-foot-long strip out of the pack and brandished it over their table that she realized it was a strip of condoms. Extra large. She slammed the offending articles back into the pack, her face burning, as laughter exploded from the three at the table.

"You guys are so, so dead," she said, plopping down in her chair again. "Not to mention insane."

"Oh, come on, Maggie," Rachel said as she tried to stop laughing, "you've got to admit it was funny!" They dissolved into hysteria again while Maggie glared.

"Not that you'll probably ever need them," Allie said dryly.

Maggie started to tell her little sister that she was right, she wouldn't need the condoms because she had started taking birth control pills five months ago. Her gynecologist had suggested it to regulate her periods, and the birth control was just a bonus. Like it mattered. She hadn't had a boyfriend in years, and at the ripe old age of thirty-two, she was unlikely to find Mr. Right anytime soon. Maggie sighed. Allie was right. She wouldn't need them.

"Okay, enough humiliation," ringleader Allie said. She picked up the large envelope on the table and handed it to Maggie. "Your second gift."

"What is this?" Maggie took the envelope and held it gingerly between her fingers.

"Open it and find out," Ellie said.

"I don't think so." Maggie hefted the envelope in her hand. "Feels heavy. What is it? Stink bomb? Superglue? C'mon, girls, don't mess with me. It's my—"

"Trust us," Allie murmured.

"Right. When have I heard that before?"

"And don't even think about saying no," Rachel said, her gaze suddenly intense as she leaned toward her, glass in hand. "We've got it all arranged and it's a done deal."

Maggie closed her eyes. "Oh, great. Please don't tell me it's another round of skydiving lessons." Her eyes flew open. "You guys are *not* getting me back up in one of those little planes!"

"Don't be silly," Allie admonished. "Besides, the pilot refused to ever take you up again, remember?"

"Besides," Rachel reminded her reproachfully, "your parachute opened,"

"Yeah, after the instructor finally caught up with me and unjammed the cord!" Maggie handed the envelope back across the table. "Maybe I'd better just pass on this 'surprise'."

Ominous, silent stares were her reply.

"Or not." Maggie sighed and tapped the envelope against the table. "Okay, fine. But there'd better not be anything inside of this that involves ink, smoke, free-falling through space, or anything else that will be likely to tear me limb from limb or put an unremoveable stain on my clothing."

"Trust us," Ellie said, lifting one black eyebrow.

"Trust us," Allie echoed, arching one tawny, perfectly waxed brow.

"Where did that waiter go?" Rachel said, staring down into her empty glass.

"Fine. Sure. Whatever." Maggie unbent the metal clasp holding the flap of the brown envelope together, opened it, and reached inside. "Just wait until your birthdays. I'm going to come up with something that—"

Maggie stopped talking as she pulled out a sheet of paper with an impressive monogram embossed across the top.

"The Archaeological Foundation of Western Scotland?" Her mouth went dry with sudden, ridiculous anticipation. "What did you guys do?" she asked, afraid to hope.

"Just read it," Allie said.

"Yeah, read it," Ellie said.

Maggie smoothed the sheet of paper out on the table

and cleared her throat. The words danced in front of her eyes as she read them aloud.

" '*Dear Ms. Graham:*

On the basis of your application and outstanding résumé, you have been chosen to join the crew of my newest archaeological dig in the Highlands of Scotland. We will be exploring the history and archaeological significance of a cairn recently discovered near the village of Drymen. Please see the enclosed brochure for more information. I look forward to greeting you personally when you arrive.

Sincerely,
Alexander MacGregor, Ph.D.' "

She lowered the paper.

"Ohmigosh," Maggie said softly. "Is this for real?" Then she remembered with whom she was dealing. "Ha, ha. Very funny. You guys are hysterical." She tossed the sheet of paper to the table. "Drymen. Couldn't you even come up with a Scottish-sounding name for the village? Lame, girls, really lame. Okay, where's my cake?"

"It's not a joke." Allie frowned and picked up the paper, handing it back to her. "Honest, Maggie. We set it all up and you're going to Scotland."

"It's *true!*" Ellie said, her voice twisting a little. "Oh, Maggie, we're sorry. We shouldn't have teased you, it's just that you're so—so—"

"Gullible." Rachel slurred the word a little. "But this is for real!"

"We've been saving money for years for this—" Allie began.

"We found this Professor MacGregor on the Internet—" Ellie interrupted.

"And we sent off your résumé and wrote a letter—" Rachel added.

"And if you'll check that envelope again, you'll find a nonrefundable airline ticket to Inverness, parachute included, leaving next Tuesday—" Allie said.

"And a reservation at Hotel George for the first night, and a tour of where Rob Roy MacGregor lived—" Ellie said.

"Rob Roy?" Maggie said faintly, interrupting Ellie.

"And *none* of this is dangerous or risky," Rachel said with a sigh. "Just extremely boring, at least the digging in the dirt part." She paused thoughtfully and took a sip of Maggie's whiskey. "Unless Professor MacGregor happens to be a hottie, in which case, maybe you'll get the opportunity to take a chance for once in your life!"

All three sat back triumphantly as Maggie stared first at each of them, and then at the paper in her hands. "It's real?" she whispered.

"Bonafide," Allie said.

"Done deal," Ellie agreed.

"It's your turn, Maggie," Rachel said softly.

Maggie felt the smile beginning, felt it stretch her mouth, felt it fill her face, and suddenly she was on her feet, and it didn't matter that everyone in the pub was staring as she climbed up on the table and raised her arms in triumph, swaying a little, as her sisters and her friend grinned up at her.

"I'M GOING TO SCOTLAND!" she shouted.

two

"Margaret!"

Maggie ignored the sound of the deep, manly voice calling her name, and smiled as she continued to carefully whisk a soft brush over the clay pot in her lap.

In the three days she'd been in Scotland, she'd discovered that: one, the "dig" was little more than a glorified tourist attraction, meant to entertain aficionados of Indiana Jones movies, and two, her daydream of a Scottish hunk who wanted to ravish her had finally come true. Strangely enough, she was more interested in the phony dig than the phony hunk.

Professor Alex MacGregor was quite possibly the most handsome guy she'd ever seen up close, real, and personal. At six foot one, Alex was a man among men—at least at first glance. His hair came to below his shoulders and was dark golden blond with natural, sun-bleached highlights. His eyes were a deep blue, fringed in long, dark lashes below perfect tawny brows.

In fact, everything about Alex was perfect. He had the perfect jaw, the perfect chin, and the perfect sexy mouth that tilted to one side and invited any and all women to partake of the sensual buffet his sensual smile promised. His body was almost exactly like that of the men in her fantasies—bulging biceps and rock-hard abs (she knew because he'd taken his shirt off on the first day to work in the sunshine) and broad "let me carry your problems for you" shoulders. And to top all of that charisma off, he claimed to be a direct descendent of Rob Roy MacGregor.

She should've been swooning in his wake like every other woman on the dig. "Should've" being the definitive word. Rachel would have a fit if she found out Maggie wasn't in the least attracted to the handsome archaeologist, not that she was sure by any means that he actually *was* an archaeologist. Maggie had pegged the hunky hunk for the player he was, and had dismissed him in favor of enjoying the pseudodig.

So what in the ever-loving world was wrong with her? She could just hear what Rachel would say: "Why aren't you taking this guy up on his innuendoes and suggestions?"

Maggie didn't know. Maybe something was wrong with her. Maybe she had low hormones. Maybe that was the real reason the gynecologist had put her on the birth control pills and just didn't want to make her feel bad. *Maybe she was going into menopause.*

For pity's sake, she told herself, *get a grip.*

She was still having a wonderful time in spite of Alex, and in spite of the the fact that most of the real excavation work had been done before the "crew"—gathered mostly from applicants on the Internet from the States—had paid their money to participate in a real archaeological "find." The "helpers" were reduced mostly to cleaning crockery and hadn't been allowed in the cairn all that much.

But she was in Scotland, and for the first time in more than a decade, responsible only for herself. That alone made her feel absolutely giddy with pleasure.

"Margaret!" Alex called again, and with a sigh, Maggie looked up to see him striding toward her, his carefully cultivated boyish grin firmly in place.

She'd told him ten times on the first day that her name wasn't Margaret. It was Maggie. He told her that a woman as "bonny" as she was had to have a prettier name than merely "Maggie." With a sigh, she brushed the dirt on her hands onto her already filthy jeans and smiled.

"Good morning, Professor Alex," she said.

"Ah, ah, what did I tell ye about that?" he asked with feigned sternness. "Ye are my special student and as such, may call me Alex."

Great. She was special. Like a hundred others he'd used that line on.

Maggie brushed a lock of hair back from her face and gave him a halfhearted smile. "Right. Alex. Did you need me?" she asked without thinking.

His smile faded into a sultry pout as his blue eyes swept over her. "Aye," he said, "I need ye with a need that burns deep within my soul. I need ye with—"

Maggie cut him off with a laugh. "Let me rephrase that question. Were you looking for me?" Alex knelt next to her, so close she could count his long lashes.

"Aye, lass," he said softly, "I've been lookin' for such as ye all of my life. I've looked from glen to glen and from loch to loch and from—"

Maggie rolled her eyes. "Enough. I've told you this isn't going to happen, remember? I'm here to explore ancient Scotland, not have a Highland fling."

He slid his eyes half closed, and as if on command, they began to smolder. Maggie gazed into them, amazed that someone could actually do that in real life. Maybe she could get him to teach her how. It might come in handy if she ever found someone she actually wanted to turn on. However, since Alex's burning gaze was doing nothing for her, maybe he shouldn't be giving lessons.

"Och, lass," he said, his voice smoldering now, too, "all I wanted was to ask if ye will go with me to the Faire?"

Maggie considered the invitation. He'd already asked her twice since her arrival to go with him to the Renaissance Faire in nearby Drymen, but she knew to agree would be agreeing to more than the Faire. At least in his mind.

"I told you, no Highland flings."

He moved one hand to his chest. "Lass! Ye wound me to the heart. Do ye think I am so insincere, so shallow, as to want only a one-night stand?" He reached out and stroked one finger gently down the side of her face.

Maggie smiled up at him. "Of course that's all you want." She took his hand and placed it on his knee, giving it a halfhearted pat. "And actually, I have a headache."

He gave her a disbelieving look.

She laughed. "Really, I'm serious." Just before she left Texas she'd gotten a sinus infection. The antibiotics were in her pack but she kept forgetting to take them. "Now, if there's nothing else," she said, "I have some dusting to do."

"Och, but there is," he said. He grabbed her hand and stood, pulling her along with him, the flirtatious tone suddenly gone from his voice. "Lass, I have something to show ye—a real discovery!" His eyes were shining with what appeared to be real excitement, and for a moment, Maggie wondered who he really was beneath the façade.

"A *real* discovery? You mean all of these fascinating pieces of clay pottery weren't real discoveries?"

His eyes slid to one side and then the "ya gotta believe me" smile was back in place. "Of course, darlin', but this is different. I've made a new, amazing find, and ye are the first one I want to show it to!"

Maggie shrugged. "All right," she agreed, pulling her hand away from his. "Lead on, MacDuff."

"The MacGregors are no part of the MacDuff clan, lass," he said with a frown.

"Right, right," she muttered. "It's just a figure of speech."

"Speakin' of figures, lass—"

"Alex! One more line and I swear I'll report you to— to . . ." She frowned. Did Scotland have a Better Business Bureau? "Well, I'll report you to somebody. Now, this is your last chance to show me your big discovery." He opened his mouth, and she held up one finger. "Don't—you—dare."

He grinned and shrugged. "All right, lass. Your loss."

At the base of the hill, they passed about twenty tents that made up the camp of those "chosen" for the archaeological dig. The site was rustic and devoid of any frills, which she felt almost sure was part of "Professor Alex's" attempt to give his customers a "real" experience.

The cairn was situated on top of a hill, and as she trudged behind Alex, Maggie enjoyed the sight of the Scottish countryside around her. Blue green glens and faded purple mountains in the distance, rolling green and russet hills divided by babbling "burns" and dotted with Neolithic rocks and brushy copses of alders and oaks. Even in this present day, the land was ancient and untouched in comparison to the rest of the world.

Oddly enough, Maggie felt as if she'd come home. For the first time since her parents had died, she found that she could relax. That alone was worth putting up with Alex MacGregor.

"Come on!" he called, pausing on the hillside and gesturing for her to hurry. Maybe she'd misjudged him. He looked so happy, so eager. Maybe he wasn't completely hopeless. Maybe all he needed was the right woman to love him to give him the confidence to drop the act and be himself. He gave her another dazzling smile.

And maybe she'd grow bigger boobs and longer eyelashes before Christmas.

Alex waited impatiently for her at the curved doorway to the cairn. The cairn itself was quite unusual, Maggie knew. Most of the ancient mounds, built from stone or dried bricks and then covered by eons of dirt, were no more than about a meter in height and had long ago collapsed inward. There were a few that were very tall, but with a small circumference.

This one was intact and huge in comparison to most at about sixty feet in diameter and fifteen feet in height. Alex had told her it was second in size only to the Newgrange cairn in Ireland. The two were also similar in that neither showed evidence of being used as a tomb. Very unusual.

As they entered the cairn, Alex had to duck down to miss the top of the doorway, and then he straightened and grinned. She was getting very tired of that grin. But she tried to be polite.

"Okay, what's the big surprise?"

"Look, lass!" Alex took her hand. For once the gesture seemed innocent. He led her to a spot on the curved walls and pointed. "This could be the discovery that finally makes my career!" he said.

Maggie took a closer look at the wall. The rest of the cairn had been built from individual, smaller stones, but at this one section in the curved wall, a huge Neolithic stone had been incorporated into the structure. The stone stood flush with the wall, but its edges protruded slightly on either side.

"Wow," she said, "this is unusual isn't it?"

"Aye, but even more amazing is this." He pointed to the edge of the standing stone.

Maggie leaned closer to examine a series of lines carved into the surface in different numerical groupings and her eyes widened. "An ogham," she whispered in awe.

Alex's smile widened. "Och, lass, I knew ye wouldna disappoint me. Ye are the only one of this motley crew that has any kind of understanding of what we're doing."

Maggie straightened and gave him a genuine smile. "Thanks. I think. Okay, I know what it's called, but give me the basics again of what it actually means. It's been a few years since I studied this."

"An ogham is a kind of ancient alphabet used by the Celtic people ages ago." He pointed at four lines carved closely together. "Each grouping designates a letter of the Celtic alphabet."

Maggie reached out to touch one of the lines. A quick thrill of excitement raced through her blood. "A message from the past," she said softly. "Amazing."

"Aye, and what's more amazing is what the message says!"

She glanced over at him and arched one brow in suspicion. "What does it say?" she asked, her tone flat. " 'What's a nice girl like you doing in a place like this?' "

Alex laughed. "Nay. Does that line really work in America?"

"No."

He lifted one broad shoulder in a shrug. "Nay, lass, its message is more cryptic than that."

Surprised that he didn't take the opportunity to make more of her comment, Maggie watched as he pulled a piece of paper out of his faded blue jeans' pocket, unfolding it carefully.

"As near as I can translate it," he said, reading something on the paper, "I make it out to say, 'Follow forward, follow back, ages lost, ages found.'" He looked up and smiled at her in delight.

Maggie smiled back, suddenly equally delighted. Ancient messages hidden in stone. How cool was that? "What does it mean?"

He spread his hands apart. "Who knows?" he said, beaming. "But isn't it wonderful?"

"It really is." She patted him on the arm. "I'm very impressed."

Alex covered her hand with his before she could move it, and pulled her against him. "Enough to grant me a kiss?"

Maggie looked up into Alex's lazy, teasing eyes and pushed him away.

"Nope. Not even close. But thanks for sharing your discovery with me." She smiled. "That was nice of you."

"Nice?" His handsome face registered a depth of despair over her rejection that she knew was entirely false.

"Very nice." She turned to head for the curved doorway. "It's really fascinating that—OW!" Maggie stumbled and fell to her knees. Alex rushed to her side, and for once, his concern sounded sincere.

"Are ye all right, lass?"

"I'm fine, just clumsy." She sat up and dusted off her hands, searching the floor for what had made her stumble. "But what did I trip over?"

Alex knelt next to her and began running his hands over the uneven surface. After a minute he pointed to a bump on the floor. "I think this is the culprit. Just a bit of stone."

Maggie leaned closer to look at the raised lump, and then reached out and brushed a layer of dirt off of the top. She blinked as she saw that the stone continued, curving to the right. "Hey, this isn't just a misplaced rock. I think this is a carving."

Alex practically flung himself to the floor. Taking a soft brush from his shirt pocket, he began sweeping the dirt away in a circular motion, his efforts quickly revealing more of the upraised stone. "Brilliant," he whispered, his blue eyes luminous.

"Me or the stone?" Maggie quipped.

"This could be it," he murmured, ignoring her words as he rose from the floor. "The ogham was good, but this could finally get me out of this dung heap existence."

"What?"

His gaze was distant, almost feverish. "I've got to get to work!" With that, he hurried toward the doorway, stepping gingerly on the mysteries beneath the dirt, leaving Maggie behind.

"You're welcome," she said crossly.

In a matter of hours, Maggie was even more disgruntled when it became apparent that Alex planned on taking credit for what was probably the archaeological find of the century. The crew had attacked the floor of the cairn, armed with brushes and cloths, and now an immense stone carving lay exposed—one that would guarantee fortune and glory to the one who had discovered it.

The carving was a tri-spiral, also known as a triskele, the size of which had never been found anywhere in the UK, Ireland, or as far as Maggie knew, the world. In fact, only a few tri-spirals had ever been found, period, most at Newgrange. This particular triskele covered the entire floor of the cairn, its three arms curving outward from the center to create three separate spirals.

As she stood in the doorway of the cairn taking photos with her digital camera, she tried to control the irritation coursing through her. Of course, *technically* Alex *had* uncovered the bump that tripped her, but she'd been the one to bring his attention to the fact that it wasn't just a lump of stone.

Whatever. She wasn't going to lose sleep over it. After all, she wasn't an archaeologist, she was a history teacher. This was just an interlude, so what did it matter if she got to share the credit or not? She'd be leaving Scotland in another week and going back to Texas to get ready for another year of teaching bored teenagers why they should care about history.

With a sigh, she went back to work.

Quinn was having fun.

While raiding the carriages of lords and ladies had been both exciting and lucrative, his decision to start attacking the duke's personal shipments was much more satisfying.

So far he and Ian had taken a wagonload of expensive fabric, one filled with eight sacks of oats, a wagon full of vegetables, and a barrel of whiskey. Small things to a highwayman, but large to a Scotsman waiting for his porridge and his drink, and they also meant a great deal to the ladies the duke sought to entertain and entice.

Montrose was not amused by their attacks, but he was still running true to form. He'd assigned two guards to protect his shipments and had put a price on the head of the mysterious "Piper." Quinn was thrilled, even though the price was a mere fifty pounds.

Quinn and Ian had no trouble overpowering Montrose's new guards, again and again. The highwaymen were making less money this way, but the satisfaction of duping Montrose and depriving him of his evening shot of whiskey made it all worthwhile. Besides, this night Quinn had learned that a carriage full of aristocrats bearing a gift to the duke from the Queen herself would arrive.

Now he and Ian lay in wait on the side of a rocky hill, listening for the sound of wheels turning over ruts and stones. The carriage was due to pass them after the moon had risen, but fortunately, the night was overcast and rain was in the wind.

"I have a strange feeling this night," Ian said as they knelt beside their horses.

Quinn was watching the roadway, but something in his friend's voice made him turn toward him. "What sort of feeling?"

Ian started to speak, then frowned and shook his head. "I dinna know how to explain it. It's as if something—" He shook his head again. "'Tis nothing. Too many boiled turnips most likely."

"Aye, well, I told ye that yer eyes were bigger than yer stomach." He glanced up at the sky again, pleased to see more clouds gathering. "No one will recognize our faces this night," Quinn said almost to himself.

"'Tis more to a man than his face," Ian said absently, "and while the lassies like a handsome man, 'tis not the face they are most interested in, my friend." He smiled at Quinn. "Nay, 'tis something much lower on a man's body."

The familiar sound of hooves and wheels interrupted his speech, and the two men fell silent, focusing on the plan. Quinn mounted his horse and looked down at his friend.

"Are ye ready?"

"Aye," Ian said, swinging into the saddle easily. "I'm a MacGregor."

"Dinna brag. Come on, lad!" Quinn vaulted into his saddle and drew his sword, then touched his heels to his horse's sides and plunged down the hillside. Ian headed in the opposite direction, in order to come at the carriage from the rear.

Quinn pulled back on Saint's reins, and came to a dramatic stop in the middle of the dark roadway, allowing his horse to rear up on its hind legs. The carriage rumbled to a halt.

"Throw down your weapons!" he cried in a perfect English accent. The driver seated on top of the carriage tossed down a musket, and the man beside him a sword. The two guards were quickly disarmed as well.

A fine mist had begun to fall and Quinn had a sudden sadistic urge to expose the aristocrats within to the elements that every Scotsman outside of a castle had to face each and every night. Quinn sidestepped Saint until he was in arm's reach of the driver sitting on top of the carriage. With one slicing move, he thrust the point of his sword to the man's throat.

"Have the passengers disembark," he said softly.

"Aye, aye," the driver muttered. He slid down from his seat and jammed his shapeless hat down on his head a little harder before opening the carriage door. Quinn grinned as an immediate chorus of voices lifted in protest.

There were two men and two women, all wearing clothing in the latest fashions, made from velvets and silks. The men had cravats tied around their necks, and the low-cut necklines of the women's dresses throbbed with flesh and the jewels strung around their chubby necks.

As they all gazed balefully up at him, Quinn had a moment of satisfaction in knowing that these luxurious garments—the cost of which would feed a family of six for a year—were now being ruined by the rain. The women were both young, dark-haired, and buxom, with a coarseness to their faces that made Quinn surmise they were mistresses or whores, not wives.

Ian had stayed behind the carriage to make sure neither of the drivers intended to pull a gun or sword and strike against them, but once all four of the passengers and the drivers stood on the ground, he guided his horse over to Quinn.

"Sink me, Siegfried," Ian said loudly in the same English accent as Quinn, "but I do believe we have some soggy pigeons this night."

"Aye, Bartholomew," Quinn answered, "but look at how brightly these pigeons' feathers shine. They simply beg for us to pluck them." He pointed at the jewels around one woman's neck.

"See here!" the stouter of the two men shouted, his soaked wig askew on his bald head. "We are guests of the Duke of Montrose and I demand that you let us pass!"

"Guests of the duke? Well, why didn't you say so? In that case"—Ian tapped his chin and pretended to consider the request and then laughed and cocked his head to one side—"instead, I think that we shall have to kill you. What do you say, Siegfried?"

"Indeed," Quinn said, as a rush of anticipation surged through his veins. "I wholeheartedly agree."

The women began to scream.

Maggie couldn't sleep. The little cot she'd been assigned was fairly comfortable, but she was freezing. She shifted to her side and shivered. Even in the summer, Highland nights were chilly, and apparently there was still no controlling the twins and Rachel's insane need to pull practical jokes on her.

The first night there she'd discovered that the heavy jogging pants she'd packed to sleep in at the camp had been replaced with her favorite threadbare pair of Hello Kitty pajamas. Very funny. Someday she would find a way to pay them back, and then she'd see who had the last laugh!

Maggie closed her eyes. Even with three pairs of socks on, inside her down sleeping bag, she was too cold to sleep. Maybe she could count sheep. There were lots of sheep in Scotland. Or how about spirals? Yeah, spirals, count 'em, three. Being hogged by Alex MacGregor.

Maggie turned onto her back, releasing her pent-up breath in one long, slow sigh. Her dream had been to travel the world, exploring ancient ruins, studying under noted archaeologists. Now, after all these years, at the ripe old age of thirty-two, here she was, ready to finally go back to the Original Plan for Her Life.

A little rush of anticipation trickled through her veins, followed by a more solid flood of adrenaline. She was free now, really free. Not that she'd forget her sisters—she'd always be there for them—but they were adults, on their own! It was finally sinking in that she could do anything she wanted. Anything!

So why did she feel so hesitant?

The answer hit her with the impact of a rock to her solar plexus and Maggie sat up and shoved her feet out of the sleeping bag, swinging them to the canvas floor. Her long red hair, free of its braid for once, tumbled around her shoulders as she forced herself to face the truth.

She was afraid.

For the last ten years she had focused all of her energy on Allie and Ellie, and now that she had the chance to put the focus back on herself, she was just afraid, pure and simple. Maggie drew in a deep, ragged breath and dragged her hair back from her face with one hand.

"Ridiculous," she said aloud. "There's nothing to fear but–but—Alex MacGregor."

Silly. There was nothing to be afraid of. She just needed to make a new plan. She always felt less afraid when she had a plan. Suddenly the little tent felt claustrophobic. Her life felt claustrophobic.

She leaned forward, unzipped the tent, and took a deep lungful of the cold night air. Shivering, she reached for her heavy jacket and pulled it on. Too bad it was too bulky to sleep in. A walk was what she needed. An envigorating walk in the brisk night air.

Maggie dragged her Doc Martens from under her bunk and put them on, laced them up over her thick white socks, and picked up her flashlight and backpack. She'd go up to the cairn and look at the ogham and spiral again. It had been hard to concentrate with Alex making his not-so-veiled innuendoes. He was cute, but hopeless.

Maggie ducked through the tent opening and straightened into the Scottish night. The moon was just rising and she took a moment to gaze up at the sky. It never really got dark during the summer in Scotland. Tonight there were no clouds—an amazing fact in itself—and stars studded the grayish sky above her like dazzling diamonds.

The rising moon combined with the not-quite-dark sky had already made her flashlight unnecessary, and she put it away to climb the craggy hillside toward the cairn at the top. But when she reached the summit, the thought of going inside the structure alone made her feel suddenly uneasy. She shook her head over her own foolishness.

"Don't be silly," she said aloud. "There are fifteen people at the bottom of the hill. Besides, who do you expect to find in there, Freddy MacKruger?"

But it was still creepy.

She paused at the doorway and swallowed hard, then laughed. "Come on, Maggie, it's just a big upside-down bowl that's been around for a really long time. Nothing scary. Cap'n Crunch container gone bad."

It would be dark inside. She needed her flashlight. A quick rummage in her pack produced it once again. She ducked under the low doorway, planning to turn on the flashlight as soon as she entered the cairn. But inside, the hollow structure was already glowing, and Maggie's fear disappeared as the scientist inside of her kicked into high gear. There were holes in the "roof" of the cairn. Moonlight poured through them and created a trail of lights, marking one of the arms of the triskele on the floor.

"Wow." Maggie moved toward the ogham stone, but stopped beneath the streaming moonlight and looked straight up. Through each of the holes, she could see a star, lined up exactly. What could it mean? Something to do with the summer solstice? Maybe this was some kind of observatory!

She grinned, mentally hugging the discovery to herself. This was a find she wouldn't share with Alex MacGregor! Maybe she could write a paper about it!

After gazing her fill for several long minutes, Maggie moved to the ogham stone and ran her fingers over the grooved lines. "Follow forward, follow back, ages lost, ages found," she said aloud.

Maybe that was really the crux of her problem. Maybe she just didn't belong in modern times. Maybe if she'd lived in the days of—oh, say—Rob Roy MacGregor, she'd have already found happiness with a hunky Scotsman. As Maggie turned, still musing over the cryptic message, she froze in place.

For a moment, it was as if she had stepped into some other world. The moonlight streaming through the holes had collided with dust particles in the air, making them glitter and dance like fanciful fairies. It was all so surreal. Maggie took a step forward, drawn to the three stone spirals joined at the center. Choosing the one beneath the moonlight, she began to walk beside the grooved "path."

As she followed it, she wondered if anyone had known about this cairn during the days of Rob Roy. "Follow forward, follow back, ages lost, ages found," she muttered. Something sparkled in her peripheral vision and she jerked her head toward it, her breath catching in her throat. The ogham, the lines carved into the standing stone in the wall of the cairn, were glowing.

"Follow forward, follow back," she whispered, and began to walk beside the spiral again. She took one step, and then another, reciting the words Alex had translated. "Ages lost, ages found."

Maggie reached the end of the single spiral and stopped, mesmerized by the conflicting sensations coursing through her body. She was dizzy, elated, scared, amazed. Light flooded in from above, and she looked up again to find one of the "star holes" directly in line with her gaze.

Suddenly Maggie had no breath, no words, no thoughts. She had only that one star above, suspended in space, holding her in some kind of mindless limbo as the spiral below her feet began to slowly turn—just before everything exploded in a dazzling blaze of light.

three

The rain had stopped. The two women beside the carriage looked like bedraggled hens and were crying and screaming, begging for their lives, while the men with them, their wigs soggy and ruined, shook their fists and shouted at the highwaymen.

Quinn shot Ian a grin. "I believe your threat to kill someone has upset the ladies," he told Ian.

Ian feigned horror. "A pox upon me! Surely not!"

Quinn bowed toward the women as he explained, "'Twas a jest, ladies," he said. "Do forgive us."

"In any case, dear ladies"—Ian tossed a cloth sack to one of the women, and she caught it against her generous bosom with a gasp. He smiled again and gestured toward the sack with his sword, falling into his usual brogue—"if ye would be so kind as to fill this bag with yer jewelry, it would be much appreciated by those less fortunate. Us, to be exact."

The women lost their tentative smiles and began to whine again.

"Scottish bastards!" The bald man shouted. "I knew you could not be Englishmen!"

"And I dinna think ye could be any kind of man," Quinn said. His eyes narrowed. "Dinna push me, for I am known to push back."

A harsh wind swept suddenly across the glen and Saint whinnied, moving restlessly beneath him. Ian's horse and the horses tied to the carriage began to shift their feet and snort and Quinn glanced around, suddenly uneasy.

"And which one of ye possesses the gift sent by the English queen to Montrose?" he asked, his voice falsely cheerful again.

"She is your queen, as well, you Scottish bastard!" the bald man cried, shaking his fist again.

Quinn lowered the point of his sword to the man's throat. "I have no queen," he said.

Maggie's eyes flew open. She lay flat on her back on the floor of the cairn. Her head ached and her mouth was dry and she stared up at the roof of the mound blankly.

What in the world had happened? Her heart was beating rapidly and a cold chill swept down her body. Why was it so cold? She blinked and took a deep breath, relieved to find that she was still alive. For a minute, she'd had her doubts.

Don't panic. She was in the cairn. Everything was fine. Just because she couldn't remember how she'd gotten there was no need to panic. Suddenly Maggie felt as if the cairn was closing in on her and she began to tremble. She had to get out of there—*now*.

It took a minute before her legs would cooperate with the orders her brain was giving, but finally she was able to stand. She crossed to the opening, aching all over, only to suddenly stop in her tracks. Her eyes widened. The opening was sealed. With stones.

Maggie stumbled back a step. "What in the world?" she whispered. Disoriented, she turned in a circle, gazing at the narrow stones forming the inside of the cairn. Everything looked the same—dusty floor, standing stone with the ogham engraved, the raised tri-spiral on the floor.

Her backpack lay crumpled on the floor on the other side of the cairn, her flashlight beside it. A moonbeam played across the dirty leather surface of the backpack, and she watched as a dozen other dots of light danced across the floor. Glancing up, she saw moonlight streaming through the "star holes" she'd discovered last night.

Last night. No. Tonight? A wave of dizziness rocked her. How long had she been unconscious? She glanced down at her wrist and realized she'd left her watch back in the tent. Maggie walked to where her pack lay and bent to pick it up, along with her flashlight. Okay, no problem, her practical side said. Someone had sealed up the opening, not knowing she was inside. She switched on the light and let it play around the empty cairn.

"Right," she said aloud. "In the middle of the night, someone sealed up the cairn, right after Alex made his big discovery. That makes sense." She shook her head. "Something is very, very wrong."

She slid the strap of her backpack over her shoulder. "Alex?" she called. Her voice broke in the middle of his name. She cleared her throat and tried again. "Alex! What's going on?"

After thirty minutes of screaming her lungs out, Maggie was exhausted and thirsty. Luckily she had the bottle of water she always carried in her pack. She took it out and unscrewed the lid, taking a small sip as her heart pounded. Who knew how long that water might have to last her?

Don't be ridiculous, she told herself. *There's no way they blocked up the door and took off in the middle of the night in the middle of a dig!*

Maggie took another small sip and then put the bottle away. She had already switched off her flashlight. The moonlight streaming through the holes in the ceiling lent quite a bit of light to the space, and she might need the flashlight later.

With a sigh, she sank down to the floor and pulled her knees to her chest, leaning her head back against the wall. Long tendrils of hair whispered around her face. She ran her fingers through her hair, massaging her scalp lightly, the pain in her head easing as she tried to think.

This was crazy. A joke? No one would pull this kind of elaborate hoax, not even her sisters. Okay, they probably would, but they were an ocean away. She leaned her head on her knees, her hair covering her like a cloak.

Calm down. She'd take the scientific approach and re-trace her steps. She'd been restless and come to the cairn, where she discovered the holes in the ceiling, and the stars lined up in them. Maggie lifted her head from her knees and watched the moonlight flicker across the triskele carving on the floor.

The spirals! She straightened. Something had happened when she walked around one of the spirals! Stumbling to her feet, she moved to the spiral. She'd walked along the raised stone carving and had spoken the words of the ogham aloud. The rest of the memory flooded back. Yes! There'd been a flash of light and then—

Maggie began to tremble. She remembered being somewhere—terrible. Trapped somehow. Drifting from her body, her soul. She had seen herself in a bubble, but she couldn't reach her own body. Maggie shook her head. It was all muddled and hazy and she forced her thoughts away from the horrible memory and back to the situation at hand.

Okay. The door to the cairn was blocked. She couldn't get out. No one was coming to save her, so she'd just have to save herself. But how? The stones of the cairn were very solidly packed together, and besides, the archaeologist in her did not want to damage this find.

During the excavation of the cairn, Alex had discovered a place where the stones had either caved outward on their own, or been pulled out by someone at some point in the past. Maggie moved quickly to the north side of the cairn, and knelt down, expecting to see the hole. She sat back on her heels and the panic returned full force.

There was no hole.

Maggie stood up, hands on her hips, and glared around at the thousands of stones making up the cairn, stones that were keeping her in.

"Well, okay then," she said. "I'll just have to *make* a hole!"

Quinn got off his horse.

He walked toward the two men, swinging his sword back and forth, slicing the air. "If ye call me a bastard again," he said, his voice as sharp as the blade he held suddenly to the taller man's throat, "I will split ye from here"—he lifted the aristocrat's cravat with the tip of the blade and then slowly brought the point of the blade down to rest against the man's crotch—"to here."

The bald man gulped and shuddered, his eyes round with fear, as the shorter man beside him apparently found his nerve.

"The duke will not stand for this treatment of his guests!" he said, his mustache drooping from the rain, his words laced with terror. "Do you know who I am? I am the Earl of—"

"Ye are the Earl of Nothing," Quinn said flatly, his gaze never moving from the terrified eyes of the man in front of him. "Ye are in Scotland now, and we dinna care what titles an Englishman may hold."

"I am sorry, my lord," the tall man said with a distinctive Scottish accent. "I promise that the duke will not allow this to go unpunished!"

Ian had circled his horse around the carriage, and now came back to Quinn's side. "I have a fair bad feeling, lad," he said. "And the clouds are passing from the moon."

"Gentlemen," Quinn said, as he walked back to his horse and mounted, sliding easily into the saddle, "your wallets, please, and the Queen's gift, before things become . . . unpleasant."

"Scalawags!" said the taller man, pulling out a velvet bag and a small box.

"You bloody bas—" The bald man swallowed the word hastily. "Ye bloody black weasels!" he shouted as he tossed his wallet to the ground. "The duke will have ye hanging on the gallows by Hogmanay!"

Saint pranced beneath Quinn. "Do you hear that, lad?" he asked Ian, and gave a short laugh. "The Black Weasels! I had hoped for a name slightly more intimidating, perhaps the Black Wolves or the Black Foxes."

"Even the Black Hounds would be better," Ian agreed, casting a glance over first one shoulder and then the other. Quinn had known his friend long enough to know when he was growing anxious.

The women giggled. "Nay," said one, "they call ye the Piper. Which one of ye is he?"

Quinn and Ian exchanged glances and grinned. "We take turns," Quinn said, and glanced at the moon, now peeking out once more from behind the skittering clouds. It was time to go. He directed one of the women to gather up the items on the ground, and when she handed them to him, she smiled. Quinn took the bag from her and bowed from the saddle.

"We do apologize, ladies," he said, "but we do assure you that your jewelry—which no doubt these good fellows will happily replace for you—is going to a good cause."

"And what cause would that be?" the stout man demanded.

Quinn smiled. "Making me rich."

Suddenly Ian straightened in the saddle and turned his horse around, moving next to Quinn. "We'd best be away."

"Aye." Quinn sheathed his sword and bowed to the ladies. "Remember that this night ye were spared by the Piper!" He wheeled his horse around as the sound of sudden thunder shook the earth.

Saint reared back, as did Ian's horse. "That is not thunder!" Ian cried as he tried to bring his mount under control.

"Nay, 'tis at least two dozen men on horseback!" Quinn kicked his heels into Saint's side. "Ride, laddie, ride!"

After painstakingly examining the curved surface of the cairn's wall, Maggie finally found a weak spot where a few stones had crumbled and left a small hole. It took about an hour, but Maggie finally managed to push enough stones out of place and was able to squeeze through to the outside. Once free of her tomb, she stood and took a deep breath of fresh air. It was dark outside, at least as dark as it was likely to get. She could see shapes in the shadowy twilight, but she switched on her flashlight and started down the hillside, slipping and sliding in her haste to reach the bottom.

Her head was pounding again as she struck out toward the glen that had been an ideal spot to pitch their tents. It had rained, of course, and only a few clouds were left in the sky, drifting across the face of the moon.

"Alex, my darlin'," she muttered as she hurried around a copse of bushes, "you are in such deep—" Maggie stopped in her tracks. She flashed the light around the meadowlike clearing where the "archaeologists" had slept for the last week. The tents were gone. Her head began to throb and the world spun around her.

"Alex! Damn you, Alex! Where are you? Where is *any-body*?!" Her words echoed back to her as she looked around, arms spread wide, the twilight sky above, the deep green below, and no one, not a soul to answer her.

What had happened? The tents had to be around here somewhere. She'd just gotten confused and gone in the wrong direction. She retraced her steps to the bottom of the hill and looked up at the cairn, shivering. No, she'd come down the right way. Obviously the tents had been taken down and everyone had left!

Maggie groaned out loud. Now she'd have to walk into the village, which was about fifteen miles away. Or she could spend the night there and hope Alex showed up in the morning. She turned away from the cairn. There was no way she was going back in there tonight.

The sensible thing to do would be to just sit down until morning, but she was too restless. She had to keep moving. Maggie walked toward the rising moon and climbed up another rocky hill. At the top, she stopped to stare out over the Scottish countryside. The moon was peeking out from behind the clouds, but more were gathering above her.

Maggie stood for a moment, drinking in the sight before her. Scotland was a mystical place at midnight, she thought, as she gazed at a world of silver stones and ebony shadows below. For a moment, she felt as if she were in some other dimension, a fairy realm filled with magic.

She shook her head at her whimsy and moved the beam of her flashlight to trace the stony slope stretching down. At the bottom was what looked like the tracks of wheels in the mud.

A road—or what passed for one in the Highlands. Relief swept over Maggie. She could follow the road and at least eventually get somewhere!

An owl hooted from somewhere nearby and Maggie turned toward the sound, just as a strong wind swept down from the north and blasted against her. Her thick jacket protected her on top, but her thin pajama pants were like paper. Then the skies opened up and the rain poured down.

"Great!" she said, lifting her head to glare up at the storm clouds. "Perfect! So now I get to be abandoned, cold, *and* wet! Alex MacGregor I am so going to kill you."

Then she heard it—voices shouting. It had to be Alex and her group. Maybe she'd been too hard on Alex. Maybe something bad had happened. Maybe something bad was happening right now!

"Hang on, Alex!" she cried. "I'm coming!" She half slid, half stumbled down to the bottom of the slope, her momentum carrying her forward several yards across the flat ground, and straight into the middle of the narrow, muddy road.

As Maggie stood still, trying to regain her equilibrium, the world spun around her again, making her feel nauseated and disoriented. Then a shot rang out, and she turned, startled, to see a man on the back of a huge black stallion riding straight toward her. The problem was . . . she couldn't move.

Quinn was ahead of Ian by several furlongs when the rain began pelting down again and shouts came from behind. He looked back through the rain to see Montrose's men gaining on them, swords drawn. A shot rang out and he put heel to his horse.

The rain was turning the ground to slush, and Quinn could only hope that their Highland ponies could keep their footing better than the nags the duke's men rode. He glanced back again, to make sure Ian was all right—and saw a figure standing directly in the path of his friend's horse.

For an instant, Quinn thought he imagined her, that the

ancient magic of the land had reached out and twisted his
mind. She looked like a faery, or a moon goddess, but no,
she was real. Slim, small, the woman stood in the path of
the charging stallion as if she were frozen, her long hair
dancing in the wind as it whipped around her with a fren-
zied haste. Only her eyes revealed her terror, glistening in
the summer twilight as Ian rode straight toward her.

"Ian!" Quinn shouted.

The woman jerked her head in the direction of the horse
and rider pounding toward her, her mouth open in wordless
fright. But Ian was looking over his shoulder and didn't see
her. He would unknowingly ride straight over the lass, and
apparently she hadn't the sense to get out of the way.

Quinn wheeled Saint around and headed back across the
muddy expanse toward Ian. He cut across his friend's path
and, without stopping, scooped the woman up and dumped
her across his saddle before whirling his horse around and
heading the other way, almost colliding with Ian's mount.

His action spooked Ian's horse, and as Saint carried him
forward, Quinn looked back to see Ian's mount rear up on
its hind legs, slip in the mud, and go down with Ian still on
its back.

"Ian!" Quinn shouted again, this time a cry from his
heart. His friend staggered to his feet and stumbled toward
Quinn as Montrose's men bore down on him.

"Go on!" he cried. "Ride on!"

But Quinn spun Saint in a half circle and charged back
toward his friend. In a matter of moments, Ian was surrounded by the duke's men, and for the second time that
night, Quinn had to make a split-second decision. He
pulled up, making Saint dance back and forth as his mind
raced. There were too many of them—over twenty by his
count—and to try to free Ian would probably mean the end
of them both. He tightened his jaw. He would have to take
that chance.

At that moment, the woman facedown across his saddle moved, pressing her hands against the side of his horse, lifting herself, turning her head to look up at him, her bewildered gaze colliding with his. Suddenly Quinn could not breathe, could not move. He fell into the depths of those almond-shaped eyes and plunged downward into an ocean of confusion and fear.

"Where am I?" she whispered.

"There's the other one!"

Quinn jerked his head toward the shout, shaken from his stupor.

"No!" He heard Ian's shout, and watched as his friend threw himself against three of the guards, taking them down. He got in a few good punches, and then staggered to his feet and shouted again, "Ride on!" before pulling a gun from the holster at a fallen guard's side.

"Ian, no!!" Quinn heard his own cry, as Saint danced beneath him, but the words came to him from far away, as if in a dream.

The next thing he knew, another guard had drawn his pistol and fired it at his friend. Ian collapsed to the ground. With a roar of outrage, Quinn dug his heels into Saint's side and sent the horse plunging forward, toward the enemy.

"No!" It was a woman's protest—the woman across his saddle. He'd forgotten her. She was in the way—he needed to draw his sword, to avenge his best friend.

She stared, wild-eyed at the meleé in front them, soldiers and guns and smoke and death. Quinn welcomed it. Ian had died like a man. Quinn would not disgrace him by turning tail and running like a coward. But the woman looked up at him, pleading in her voice and her shimmering eyes.

"Please," she said, "please don't let me die. I've just begun to live!"

Her words struck him in the heart and, without conscious

decision, Quinn pulled back on the reins, his arms shaking from the task. Saint fought the abrupt stop and almost went down, but quickly found his feet again. Quinn laid the rein across his neck and turned him. The black horse stretched into a long, lean gallop that carried Quinn and the woman away from danger, leaving Ian behind, without even a piper's lament.

four

Quinn gripped the flask of whiskey and took another drink, closing his eyes as the burn trickled down his throat. He and Ian always had a drink together after a job well done. Now that heady pleasure would never take place again. Ian was gone. He opened his eyes and turned his gaze to the woman responsible for his best friend's death.

She lay silent on the ground, sleeping or unconscious, he didn't know and didn't care. Dispassionately, he watched her lie there, his plaid beneath her and draped around her—he couldn't let her freeze—curled on her side, her hands folded beneath her head like a child. She wore the strangest clothing—a heavy, short coat on top, and thin, odd breeches on the bottom.

Her long hair waved along her back and over one shoulder like a waterfall at sunset, red gold and glorious, and her long lashes made dark crescents upon her porcelain skin; the few freckles dotted across her nose and cheeks made her look almost childlike, but the lush curves of her body he had inadvertently felt as he carried her proved she was no child.

She was beautiful, and Quinn hated her with every fiber of his being.

Ian's death was her fault. His hand tightened around the whiskey flask. And it was his fault, as well. If he hadn't ridden to her rescue, if he had just let Ian run her down, none of this would have happened. He put the flask down beside him and reached for a large leather bag at his feet. He lifted it to his lap, drawing a cumbersome object from the depths of the satchel. Ian's bagpipes.

When the two had first met at MacCrimmons School of Piping, Quinn, along with everyone else, had immediately assumed the son of a wealthy landowner was a rich, spoiled brat. All had heard that the ten-year-old boy was something of a prodigy on the pipes, and expected him to be vain and arrogant. Quinn had fallen right in with the general consensus, basing his assumption on his resentment of aristocrats, something his father had instilled in him from a young age, and also on Ian's somewhat foppish appearance.

Ian had been tall for his age and thin, with shadows under his long-lashed blue eyes and waving blond hair pretty enough for a girl. But during the second week of school, everything changed. Four of the bigger boys had jumped Ian after finding him walking through the court-yard alone.

Or so they had thought. Quinn had been practicing his pipes in a secluded corner of the commons and when he heard the commotion, ran to join the fray—until he saw the terror in Ian's eyes. Instead, he came to the younger boy's rescue, and after the fight had been broken up by two of the school's instructors, Ian had vowed his undying loyalty to his new friend.

In the days that followed, Quinn found he had been

completely wrong about the rich man's son. Ian was actually a down-to-earth, good-natured boy who had been ill most of his life. The two quickly became friends, and as their common love of music bound them closer together, Quinn taught Ian how to defend himself and how to hold his own in the rough-and-tumble sports the boys liked to play. In return, Ian taught Quinn more than one of his amazing techniques on the pipes. Ian's frail muscles began to strengthen and the shadows beneath his eyes faded. Soon the lad became one of the most well-liked students in the school.

They had both planned to be pipers. Music would be their lives. But in the days that followed their last year at MacCrimmons, the two friends had lost that dream, along with everything else they'd held dear, except for each other.

And now, because of a stupid woman's blundering, Ian was gone.

As Quinn fought the new wave of sorrow sweeping over him, along with the need to shout out his loss and his anger, he realized he was very drunk. He dragged the back of his sleeve across his eyes and picked up the bagpipes. For the first time in a very long time, he began to play.

Maggie came back to consciousness slowly, swimming up through layers of fog and confusion and—bagpipe music? A haunting melody pushed through the rest of the fuzz surrounding her brain and she reached for the thread of music, letting it draw her up to full awareness. She opened her eyes and found she was lying on the cold, rocky ground, staring up at a sky lightening with the dawn.

Where am I?

Fear swept over her, but Maggie forced the emotion down as her mind searched for something concrete to latch on to. The soft music of the pipes stirred her memory. Scotland. She was in the Highlands and something bizarre had happened to her . . . but what?

As the bagpipe music continued, she opened her eyes and drew in a quick breath. She was not alone. The man sat on the other side of a small campfire, his back against a large stone, one leg cocked, the other straight in front of him. His arms cradled what looked like a half-deflated jellyfish with little tubes poking out of it—no, pipes. One smaller pipe was held between his lips.

Bagpipes. She'd always loved bagpipe music and that alone would have made her feel warmly toward the stranger, but one look at his face chased that thought away.

His eyes were closed as if against a raging storm. Pain was etched across his features as if with a demon's hand. Maggie closed her own eyes against the sight as she tried to get her bearings.

She'd been standing on a hill and had run down to the road below. There'd been a man on horseback, charging toward her. Another had saved her from being run down.

The sound of the pipes faded away and she opened her eyes, her gaze locking with two angry green eyes. The long tube slipped from between the man's lips as he stared at her. A shiver danced down Maggie's back as she stared back, unable to look away.

Ragged dark brown hair that came to just above his shoulders waved around his ruggedly handsome face, tossed by the Highland wind. His nose was straight and a little large, slightly dominating his face, and beneath it was the most amazing mouth Maggie had ever seen, full, yet firm, a mouth she could imagine pressed against hers.

A wave of dizziness swept over her. What in the world was wrong with her, having such thoughts? The man was a stranger. Possibly a serial killer. But somehow Maggie couldn't look away from him, from that chiseled face rich with dark beard stubble, from the lines curving around the corners of his lips and radiating out from the corners of his eyes, evidence that once he had liked to laugh.

He wasn't laughing now. No, right now his square jaw was locked tightly together and his chin, strong with a slight cleft in the middle, was lifted arrogantly as he glared at her from beneath dark brows that clashed above those piercing, haunted eyes.

Holding her gaze, the man reached for a sword lying on the ground beside him, hesitated, and then moved his hand to close around the flask next to it.

Sword? Maggie drew in another sharp breath. He had a sword.

He took a long drink, then dragged his black sleeve across his mouth. He was dressed all in black, slim black trousers, knee-high black boots, a black shirt, and a long black cloak. Maggie frowned. A cloak? Who did this guy think he was, the vampire Lestat?

A sudden image of the man riding across the Highlands on the back of a black horse, his dark cloak flying behind him, flooded her mind. He was the one who had saved her from the path of a charging stallion.

"So, ye're awake," the man said, his heavy brogue slurred and somewhat menacing. Panic sliced into Maggie. He was drunk, and apparently very angry.

Her hands clenched and closed around something rough and warm. She looked down and found she was wrapped in a blanket, a faint gray and green plaid pattern woven into the material.

"Y-yes," she stuttered, grabbing the blanket and pulling it up to her neck as if the covering could protect her. She lifted one hand to her head and found her braid had come undone and her hair hung in long waves down her back. "I—I—how long have I been asleep?"

He took another drink from his flask, his eyes never

leaving her. "The night," he said. He gestured with the container toward the sun, just beginning to peek over the distant purple hills.

Maggie nodded, running her tongue across her dry lips. His steady gaze followed her movement and she put her tongue back where it belonged. "Oh, yes, well, I—I'm so sorry. I must have ruined your evening. Were you on your way to a costume party?"

He didn't answer, but the anger in his gaze quickened. She swallowed hard and then rushed on.

"Listen, I can't tell you how much I appreciate your help, I mean, you probably saved my life! You pulled me out from in front of that man's horse. I guess he didn't see me."

He still didn't answer, just took another drink. Maggie laughed uneasily. "Saying 'thank you' isn't enough, I realize, but I do thank you, very much. When I get back to my friends, I'll be happy to pay you for your trouble."

The man froze, the flask still held to his lips. As he slowly lowered it, the emotion in his eyes changed from fury to disbelief and back to fury again. Finally looking away from her, he stumbled to his feet and dragged one hand through his dark, tousled hair. He began to stride back and forth beside the fire, his fingers still curling around the neck of the flask, the black cloak whipping around him in the wind as he paced, the heels of his boots biting into the frozen earth.

" 'Trouble,' she says," he muttered. " 'Thank ye and I'll pay ye,' she says." His voice got louder. " 'I must have ruined yer evening,' she says!"

He flung the flask against the large stone behind him, and Maggie jumped as the container shattered and the sound broke the still softness of the morning. Before she could recover from that shock, the man had crossed to her side and fallen to his knees beside her, his large hands digging into her shoulders as he wrenched her up to face him.

"Do ye have no remorse, woman?" he demanded, giving her a shake, his voice deep and hoarse. "Do ye have no shame? A man is dead because of ye, and ye blather on about parties and payment for my help!"

Maggie's heart pounded as she was forced to look into his face. His furious, burning eyes were too close to hers, and all at once, the rest of the night's memories rushed into her mind. The other man, the one who had almost run her down, had been thrown from his horse when it reared backward. Her man—no, no, bad thought—the man beside her now had swung his own horse around and headed back to help his friend.

But his friend was being held by a bunch of guys in uniform and had shouted for them to ride on. There'd been a gunshot, and the other man had fallen to the ground. She'd begged her rescuer to turn tail and run, to save her life. And he had.

"The man that was shot—he was your friend," she whispered, feeling stunned.

"Aye, he was my friend," the man spat out. "Now *dead* because of ye." He shoved her backward and Maggie sprawled against the ground, her head whirling with the implication of his words. He stood and staggered back to the fire, one hand to his head.

Horror rushed over her. "Why did they shoot him?" she cried as she scrambled to her feet, holding the blanket around her. "*Who* shot him? Where are the police?"

She'd heard that men in the more isolated parts of the Highlands had sometimes been known to take the law into their own hands, but surely even here there would be a police investigation of a murder! Murder. She slid the man an uneasy glance. She was alone in the middle of the night in the middle of nowhere with a drunk stranger. Not good.

The man stopped in his tracks and turned. In his black outfit and cloak, with the sword at his side, all he needed was a flat-topped black hat and mask and he could have passed for Zorro. *A mask.* When he had grabbed her and dragged her across his saddle, he'd had on a mask, and so had the other man they'd left behind.

Maggie clutched the blanket more tightly around her shoulders, new fears lacing through her. What was a guy dressed like someone out of a horror flick or some kind of cheesy adventure film doing in this part of Scotland? And why had he and his friend been riding like every demon in hell was at their heels when she stepped into the road? And *why* had someone shot his friend?

"Who are you?" she said, brushing one long strand of hair back from her face as the wind whipped against her. "What are you doing out here dressed like some kind of bandit?"

In two long strides he was next to her again and she gasped as he grabbed her, this time pulling her full against him. "Who the hell are *ye*?" he demanded, the smell of whiskey on his breath, his chest hard beneath her hands. "Ye appear out of nowhere and in one moment, ye destroy Ian's life and mine as well!"

Maggie closed her eyes, fighting sudden hot tears burning against her eyelids. What if it was true? What if she'd been responsible for someone's death? She opened her eyes and let the tears spill down her cheeks.

"I—I'm sorry," she said. "I'm Maggie Graham. I'm from the U.S., Texas actually." He stared at her blankly. She rushed on, "You know the colonies. I'm very, very sorry if I caused your friend to fall off his horse, but you know, I wasn't the one who shot him!"

She was close enough now, and the sky light enough, to see that his eyes weren't black, as she'd thought, but a dark forest green. She stared into them, trying to keep her panic under control by focusing on the thin band of blue green that edged his irises and the flecks of that same color near the center.

"Nay," he said, "ye dinna pull the trigger, but when ye rushed into the pathway of Ian's horse and he went down, ye gave him over into the hands of the duke's men!" He pushed her away from him, and she stumbled back a step, stunned.

Maggie opened and closed her mouth a couple of times before she could respond to that statement. The Duke? Wasn't John Wayne dead?

"Look," she said, fighting her need to cry while trying to sound confident, which made her voice a rather stern croak, "do you have a cell phone? Let's call the police. I'll tell my part of it. You obviously know who shot your friend, so the sooner you call the authorities, the sooner you'll find out what happened to him."

He shook his head. "Yer words have no meaning to me."

Her temper flared and she glared back at him. "Look, you stubborn"—she tried to think of a good insult, but her nerve faltered as he continued to face her down—"man," she amended. "You know, blaming me isn't going to absolve you of your part in this. You were the one who made his horse rear back like that, when you—uh—rescued me."

Which technically still made it her fault. Maggie lifted her chin, quivering inside. The man's face went ashen, and Maggie remembered why she never stood up to people. It always seemed to backfire and make her feel worse than ever. And guilty. Then the color returned to his face and he nodded.

"Aye," he said softly as he took a step toward her, his eyes like emerald glass. "T'was my fault. I should have let ye been run down, and then none of this would have happened."

Maggie felt heat rise to her cheeks, even as fear gripped her by the throat. "I didn't do anything—at least not on purpose! I was confused and lost and I ran into the road looking for help. How was I to know that you and your friend were—having a race?"

He laughed shortly and shook his head, turning abruptly to walk back toward the fire. "A race!" He dragged one hand through his hair and looked back at her, his features now somber, though framed in disbelief. "Aye, a race for our lives."

He sat down on the huge stone and folded his arms across his chest. Maggie hesitated but, determined to get to the bottom of his accusations, took a step toward him, still clutching the blanket around her shoulders. "You had on masks last night, didn't you? You and your friend."

He shot her a sharp look and then shrugged. "Aye."

"Why? Were you on your way to a costume party?" she repeated. "Or some kind of equestrian-Zorro-vampire-look-alike thing?" She smiled faintly at the absurdity of her words and received a frown in return.

"Ye talk and ye talk, but yer words make no sense," he said, shaking his head. He picked up the bagpipe lying on the stone beside him and began to carefully place it into a leather bag.

"It was you playing the pipes," Maggie said. "I thought I was dreaming."

"Aye," he said, his voice almost gentle, "'twas all just a dream. I hope *yer* dreams are filled with remorse and shame."

"Well, that's not a nice thing to say," Maggie said.

"I am not nice."

He continued to almost reverently put the instrument away. When he seemed sure it was covered properly, he reached into another leather satchel and took out an earthenware bottle.

"What is that?" she asked.

"Whiskey. Do ye want a drink?"

Maggie took a deep breath. She'd wanted adventure and excitement in her life—well, here it was in spades. At that moment the morning mist rose up and she shivered. A shot of whiskey sounded pretty good and she opened her mouth to say yes, when her practical side thrust itself front and center.

She didn't know this guy, didn't know what was in the bottle, and keeping her wits about her was the only smart thing to do. She reached for her backpack at her feet.

"No, that's okay. I have a bottle of water." She took out her Ozarka and took a long drink. "Ah, that's good."

He didn't answer, and Maggie looked up to see him tip the earthenware bottle to his lips and take a drink that seemed to go on for minutes.

"Uh, don't you think you've had enough, maybe?" she asked.

He shook his head and took another drink, his voice growing more slurred, his eyes unfocused. "T'will never be enough. Never enough whiskey to wash away my guilt." He stood and lifted the bottle in her direction. "Here's to ye, lass. To the only woman who could break up a beautiful friendship."

"I'm sorry," Maggie whispered.

"Aye," he said, his voice almost gentle, "so am I." He hefted the bag onto his shoulder and then turned and walked away from her, his gait unsteady.

After watching him for a moment, Maggie realized he didn't intend to come back.

"Hey!" she yelled. "Wait a minute!" She hurried to catch up with him as he continued to stride away from her. "Where are you going? What about the police?"

He stopped abruptly and she ran smack into his back. Her head began to throb again and she wavered as the man turned around, a scowl on his face.

"I dinna ken what this 'police' is that ye keep babblin' about," he said. "Ian is dead and I must plot my revenge."

"Of course you must," Maggie said faintly. A new wave of dizziness hit her, and she instinctively held out her hand for support. Alarm darted across his face and his arms went around her waist, just as her knees gave way. She leaned against him, breathing deeply, the rough wool of his cloak scratching her face, the smell of whiskey and rain and something definitely male permeating her senses.

"Are ye all right, lass?" he asked, almost kindly, his voice liquid, his lips so close to her cheek that all she would have to do was turn her head and his mouth would be against hers.

She didn't dare, but oh, how she wanted to. Wanted to lift her face to his and feel the warmth and the passion of his mouth as their lips met and their tongues touched and—

Maggie blinked and shook her head. *Okay, I must have a concussion.* Maybe she had hit her head during that mad ride across the heather. With effort, she lifted her face from his chest and looked up at him, then drew in a sharp breath at the unexpected concern in his eyes.

His gaze locked with hers, and drifted to her mouth. He lifted one hand from her waist to cup the side of her face, his thumb smoothing her cheek and stopping just short of touching her lower lip.

You don't even know his name. Oh, and let's not forget—someone just killed his friend! He may be next. Get out of the line of fire.

Sense returned to Maggie like a wave of salt water, washing over her, sending strength back into her legs. She straightened away from him and ran her tongue across her lips. Something glinted in his gaze, and this time it wasn't concern.

"Thank you," she said hoarsely. No, that didn't sound right. She cleared her throat. "For catching me. I was dizzy, but I'm okay now. Except I'm still lost." She took another breath and added, inanely, "I got separated from my group somehow."

He frowned and took a step back, as if he had come to

his senses as well. "Yer group? I dinna ken what ye're talking about, lass, and I have no time to care for ye." He shook his head. "I must go to Rob Roy and tell him of Ian. He will be sore unhappy to hear such dismal news."

He turned away, but Maggie reached out and stopped him, laying one hand on his arm. "Rob Roy? MacGregor? The outlaw?"

His brow darkened again, and she quickly backed away a step. "He is no outlaw. The accusations against him are false!"

"Okay, okay, just calm down." Maggie thought quickly. This was worse than she'd thought. The guy had either gotten so drunk that some major brain cells had been fried, or he was nuts.

But maybe it was just a too-many-tequilas-too-many-nights-without-sleep kind of nuts. She'd known some Scottish history majors in college who had partied so hard after finals that they started talking Gaelic, even though they were all from Amarillo. And wasn't there some kind of Renaissance Faire this weekend? Sure, Alex had invited her to it! Maybe this guy was just a little too into the persona he'd chosen.

Maybe.

Okay, so she was a little scared, but if the man was going to hurt her, he'd had all night to accost her, and he hadn't. She needed help getting back to Alex and the others, and like it or not, this guy was it. He was probably harmless.

Yeah, right. So why did her blood pressure go up ten points any time she got within two feet of him? *That has nothing to do with fear,* her wiser self noted.

"Okay, I'm in total agreement with you," she said, trying to sound soothing. "Rob Roy is the best, without a doubt. My personal hero, hands down."

She must have imagined that previous look of concern,

because now his eyes were as hard as steel. No way he felt anything for anyone—except maybe his friend, Ian.

"I must go," he said, turning to do just that.

"Wait!"

He looked back at her, his eyes bleary.

"Look," she said quickly, before he could walk away again, "I need your help. I'm lost. Please don't leave me out here alone."

"Why should I help ye?" the man asked.

"Um, because you're a gentleman?"

"I am no gentleman," he said.

"Because you're a nice guy?" she said, getting exasperated.

"I told ye before, I am not nice."

Maggie released her breath in frustration. "Fine. Then who the hell are you?"

He stopped and swung back around, the black cloak arching like Batman's cape behind him as the wind lifted it, his lips curved up in what could only be called a sardonic smile. He bowed, one hand to his chest, his tone sarcastic.

"They call me the Piper, and I, dear lady, am a highwayman."

five

After his dramatic pronouncement, the man turned and walked away *again*. Tears burned in Maggie's eyes and she brushed them quickly away with the back of her hand. She refused to give in to the helplessness that rushed over her at the thought of being left alone in the Highlands.

"Well, that's just fine then!" she shouted after him. She searched her mind for something really bad to call him that wouldn't make him want to come back and do her bodily harm, but would make her feel better. A scene from one of her favorite movies gave her the ammunition she needed.

"Do you know what you really are, Mr. Piper? You're a—a Mondo-dizmo—that's what you are!"

He kept walking.

"And by the way," she shouted after him, "love your fashion statement for the undead!"

A highwayman. The guy was delusional all right. That explained the mask, sort of, and the attitude. Too bad, because he sure was cute.

She turned away and surveyed the dying campfire. The

problem was, the "highwayman" had been her only apparent hope of getting back to civilization. She ought to go after him. Rachel would.

Heck, Rachel would have already tackled the guy and kickboxed him into next week. The thought cheered her, only to be followed by an immediate letdown. She wasn't Rachel. She was a chicken.

Maggie took a deep, ragged breath as the practicality that had seen her through Allie's first date and Ellie's first tattoo began to calm her down. Maybe it was better just to let the guy go. She'd report him to the cops or Scotland Yard or somebody, as soon as she got to a phone. After all, there couldn't be that many guys in the Highlands dressed all in black, wearing a vampire cloak.

With his dark hair and mesmerizing green eyes, he reminded her of one of the heroes in her favorite paranormal romances. Of course, this wasn't a romance novel, and just because he was a really sexy rogue, alpha-male type, it was always good to remember that in real life those kinds of guys were not usually heroes. They were usually the bad guys.

Which he obviously was, since he'd admitted to being a thief and had refused to help her and then left her to rot in the Highlands. Of course, he *had* caught her when she almost fainted.

And then left her to rot.

Maggie sighed. Yeah. Right. So maybe she should just forget about vampire boy and find her own way back to civilization. There were no heroes in real life. Well, not many. The ones that did exist sure weren't lining up to do her any favors. She was on her own. As usual.

She gazed around at the beautiful wilderness surrounding her, and then looked up at the breathtaking sky, feeling infinitely insignificant. From the looks of the clouds gathering above, her insignificant self was about to get drenched. Again.

Suddenly drained of energy, Maggie sank to the ground and tried to think. How, in the space of a few hours, had she gone from enjoying a dream-come-true trip to Scotland to getting completely lost while standing still and becoming responsible for a man's death? She leaned her head against her hands, her elbows propped on her knees.

Had it been her fault? And if so, how could she live with herself, knowing she had caused the death of another person? But he'd been shot—surely the man who had saved her couldn't truly blame her. The memory of his irate, handsome face came back to her clearly.

Oh, yeah, he could.

Maggie sighed and glanced up. The sun might have risen, but its light had barely penetrated through the gray clouds above, casting a melancholy pallor over the land. She gathered the plaid blanket around her shoulders as a host of questions reverberated through her mind. She had almost fallen asleep, when the soft nicker of a horse permeated the fog around her mind and Maggie looked up. She grinned.

The drunk vampire had left his horse behind.

Quinn hadn't gone far from the woman, just around several large stones, before he stumbled and fell facedown. He had a fleeting thought about leaving his horse behind before he passed out entirely, but wasn't worried. Saint would never go far from him.

When he opened his eyes again, he felt as though a horse—a huge horse from the bowels of hell—had found him and kicked in his head, so miserably did it pound as he lay watching the red gold sun balance upon a distant

mountain peak. For a moment, he had no idea how he had
come to be in such a state, then he remembered—Ian and
the woman and the despair that had driven him to his foolish overindulgence.

It was the woman who stood out in his mind. He remembered some of the things he had said to her and was
slightly ashamed. The girl had been scared to death and
had turned to him for help, and he had frightened her all
the more and then abandoned her. She was probably crying
her eyes out right now.

Quinn sat up then, too quickly, and reached up with
both hands to steady his head, feeling if he didn't, it might
fall off his shoulders. When he was fairly sure it would stay
attached, he drew his legs up in front of him and leaned his
forehead carefully against his knees. As soon as he could
stand, he'd go back to the woman and retrieve his horse.
She was certainly too timid of a lass to try and mount the
stallion by herself.

He closed his eyes, and without warning, an image of her
face when she'd first awakened danced through his mind.
Blue eyes, the shape of a cat's, the color of the Scottish sky
on one of its rare days of sunshine, had gazed back at him,
startled, afraid. And that mouth. That beautiful mouth.

What had she said her name was? Ah, yes, Maggie. Well,
Maggie was lovely and scared and he had tried to punish her
by frightening her with his drunkenness. A cloud of melancholy settled over him. Who was he trying to fool? The lass
was not to blame for Ian's death, he was. He raised his head,
his breath catching in his throat as a sudden thought struck
him.

He had only heard the gunshot and then seen Ian col-
lapse. The lad might have survived. It was possible. Montrose's men could have dragged him back to the duke's
well-known dungeon and left him there to die from his
gunshot wound. The thought had the power to sober Quinn

quickly. His heart began to pound harder as he dared to hope.

It would take time for information to leak from the hallowed halls of Montrose's manor to the glen, time that was too precious to waste. Perhaps he could sneak inside the laird's household and find out what had happened to Ian. He shook his head.

Quinn MacIntyre was no more welcome in Montrose's home than if the man had known he was the Piper. If he was seen on the duke's property, he'd be arrested. And getting thrown into the gaol with his friend would only ensure Ian's certain doom, and his own, though he would prefer being in prison with Ian to doing nothing.

He rose from the stone and began to pace in spite of his throbbing headache. The satchel holding Ian's bagpipes rode over one shoulder and bumped against his hip as he walked. He was getting ahead of himself, he knew that. Ian was probably dead.

But what if he wasn't? What if God in His infinite mercy had deigned to save his friend from death and give Quinn the chance to make things right?

All right, then. If Ian was alive, Quinn would need someone inside the manor, someone who wouldn't raise suspicions. A woman possibly. A maid or cook.

Quinn slowly came to a stop. The lass had felt badly about Ian, he could see that, in spite of her harsh words. She wanted to make things right and if he gave her the chance . . .

Quinn smiled and headed back the way he had come.

Maggie lay under a big, black horse.

Using the wannabe vampire's horse to make her escape back to civilization had seemed like a good idea, but the animal was taller than she'd realized, and when she put her foot in the stirrup, the dumb horse had started walking away.

Her foot wouldn't come out of the stirrup. She'd had to hop sideways to keep from falling, and finally her foot came free and she fell flat on her back anyway.

The big animal decided to do a two-step back to the left and suddenly Maggie found herself staring up at the underbelly of the beast. Where she lay now, too scared to move, getting up close and personal with parts of a horse that should be housed in a very large pair of horse pants.

Great. This was just terrific. She closed her eyes. Maybe this was her payback for what had happened to Ian.

"So ye feel badly about my friend's untimely demise?"

Maggie's eyes flew open. The man in black knelt beside her, gazing at her. He looked a little more sober than he had an hour or so ago, but looks could be deceiving. And he must have switched into ninja mode, because she hadn't heard even a footstep.

A crazy ninja-vampire-outlaw who could read her mind. It was official: She was losing it.

"Wh-what?" she stuttered.

"Before I left, ye said ye felt badly about your part in what happened to Ian."

Oh, yeah. Good. No supernatural powers at work here. Maggie cleared her throat. "I do feel bad—badly—about the accident," she said, looking up at him earnestly. "Get me out from under your horse, please?"

A glimmer of humor danced through his eyes and he stroked the stubble on his face with one hand. "Well, I dinna know about that, lassie. I think I need a few assurances first."

Great. Chivalry really was dead. "Look, please believe me, I didn't run out in front of your friend on purpose. I was lost and I stumbled down that hillside and straight into his path. If there is anything I can do to make amends—"

she broke off, realizing how lame that was. What could she do that would ever make up for inadvertently causing another person's death?

"What would ye do?" he asked, his dark brows knitting together, not in anger this time, but in thoughtful consideration. He gazed down at her, his green eyes unreadable.

She shook her head. "I don't know. Anything. Whatever I could." Maggie felt the tears start again. Darn, but she was a crybaby!

He frowned. "Ye would do anything?"

Maggie took a deep breath and swallowed hard. Next to her head, the horse's feet shifted, and she hurried to answer. "Yes, I mean, anything within reason, but no matter what I might do, I can't bring him back. I wish I could."

"Ah, lass, ye might just be surprised at what the power of a willing heart can do." He unfolded his arms, and his black cloak billowed behind him as he reached down and grabbed her by the wrists. His fingers were long and square, the skin roughened, callused, the hands of a man who worked for a living.

"Be still, Saint," he said to the horse. The shifting of Saint's feet immediately stopped and the animal stayed immobile for the few seconds it took the man to pull her from underneath its belly. He helped her to her feet and his hands lingered for a moment at her waist.

"Er, maybe I need to rephrase that," she said. "When I say I'll do anything within reason, I mean—"

His hands fell away from her. "I know what ye mean, lass. I am no a blackguard, for all ye may think me one."

Blackguard? Now that was a word you didn't hear every day. But this was Scotland, after all.

"Now," he said, staring down at her, looking much too tall and much too handsome, "if ye meant what ye said, I would like to apologize to ye."

"Yeah?" she asked suspiciously. "Really?"

"Aye. I think I may have misjudged ye," he said.

Maggie felt a wave of relief sweep over her. "You have? I mean, yes, you have!"

"Aye." He took her hand, and she blinked as he brought it up to his chest, cradling it there, his gaze burning into hers. "I see now that ye are simply a damsel in distress, one with a gentle heart," he said. "My apologies for my drunken behavior earlier. I was distraught."

Maggie stared up at him, a ripple of something very nice dancing under her skin. When he finally released her hand, the loss of his touch was like the absence of the sun.

Aw, heck no, Maggie, you don't like bad boys, not one little bit.

"That's all right."

"Ian and I have been friends for a very long time. He is like a brother to me. Ye can understand how seeing him shot down like a dog would be upsetting."

Maggie nodded, all sympathy now that he was being nice. "Of course. Sure. I really understand. It was an awful thing."

His green eyes shifted to the side and a muscle just above his jaw twitched. "I must ride and seek counsel from Rob Roy."

Maggie hesitated before she spoke. "MacGregor? Rob Roy MacGregor?" He had mentioned the name of the historical figure earlier, pouncing on her in anger when she called the man an outlaw.

"Aye." He nodded to himself, his eyes burning with a fanatic intensity. "Rob will know what to do."

She blinked. "You're talking about *the* Rob Roy MacGregor."

A sudden smile lit his face, and Maggie's knees melted. "Och, lass there is only one Rob Roy MacGregor."

"The one who had a little tiff with the Duke of Montrose?" she asked, trying to ignore how green his eyes were—like the distant Scottish hills.

He laughed shortly. "*Tiff* ye call it? Montrose has accused him of stealing a thousand pounds from him! Called him an outlaw." He shook his head. "Rob is no outlaw." The man glanced back at her. "Ye will go with me."

Maggie stared. Okay, the guy thought he was living in some other time zone and was definitely cuckoo for Cocoa Puffs, but he was all she had.

Maggie smiled and started moving slowly backward, trying to put some distance between them. "You know, that sounds great, but I really need to get back to my friends. Hey, you wouldn't live around here somewhere would you? Somewhere with a phone and a car maybe?"

He frowned, following her as she continued to edge away from him. "I dinna know what ye are asking, lass." He shook his head. "So ye dinna mean what ye said, that ye would do anything to redeem yerself?"

Maggie felt the anguish wash over her again. "Of course I would, but what can I do? You said your friend was killed. I am so, so sorry."

He raised one brow, his graveled voice still a little slurred, but steadier than she'd heard it since they'd left his friend behind in the mud. "Well, lass, it occurred to me that perhaps I was hasty in that assessment. Perhaps Ian was shot, but is still alive, and the duke's men took him back to the manor for judgment."

Hope quickened inside of her. "Really? Do you think that's possible?"

He shrugged, one broad shoulder lifting beneath the thick black cloak. "We can only hope, until we find a way to know for certain."

"How can we find out?" she asked, and without thinking, reached out and laid her hand on his arm.

Now a full-fledged smile spread across his lips, and

Maggie felt stunned, melted, and destroyed, all in the same moment. He had been handsome before, but when he smiled, really smiled . . . he was simply gorgeous. Eccentric, but gorgeous.

She snatched her hand back. Maybe there was a way to find out if he wore black cloaks and masks all the time, or if this was just some kind of weekend game he played. She frowned. Maybe he just had some kind of bondage fetish. That would explain the black and the leather and the sword. Oh, yeah, *that* would make the idea of hooking up with him *lots* better!

Maggie didn't have much sexual experience, but what she did have was limited to the two fairly long-term relationships she'd had after her parents died. Both times, when things started getting serious, her boyfriends had expected her to dump her sisters and start a new life with them.

The first time, the girls were only fifteen and it was a total no-brainer. The second time, they were eighteen and about to graduate from high school. Ellie and Allie had urged her to forget about them and marry the guy, but as far as Maggie was concerned, if there wasn't room in his life for her sisters, he wasn't the man for her. In any case, neither of her boyfriends had been kinky. In fact, they'd been a little boring. This guy was anything but boring.

"Ye are following my thoughts exactly, lass," he told her, moving closer.

"Um, I hope not," she muttered. "What—what were we talking about?"

He frowned thoughtfully. "We will wait on going to see Rob. First, we must find out if Ian is alive. We will ride to Montrose's home first."

Maggie frowned and took a step back from him. Okay, things were weird, but that didn't mean she was going to just take off across the countryside with him. Maybe all of this was a scam—Ian, the accident, all of it.

"Before, when you were, er, drinking, you said you were a highwayman. You were just kidding, right?" It was getting warmer now that the sun had risen higher, and she shrugged out of her jacket.

"*Kidding?* Ye talk strangely, lass."

"I mean, were you, uh, jesting, when you said that you were a highwayman? You aren't really wanted or anything, are you?"

His hand closed around her upper arm and Maggie pulled back, startled. He gave her a broad smile and tugged her toward his horse, seeming unperturbed. "I am wanted by many—all comely lasses," he said.

Maggie frowned. "Look, who are you? I won't turn you in or anything—I mean, as long as you don't hurt me."

"Hurt ye?" His gaze softened, and for a moment Maggie couldn't breathe. Then he raised his hand and swept a few strands of hair back from her face, his fingers slipping against her cheek and then above her ears as he tucked the tendrils away. "Och, lass, the last thing I want to do is hurt ye."

Maggie sucked in a sharp breath as he held her gaze for a long moment, before looking away and dropping his hand back to his side. She swallowed hard, feeling completely bereft. "Well, good," she said into the silence, "that's good to know."

He raked his hand through his dark, raggedly beautiful hair. "The last thing I've ever wanted is to hurt anyone, though God knows, that seems to be all I do."

For a moment, Maggie couldn't speak. Her heart ached too badly for this tortured soul, this extremely sexy bad boy, this beautiful, passionate nut. It suddenly struck her that she didn't even know his name.

"Tell me who you are. Please?" she whispered.

He lifted his chin and seemed to grow visibly taller before her eyes. "My name is Quinn MacIntyre." The fire in his eyes dimmed, and he looked away from her, even as he continued to speak. "I dinna wonder that ye hesitate, lass, but I swear upon my mother's grave, no harm will come to ye."

Maggie swallowed hard. "Well, it's very nice to meet you, Quinn, but uh, I really think that . . ." Her voice faded as he cocked one dark brow and his jaw tightened.

"If ye regret what happened," he finally said, "prove it now by helping me." One corner of his mouth quirked up. "After all, I did rescue ye from a fate worse than death."

Maggie gave him a hesitant smile. "Fate worse than death?"

"Aye," he said, sounding serious, "being pissed on by an irritated stallion."

"Okay," she said. "I'll go with you to the duke's house. But I need to go back to the cairn first. Do you know where it is?"

"A large cairn? Many small stones?"

"Yes," she said eagerly. "If you'll take me there first and let me check in with my friends, I'll be happy to go with you."

"Of course," he said, still smiling, as he led her to his horse.

As Quinn helped the woman up into Saint's saddle, he once again marveled at the strange clothing she wore underneath his plaid. For one thing, she wore a pair of breeches that were pale pink, with what appeared to be a pattern of—he had to look twice—the head of a white cat. The blouse she wore with it was made of the same odd but soft material, and cut in a mannish style.

Her footwear was equally strange—heavy black boots that laced up the front—totally incongruous with the pastel clothing she wore. The heavy jacket she'd worn was too difficult to hold and too hot to wear, so Quinn tied it behind the saddle, along with the pack she clung to so fervently.

She had trouble mounting the horse, and without thinking, Quinn put the palm of one hand on her backside and pushed, the pressure lifting her up and into the saddle. She looked down at him, startled and lovely, her auburn hair unbound and waving down her pink-covered back. Meanwhile, the hand that had touched her soft and rounded bottom felt as if it had been dowsed in flames.

"Thank you for letting me ride your horse," she said. "I feel guilty that you have to walk, though."

He raised both brows. "Do ye now? Well, dinna worry on that score." Quinn placed his foot on top of the stirrup, grasped the side of the saddle, and with an ease born of long practice, slipped into place behind her. She gasped slightly as he lifted her, letting her bottom rest on his lap and her legs curve over the top of his. He drew in his own sharp breath. The cloth was very thin.

Perhaps this was not such a good idea.

"Of course, if I make ye uncomfortable, lass—"

"No," she said quickly. Her cheeks were red, but she seemed calm enough. "I've done enough to you and yours since I met you without making you walk."

Weel, not quite enough. The wicked thought danced through his mind before he could stop it. Saints above knew that it was hard enough—nay, dinna think that thought—it was *difficult* enough to be pressed beneath the lass without he himself entertaining lustful thoughts. A cloud passed in front of the sun and a cool breeze suddenly kicked up. He tossed his plaid around his shoulders and draped the rest of it around her, enclosing them, creating a heat that chased away the chill in the air.

Long tendrils of her red gold hair drifted in the wind and against his face, the perfume of the locks sending a shudder through him, straight down into his nether parts. This was never going to work. He should get off and walk.

But he didn't want to get off and walk. He wanted to stay right where he was, pressed against the softness of this strange lass. Truth be told, he wanted to take her from the saddle and bundle her away to some wee bed where . . .

"Are we going?" She turned slightly and looked back at him, her blue eyes wide with concern and a little fear.

"Aye, we are going." He slipped one arm around her waist. Her sharp intake of breath told him that she was no more immune to their bodies touching than he was, and for some reason, that made him bold. He gathered the reins in his right hand and pulled her firmly against him.

"What are you doing?" she asked, her voice wavering.

"Keepin' ye from fallin' off, lass. Of course, if ye'd rather walk . . ." There was challenge in his words and the woman glanced back at him hesitantly. Then he saw something new in her eyes that he hadn't seen before. Strength.

"No, I don't want to walk," she said, as she shifted her weight to find a more comfortable spot and sent another surge of lust straight through his body.

She leaned her head back against him and yawned. "Is it all right if I go to sleep for a while?"

"Aye, lass," he said, "go to sleep."

"You won't let me fall, will you?" she asked, her voice anxious.

Quinn resisted the urge to rub his face into her tresses, resisted the urge to slide his hand upward from her waist to cup one of the full, firm breasts above it, resisted the need growing within him, and instead answered her with a steadiness to his voice that surprised even him.

"No, lass," he said, "I willna let ye fall."

six

Maggie was bone tired and weary, but that didn't mean she wasn't aware of every movement of the man straddling the horse behind her. Every time the sure, steady hooves hit a hole or a downward slope, Maggie had no choice but to feel Quinn MacIntyre's hard, muscled chest pressing against her and his strong fingers holding her tightly to keep her safe.

Safe—that was the craziest thing of all. She did feel safe. Even though she was mounted on horseback with a guy who liked to run around the countryside playing cowboys and Indians, or the Scottish equivalent, she felt completely and utterly safe. He wouldn't let her fall.

"So tell me more about yourself," she said suddenly, as they ambled across the countryside.

"I thought ye were sleeping." His rough voice rumbled against her back, and she closed her eyes from the sheer physical joy of feeling it.

"Too bouncy. So where are you from originally?"

"Glenoe."

The silence stretched between them again.

"So do your parents live there, in Glenoe?"

He didn't answer for several long minutes. "Nay, my parents are dead."

"Mine are, too." Maggie couldn't help thinking that this coincidence gave them a common bond. She cleared her throat. "Any brothers or sisters? I have two sisters."

"Nay," he said again, "my only brother was hanged by the Duke of Montrose, along with my father."

Maggie went cold inside. Hangings? Did they do that anymore? Maybe in Scotland they did. Or maybe the guy was, as she suspected, nuts.

"I'm sorry," she said carefully. "Why were they hanged?"

"They reived the duke's cattle."

"Reived?" she frowned, and then whirled around in the saddle, sure her outrage was dancing in her eyes. "You mean stole? They hanged them for stealing cattle? That's crazy!"

"Aye, mad as a fox, that's Montrose. The day he hanged them, 'twas said he stood at the foot of the gallows as he guzzled his wine and ate a turkey leg. And laughed."

He sure sounded sane. Maybe it was true. Maybe there was some kind of "Wild West" justice in the Highlands. She decided to go along with him, for the moment.

"To think that in this day and age, a person could be hanged for such a thing—why, it's outrageous!" Maggie said. "Why don't you write your congressman, or Parliament, or whatever you have up here? Why don't you protest? Demand to see the Queen!"

A wry grin made his mouth quirk up even as he frowned at her. "I have no contacts at court, and Parliament was dissolved when they signed the Act of Union."

Maggie remained silent. It didn't seem polite to remind him that the Act of Union was signed in 1707, and the

Scots had their own Parliament now. The guy really was messed up. But so, so hot.

His fingers contracted against her waist, and Maggie closed her eyes, not wanting to feel the warmth and safety, afraid to feel the sheer, unadulterated comfort his touch promised. *And* the possibility of sex with him.

Oh yeah, he was promising that, too, or at least offering, no doubt about it. Even though she'd come to Scotland to find excitement in her life, she probably ought to draw the line at making love to delusional Scotsmen.

Probably. She tried to steer him back into reality.

"So you don't mean that the duke actually ordered your brother and father's execution? The court did, right? I didn't know Scotland had the death penalty."

"My father was no one important. The duke will kill any man caught reiving his cattle. Now, ye should try to sleep. We've a ways to go before we reach our destination."

"All right, I'll shut up," she said, fighting a yawn. She began nodding off as the steady rhythm of the horse beneath them lulled her to sleep in his arms. Some time later she awoke. They were riding over a tall hill and when they came to the top, Quinn pulled up on the reins and paused.

Groggily Maggie realized she'd spent precious little time on being a tourist since this strange part of her vacation began. Now, she sat up and released her breath in wonder. Below them a big, dark lake stretched like a crazy black opal in the middle of an emerald, with purple amethyst mountains beyond. Mist hovered over the water and across the green grass beside the loch.

"It's beautiful," she said.

"Aye, Loch Lomond is lovely this time of year."

She nodded, and then his words hit her. Loch Lomond? She knew little about the geography of Scotland, but she knew that you couldn't see Loch Lomond from the cairn.

She squinted in another direction and saw something familiar—a very large mountain. It was just in the wrong place. "That mountain," she said. "What is it called?"

"Ben Lomond."

Maggie turned, one hand unfortunately landing on his thigh as she gazed back at him, her heart pounding. "We aren't going to the cairn, are we?"

Quinn's long-lashed eyelids drifted down and then up again, and she saw regret mirrored in his green eyes.

"You said you would take me," she said, her voice shaking a little. It had been so easy to trust him. "You promised."

"I'm sorry, lass. I swear I will take ye, but first I must find out about Ian."

Don't panic, don't panic, don't panic, she thought, fighting to maintain her calm. She just had to think, decide what to do, make a plan.

Oh, to hell with it. Maggie threw her head back and screamed bloody murder, struggling with all of her strength against Quinn's tight hold until he finally pulled the horse to a stop and released her. She half slid, half fell to the ground and glared up at him.

"This is where I get off, bucko."

His dark brows collided. "Have ye lost yer wits? That screechin' will bring every man in the Highlands. Now climb back up here. We must ride on. Ye must be ready to work in the morning."

"Work?" Maggie frowned up at him. "What are you talking about?"

"Get back on the horse," he ordered, ignoring her question.

"No. I think it's time you told me exactly what your plans are." She put her hands on her hips and glared.

Quinn hesitated and then gave her a brilliant smile that lit his entire face. She stood there for a moment, feeling stunned, almost like someone hypnotized. If he told her to get on the horse again, she'd probably walk forward like a zombie and obey him. Maggie shook her head and tried to find her anger again.

"Och, lass," he said softly, leaning over the saddle horn to gaze deeply into her eyes. "I'm sorry. 'Twas my hope that I could persuade ye to pose as a scullery maid and be my eyes and ears in Montrose's manor."

"Oh, really?" She cocked her head to one side. "So you just thought you'd send me into the house where the guys with the *guns* are? Forget it. Call. The. Police."

Quinn threw his right leg over the saddle and jumped down in front of her, glowering. "Ye promised—"

"I didn't promise." She cut him off, her voice sharp, as she began to back away. "I never said 'I promise to be some kind of servant.' I just said I'd help you—*after* you took me to the cairn."

"Ye said ye would do anything," he said, advancing toward her.

Maggie started to step back again, but instead stopped and held her ground.

"I said *almost* anything. But I didn't say I'd put myself at risk. And really, this is a dumb idea. You just need to go to the police." He frowned and she sighed. "Okay. Whatever. The *law*. They'll help you."

"Why is it so important for ye to return to the cairn right now?" he asked. He stood with one knee cocked, the reins of his horse trailing from his hand. The wind swept Quinn's hair back from his rugged face, and Maggie bit her lower lip as she gazed at him. If only they could have met under less—weird—circumstances.

"My friends are at the cairn. They're waiting for me, I told you."

"Yer friends will have to wait a little longer," he said, his green eyes dark and narrowed. "If we ride toward the setting sun, we can be at the manor by nightfall and—"

He broke off suddenly and grabbed Maggie by the arm, pulling her roughly against him with one sharp tug. As she knotted her fingers into his shirt to keep from falling, she realized his chest was fast becoming her favorite place to be. Still, she ought to protest—at least a little.

"Hey, what's the idea?"

"Get on the horse," he ordered. She looked up at him, startled by the dark tone of his voice. His eyes were fixed on something behind her, and she didn't like what she saw mirrored there. Maggie swallowed hard.

"Don't order me around," she said faintly.

Without another word, Quinn picked her up and strode quickly to Saint, where he tossed her into the saddle. As Maggie sprawled over the stallion's neck, Quinn vaulted into place behind her and sent Saint plunging forward, just as a shout pierced the Highlands behind them.

Maggie craned her neck around and wished she hadn't. A dozen or more men on horseback charged after them, waving swords, some of them brandishing pistols. Old pistols. "Who are they?" she cried, clutching the saddle horn and part of the horse's mane. Quinn didn't answer.

Maggie couldn't remember ever being on a horse and going this fast, and she closed her eyes, absolutely terrified. They rode for some time, pounding across the Highlands, when all at once she heard Quinn curse. Saint lurched sharply to the right, and her eyes flew open as they skidded to a stop.

"What are you doing?" she shouted, and then lost her breath as he pulled her leg over the saddle and pushed her off the horse to the ground. She landed on her side and lay there gasping, trying to get the air back in her lungs as he thundered away from her.

Maggie stared after him in horror. He'd realized he could make better time without the extra burden and was abandoning her—leaving her for the cutthroats chasing after them! She found her breath.

"Quinn!" she screamed his name, her heart thudding so hard she thought it would burst from her chest.

He looked back over one shoulder and pulled back on the reins, making Saint rear back. "Take cover!" he cried. "I will return for ye!" He threw her jacket, pack, and the extra plaid to the ground, then dug his heels into his horse's sides and was gone, leaving Maggie to stare after him.

Another shout from behind blasted her out of her shock. Trembling in terror, she ran and grabbed the things he had tossed down and threw herself behind a nearby cluster of bushes just before a dozen or more horses came barreling up the hill in her direction.

"Quinn MacIntyre," she whispered, "you are dead meat!"

Right at the corner of her hiding place, the mountain and trees and bushes around her met. There was a narrow passage for the riders and they slowed as each man urged his horse through, giving Maggie a chance to see exactly who was chasing Quinn.

The leader of the riders was a man in a long, curling wig and a tricornered hat, like something out of the 1700s. His long, embroidered coat and knee pants were just as astonishing, and the other men surging by were dressed in a similar manner, except they didn't wear wigs; their hair was pulled back in short ponytails under their tricornered hats.

It didn't make a lick of sense, but maybe they were just the local authorities. How else could they track down criminals in the Highlands except on foot or by horseback? Right. Wearing costumes. Or maybe they were part of some kind of reenactment society and they were also the police. And maybe the pistols she'd thought she'd seen in their hands—old muzzle-loading pistols—had just been a trick of the eye. They'd probably been brandishing tasers or something. And the swords—well, this was Scotland. That well-worn excuse was losing its luster as far as Maggie was concerned.

She thought about heading for the cairn, but had no idea where she was. Quinn might be nuts, but so far he seemed to be a harmless nut. The guys chasing him hadn't looked quite so innocuous. The safest course of action was to wait for Quinn to return.

By sundown, it was apparent that Quinn wasn't coming back. The hard ground grew colder beneath her after the sun disappeared, and if it hadn't been for her jacket and the plaid, Maggie felt sure she'd have died of hypothermia. As it was, she spent the worst night of her life, shivering under a bush, half-starved, with only the half-filled bottle of water in her backpack to keep her from total panic.

When the sun came up the next morning, she'd slept little, but only too gladly dragged herself up off the ground. After taking care of a very urgent problem—she was sure she would never feel quite the same about leaves again—Maggie started walking. Only the thought of what she would do to Quinn MacIntyre when she saw him again kept her moving.

Maggie had been walking for eons. Or at least it felt like she had. She stopped at the top of yet another hill, and dragged in a deep, weary breath. Not exactly the Scottish holiday she'd dreamed of, where she'd find her soul mate and ride off into the Highlands with him forever.

She turned back toward the sun to get her bearings. Maybe she was going about this the wrong way. She'd spent her time walking away from the sun, thinking that would lead her to the cairn, but so far she hadn't seen anything familiar. Maybe it would be better to go to the manor house. If she walked toward the sun, she'd get there. She knew, sort of, how to reach it, and surely someone there would have a phone. With a sigh, she started walking again.

An hour later she stood staring at a very large, dark loch. Loch Lomond? There were a billion lochs in Scotland, she supposed. The trick was in being able to tell the difference between them, something she didn't think she'd ever be able to do. They all looked the same to her.

Maybe Quinn could teach her how to—she stopped the thought with a humorless laugh. If she ever *did* see Quinn MacIntyre again, she sure wouldn't waste time getting geographical lessons from him. She'd be too busy using his good-looking face as a punching bag. If ever there was a man who needed to be taught a lesson, it was her would-be rescuer.

She frowned as the wind picked up, gusting against her. Maybe there was another reason for Quinn's failure to return to her. What if he had been caught? No, Quinn was too smart for that. What if he'd been hurt?

A tendril of her hair blew into her face and Maggie dragged it back, ignoring the way her heart pounded at the thought of Quinn lying bleeding somewhere, alone. Or maybe he *had* been caught and was in a dank cell somewhere awaiting the dubious Scottish justice system. She was getting depressed, so she stopped thinking and drew in a deep, fortifying breath.

"Ye'd better start worryin' about yerself, lassie," Maggie announced to the hills, "and let the outlaws fend for themselves." She walked on. She'd finished the last of her water an hour ago, and so was thrilled when she stumbled across a beautiful clear stream. As she knelt beside it and refilled her bottle—surely these crystal clear waters were free of bacteria or anything harmful—a loud noise rumbled behind her. She threw herself flat on the ground, fearful the men who had chased them the day before had returned.

After a moment, the sound came again, and then again. All at once, Maggie realized what it was—someone nearby was snoring. Cautiously she raised her head.

On one hand, maybe this would be someone who would help her. On the other, this was obviously a man snoring, and she'd had enough of dealing with wild Highlanders to last her a lifetime.

Carefully easing back to her feet, she pinpointed where the sound was coming from—behind some large stones not too far from the brook. She moved quietly across the soft ground and peered around the edge of the large rock and almost passed out from surprise.

Quinn MacIntyre lay asleep on the ground, his plaid wrapped around him. Saint grazed nearby. The stones had blocked the stallion from her sight when she went to refill her water bottle. Now, as she watched the horse move farther away from the sleeping man, her need to kill Quinn faded as she saw a better way to get even.

She was lost.

Maggie sighed and stood up in the stirrups, taking the weight off of her backside. She gazed helplessly around at the beautiful countryside, trying to get her bearings, as Saint moved restlessly beneath her. She finally gave up and settled her sore bottom into the saddle again.

Maybe she had overreacted. Maybe she was losing her mind. Maybe she'd jumped to a wild conclusion, based on her own fear. Maybe Quinn had been her destiny, a gorgeous guy with edge, and what had she done? She'd stolen his horse and run away.

"Good going, Maggie," she muttered. She was just

lucky that Rachel wasn't here. She'd have delivered a sharp lecture on carpe diem, but in this case it would have translated to "seize the Scot."

Maggie still felt guilty about Quinn's friend being shot, but maybe Ian really wasn't dead. When she got back to civilization, she'd find out, call the police, or the Scottish equivalent. Maybe it would be in the newspapers.

But if Ian was robbing people, she didn't feel so guilty. She still didn't want him dead, but that was sort of the risk robbers took, wasn't it? So she would chalk Bad Boy Quinn up as an interesting experience and focus on finding a phone, a bus, a taxi, anything that would help her get back to civilization.

Suddenly, up ahead, gleaming in the hazy light of the setting sun, she saw a crumbling castle. As she watched, the fog shifted away from the ruins and sunlight lit the stones, turning them golden. For a moment she felt just like Dorothy must have as she stood in the field of poppies and gazed at the Emerald City. Awestruck and amazed. Except Oz wasn't real, and this definitely was.

Her stomach growled loudly. As real as the fact that she was starving to death. She lifted the reins again and muttered to Saint to move on. He headed downward again now, and with every jarring step, she wondered how much longer it would take before she got somewhere—anywhere? There was just a bare sliver of the red gold sun in the distance behind the dark purple hills, and too late she realized she should have stopped earlier and found shelter.

The ruins of the castle lay at the top of the next rise. She turned Saint's head toward the stones, quickening their pace. Camping within some kind of structure, even a crumbling one, would make her feel less exposed, she decided. Another night spent alone, sleeping on the cold, hard ground, with no midnight snack, was *not* her idea of fun.

But heck, she was having an *adventure*. And at least she had on her favorite jammies. She smiled, shaking her head at her lame attempt to boost her own spirits.

"Fortune and glory," she said out loud. "Fortune and glory."

An hour later, Maggie was sick of having an adventure and all she wanted was a warm soak in a deep bathtub, followed by a nice, soft bed. Instead, she had a hard piece of ground damp from an earlier rain, the kind of wet that the thickest blanket in Scotland couldn't keep out. And the ruins were not comforting, they were creepy.

After trying to get comfortable for an hour or more, she finally gave up. With her jacket zipped up tight, she leaned back against one of the tall stones to stare up at the stars brilliant against the backdrop of the summer sky. In the distance a wolf, or some other kind of animal, howled, and she shivered.

With a sigh, she stretched a little, easing the ache in her back. Instead she got a cramp in her leg. Well, she had walked a million miles that day, hadn't she?

Maggie stumbled to her feet and massaged her calf muscle. She didn't hear her attacker at all, just felt the sudden, hard sensation of a hand clamping over her mouth and another around her waist, slamming her back against a hard chest.

Her heart began to pound. This was great. Perfect. Not only had she gotten lost, now she was being kidnapped. Or worse.

"Dinna scream," said a deep voice that rumbled like a thundercloud. "T'will do ye no good for there is no one around to hear ye."

She swallowed hard and nodded. The man removed his hand from her mouth. "Wh-what do you want?" she stuttered.

He laughed, the dark, ominous sound sending a tremor

through her soul. "I have been sent to teach ye a lesson, and deliver a well-deserved punishment."

"Qu–Quinn sent you?" she quavered.

The man chuckled.

Maggie knew that chuckle. She whirled around.

Quinn MacIntyre stood there grinning like a Cheshire cat. "Good evening, Miss Maggie."

"You—you—"

"Mondo-dizmo?" he asked.

"Worse," Maggie said, trembling with fury. "You idiot! You scared the life out of me!"

Quinn crossed his arms over his broad chest, his green eyes amused. His dark, wavy hair danced in the wind, and even as Maggie thought about just how she was going to kill him, she couldn't help the way her heart fluttered at the sight of him.

He had changed his clothes. Gone was the black outfit, and in its place, he wore a kilt that was somehow pleated around him, but left enough material to loop across his chest and then his back, and his chest again, ending at the shoulder, where what looked like the antler of a deer was thrust to hold the cloth in place. He wore a wide belt and the Scottish version of a fanny pack—the sporran. Beneath the plaid was a rough-textured, cream-colored shirt, open at the neck, with full sleeves. Rough leather boots laced to his knees, golden brown and dirty.

Great. Maggie thought in disgust. *Now he thinks he's Braveheart!*

"How dare you scare me like that?" she said, her fists still clenched.

Quinn looked down at her and shrugged. "How dare ye steal my horse when I was sleeping?"

"I did not steal your horse!"

Saint, grazing nearby, nickered softly, threw his head back, and broke into a quick trot, headed straight for his master. Quinn laughed as the stallion stopped inches in front of him, nuzzling his nose against his owner's neck.

"Aye, I'm glad to see ye, too, ye old scalawag. Why did ye go with her in the first place?" The horse whinnied, and he laughed again. "I know, I know, ye never could turn down the lassies." He stroked the horse's neck with one hand and raised his gaze to Maggie's. "So, ye dinna steal my horse?"

Now he looked a little less amused. Time to do some damage control. Maggie strolled across the rough ground between them, her hands on her hips.

"Well, for your information, I've been looking for you so I could give this silly horse back to you! I found him wandering in the Highlands." She lifted her chin slightly. "Now that I think of it, maybe he was just coming to my rescue, after you dumped me."

Quinn knotted the reins together, never taking his gaze from her. "I came back for ye. Ye were gone."

A new wave of anger flooded over her. "Don't lie, Quinn MacIntyre."

His eyes sparked with answering fire. "I dinna lie. I came back for ye."

"I was there all night," she said, so furious she was shaking. "Lying on the cold, hard ground, waiting for you to show up. And you didn't. So this morning I started walking."

He shrugged. "I must have come after ye decided to leave. Montrose's men chased me the entire night. After I saw ye were gone, I went looking for ye, but when I stopped to rest Saint, I must have fallen asleep."

"Right. You were looking for me."

"Aye, I was. I am no lying." His gaze suddenly shifted back to her, once again narrowed. "So tell me, Maggie, how did you happen to stumble across Saint wandering in the hills?"

Oops. Okay, so she was lying, too. That didn't let him off the hook.

"I saw you sleeping near the stream," she said bluntly. "How did you know I took him?"

Quinn moved to sit down on a large rock. He cocked one leg and clasped his hands around his knee. "I saw yer wee footprint."

"Oh. Well, believe me, taking your horse was the least of what I wanted to do to you!" Maggie turned and walked away from him, finding her own stone to sit on. She flounced down on it and winced, then glared at him when he smiled.

He rubbed his chin. "Hmmm. What did ye want to do to me?"

Several illicit thoughts came to mind, but she managed not to blurt them out.

"Oh, I don't know, kick you where it would hurt?" She took her jacket off and put it on the rock, then sat back down. "And now I owe you twice the pain."

"I dinna hurt ye," Quinn said. "I was being . . . playful. It was a jest."

Maggie rolled her eyes. She'd had enough. "A jest. Playful. Look, jackass, you left me in the middle of nowhere and I wanted to pay you back. Also, I needed transportation, so I took your horse."

"So ye admit that ye stole my horse," he said. "I should bring ye up before the magistrate."

"But you won't do that," she said.

Quinn raised one brow. "I won't? And why is that?"

Maggie shook her head. "For some reason I think the authorities are the last people you want to see."

To her surprise, the glint in his eyes faded into a grudging admiration. "Aye, lass," he said, "ye understand the way of things. I'll no turn ye in for horse theft." His almost smile faltered and then disappeared completely. When he raised his head again, his eyes were darkly serious. "What happened to Ian is not yer fault. 'Tis mine. But I am asking ye, lass, to help me. I need someone to work in the manor house, someone who could have access to Montrose and his gaol." He looked up at her. "I am asking ye, not forcing ye, not threatening ye, just asking ye, to come with me."

"You left me," Maggie said, embarrassed at the pitiful sound of her voice. "I was terrified."

His gaze softened. "I'm sorry, lass," he said.

Maybe she was stupid, but she believed him. He crossed to her side and knelt beside her. He took her hand.

"Let us begin again. I am Quinn MacIntyre, ne'er-do-well, but I promise ye, no debaucher of innocents, and no murderer. I need yer help. Will ye help me, lass?"

seven

The lass trembled as she gazed back at him. "Well," she said finally, "when you put it that way—sure."

He smiled and released her hand. "Are ye hungry, lass?"

She laughed and brought her knees up to her chest, wrapping her arms around them. "I could eat an entire cow. Horns, hooves, tail, everything."

"I dinna think I can quite manage a cow," he said, "but perhaps I can find something smaller."

He didn't usually build a fire when he slept in the hills, but his brief experience with Maggie had taught him that she wasn't used to the cold Highland nights. He took a few precious pieces of peat from his pack and got a small fire going.

He'd had the luck to kill a hare earlier and had it tethered in a nearby stream, keeping cold. Maggie made a face as he skinned, spitted, and started roasting the hare, but smiled in delight when he took her to the stream. Under his watchful eye, she took off her heavy boots and rolled up her breeches, exposing her bare legs to the knee. As he stared, dumfounded, she pulled a bright kerchief from her pack and dipped it into the moonlit water to wash her face, arms, and legs.

After a moment, Quinn decided he had more moral fiber than he'd thought. He made a conscious choice to treat the lass as if she were his younger sister, even though she sat there displaying her limbs to him as she washed. If she had actually been his sister, he'd have given her a damn good thrashing for exposing herself in such a way. But because it was Maggie, he just wanted to kiss her from her cute little toes, up her curved calves, around her knee, and all the way up to her still-hidden secrets. She glanced up at him and smiled. Quinn's mouth went dry and he forced his gaze to the sky above.

After they returned from the stream, on an impulse, he took Ian's pipes from his saddlebag. As Maggie sat down close to the fire, his plaid once more wrapped around the pale pink—what had she called them when he asked?— aye, pajamas, he began to softly play the pipes.

She leaned back against a stone and closed her eyes. For a moment, Quinn let all of his thoughts of Ian and what lay ahead drift away while he watched her. She made a beautiful picture sitting there, pale skin, long red hair bright from the flames behind her as she listened to his music. When he reached the end of the piece, she opened her eyes and looked at him with new respect.

"That was beautiful," she said. "What's it called?"

"MacKintosh's Lament," he told her. " 'Tis a pibroch, a verra old song written by a MacIntyre."

She turned toward him, her face suddenly cast in shadow. "Tell me about your clan. About your family."

He leaned back and stared dreamily up at the stars. It had been a long time since he'd even heard the old tales, let alone shared them.

" 'Tis said that the first MacIntyres came from the isle

of Sleat. They were told to settle at the first place that their white cow lay down upon the ground."

"White cow?"

"Aye. Once the hills of Glenoe were covered with the white cattle of the MacIntyres. The old stories say that they landed in a beauteous place, near the base of Ben Cruchan, and there they were challenged by the spirit of the mountain and told they couldna stay there, but to go around the other side and there they would find solace. They did as they were told, and on the other side of the mountain, the white cow lay down."

"That's beautiful," she said softly when he had finished, gazing out across the misty valley. "So why are you here, and not in Glenoe?"

He heard the grimness enter his voice, but he could not banish it. "I was sent to foster with the Duke of Montrose when I was a lad. He heard me play my pipes at a faire and thought I had talent."

"The Duke of Montrose?" she said. "The same Duke of Montrose that's chasing you?"

"Aye. Ye must understand, the MacIntyres' fame lies in their ability to pipe. 'Twas a MacIntyre that piped for Robert the Bruce at Bannockburn. Montrose convinced my father to let him foster me, and my father, of course, was thrilled. I had a tutor, both for my letters and for the pipes, but Montrose eventually sent me to the MacCrimmons School of Piping when I was twelve years old. 'Tis there that I learned how to write music for the pipes."

"You're a composer?"

He almost laughed out loud at the astonishment in her voice. "Aye," he said, laying the pipes aside. "Though I wasn't able to stay long enough to learn all I wanted."

"What happened?" she asked softly.

Quinn stared into the fire. "Back at home, my father couldna make his rent and had been turned out, he and my mother and my brother. They asked Montrose for help, and he said he had enough burden with just one MacIntyre to support."

"Bastard," Maggie said, with fire in her voice.

"Aye. I realized, finally, that the only reason he took me on in the first place was that he thought I had a rare talent and that I would be the best piper in all of Scotland one day. It would give him great stature in the eyes of his peers if his piper was the best. My father and brother, angry at his hard-heartedness—my mother was verra ill at the time—began to reive the duke's cattle. They were caught. They were hanged."

"Quinn, I'm so sorry."

He blinked over at her. Somehow she had moved from the fire to his side, her warm hand upon his arm. He gazed into her blue eyes. "After that, I couldna stay at Mac-Crimmons, of course," he said, noting the smoothness of her skin and the arch of her brow. "I would no longer take Montrose's sponsorship."

"Where did you go?"

He shrugged. "Ian and I—"

"Ian was with you? How did the two of you meet?"

A slow grin spread across his face as he remembered the first time he'd ever seen Ian MacGregor. "Though we are distant cousins by birth, I first met Ian at MacCrimmons. He was a scrap of a lad, skinny and frail. All the lads there, it seemed, wanted to beat him up."

"Except you," Maggie said knowingly.

He glanced at her, surprised. "Aye. How did ye know? I defended him, and he will never let me forget it. We have been friends ever since."

"Did he want to be a piper, too?"

"Aye. We both shared a passion for the pipes." Quinn leaned his head back and laced his fingers over his chest, fighting the urge to reach for her. "All either of us ever

wanted was to be the piper of a clan. I begged him not to
come with me when I left, but he wouldna hear of it. I'll
never forget. He said, 'I am yer brother now.'"

For a moment he could not talk, but the silence between
them, there in the misty moonlight, was not uncomfortable, but gentle and thoughtful. Her silence encouraged
him to continue.

"That is why I must save him, lass. He is all the family I
have left." Her fingers tightened on his arm. "We lived
where we could for a time, and then Ian suggested we work
for his uncle, Rob Roy MacGregor. We were drovers of
cattle until my twenty-fifth birthday and then . . ." His
voice trailed away.

"What happened then?" she whispered, her words
edged in concern.

He frowned slightly, shaking his head. It was still a
mystery to him, how it had happened. "I was sitting on a
hillside, just like this, playing the pipes. 'Twas the anniver-
sary of my father's death and I had composed a new tune
in his honor. As I played it, suddenly a rage filled me like
none I'd ever known. And just as suddenly, I wanted revenge
on Montrose."

"Shock," she said. "You were in shock, and eventually
the way you really felt pushed through the grief and the
numbness and you had to look at it."

Quinn frowned and turned to stare at her. He'd never
met a lass who spoke with such assurance as this one. And
her words rang true, though he had never considered that
the anger had been inside of him all along.

"Perhaps so. Ian was ready for anything—his father had
disowned him when he left MacCrimmons—and so we began playing merry havoc with the duke." He shook his
head. "Only the more we have robbed him, the angrier I
seem to have become."

He blinked then and sat up, feeling Maggie's hand slip

away from his arm. What kind of fool was he, to sit and confide his innermost secrets to a lass he scarcely knew, like some schoolgirl? He'd never shared such things with anyone in his life.

"I will check the meat," he said, rising and moving toward the fire. He knelt down beside the burning peat and plucked a bit of meat from the spit and tasted it. Almost done.

"How long ago was it that your father and brother died?"

He thought about it. It had been a long time since he'd shared this story with anyone else. "I was nineteen at the time. I am twenty-six now, so—"

"You're twenty-six?" Maggie asked, her voice filled with surprise.

"Aye. Did ye think me younger?"

She shook her head, looking vastly disturbed. "No, I thought you looked about your age, I guess."

"How old are ye, lass?"

Her mouth dropped open for a moment and then she closed it and smiled, warily.

"Old enough to know better," she murmured, and then straightened. "I'm a little, er, younger than you."

"I thought so. I pegged ye for three-and-twenty. Was I right?"

Her face brightened and her hesitant smile grew into a beautiful beaming gesture. "Yes, you were exactly right," she said.

"The rabbit is exactly right as well," he said, lifting the spit from the fire and moving to sit beside her. "Just pull the meat off as ye will, but be careful, 'tis hot."

She nodded and then peeled a layer of meat and put it in her mouth, chewing tentatively. "It's better than I thought it would be," she said. "Sort of like chicken."

"Now, 'tis yer turn. Tell me about the colonies."

She glanced up at him, and once again, he felt desire curl in his loins, felt the need to reach out, to take her in his arms. He'd bedded enough women to know that she wanted him, too. Her body fairly shimmered with desire whenever she drew near him, but she had remained very demure and somewhat shy. Perhaps she was a maid, and not knowing him well, was a little afraid.

"Oh, Quinn," she began, and he blinked, for a moment thinking he must have spoken his feelings aloud, but as she continued, he released his breath in relief. "Can I tell you about the colonies tomorrow? I'm so tired."

"Of course, lass," he said. They ate in companionable silence then, until all of the hare had been eaten. Maggie sat licking her fingers, the gesture making him wish he could take her hand in his and do the licking for her.

He arched one brow. And why not? The perfect way to test the waters. He reached over and took her hand, prepared for the startled look on her face as he did. It seemed that most things he did startled Maggie.

The realization made him slow as he brought her hand to his lips, taking his time, letting his tongue slide across her palm and then capturing first one finger and then the next, the taste of the hare mingling with the salt of her skin.

"Wha-what are you doing?" she whispered.

"I have no cloth to cleanse yer skin," he said, watching her from beneath his lashes. "And so I offer myself to ye."

"You—ye do?"

"Aye," he said, his voice rumbling with pleasure as he painted a wet path around each knuckle of her wee hand. He glanced up at her and pointed to her neck. "And I believe the grease from the cooking must have splattered ye."

Her hand moved to her throat, but before she could touch her skin, he'd moved closer, slid his arm around her waist and put his mouth to her neck. She shivered at the touch of his lips and then his tongue, and when she did not protest, he kissed the sweet curve of her jaw before moving to possess her mouth.

Ah, it was like nectar, the sweetness of her lips, the gentle sigh that escaped her as he slid his hands to cup her face. Her hands curled around the back of his neck and he grew bolder, parting her lips with his tongue and delving into the warmth she offered.

"And what have we here on this bonny fine evening? A lovers' tryst?"

Maggie gasped at the sound of the low voice and clutched at Quinn's shoulders. He whirled as a man stepped out of the shadows of the castle ruins.

The stranger stood with his hands on his hips, glaring down at them, as one by one, more men appeared on either side of him. As their leader stepped closer, Quinn saw it wasn't a stranger at all, but an old friend, with anger burning in his eyes.

Carefully Quinn rose from the ground, bringing Maggie with him. He pushed her behind him protectively, keeping one hand clasped in hers. She was trembling with fear and his temper flared.

"Do ye have to scare the lass half to death?" he demanded.

The tall man took another step toward the fire and his face was illuminated, revealing a craggy countenance and a mane of auburn hair lit by the flames in front of him and the rising sun behind.

"So it *is* ye, Quinn MacIntyre," he said, his voice rough, taut. "Sitting here twiddling a lassie while my cousin lies dead and unmourned." His gaze flickered from Maggie back to Quinn. "From what I have heard, ye turned yer back and left Ian to take his chances with Montrose's men."

"You're wrong!" Maggie cried, stepping around Quinn. "That is *not* what happened."

"Maggie, stay out of this," Quinn warned, one hand lifted to keep her back.

"Wrong, am I?" MacGregor shifted his gaze to her, and Quinn tensed. "And who might ye be to question whether I am right or wrong?"

"I'm Maggie Graham," she said, her voice quavering. "Who the hell are you?"

"Graham?" His blue eyes narrowed.

"She has naught to do with this, Rob Roy MacGregor," Quinn said, feeling suddenly protective. He grabbed her by the arm and pulled her back to his side. "She is from the colonies and has no knowledge of Montrose."

"Rob Roy?" Maggie pushed forward again, her eyes wide in the firelight. "You're *the* Rob Roy MacGregor?"

The man frowned at her. "Aye, I am Robert Roy Mac-Gregor."

"Rob Roy," she said faintly. Quinn frowned and wondered why she had the look of a dazed deer. "Are you real or am I imagining all this?" she asked.

MacGregor glanced at Quinn. "What is the lass talking about?"

"I never know," he admitted. "I dinna turn my back on Ian," he went on, keeping his voice steady. "Ian's horse threw him, and before I could reach him, Montrose's guards shot him. I thought I would be of more aid to him outside the Tolbooth than inside with him—if indeed, he still lived."

"And does he live?" MacGregor asked.

Quinn looked away. "In faith, I know not."

"But it wasn't Quinn's fault," Maggie said.

"Hush, lass," he admonished. "We were just on our way to the manor to learn if Ian is being held or is—" He broke off.

"Dead," Rob finished for him.

A pain laced through Quinn's chest at the thought. "Aye," he said.

"And so why are ye still standin' here?" Rob Roy said. "When ye learn the truth, come to me at Craigrostan and we will say what shall be done."

"What will you do if Ian is dead?" Maggie asked.

Rob Roy smiled down at the woman, but there was steel in his eyes. "Ye have courage, lass, but dinna think that courage will always carry ye, especially when ye are outnumbered." He turned back to Quinn. "Come to me when ye find out."

He turned on his heel and strode away. One by one, his men followed him, disappearing into the night until all were gone.

"I think I need to sit down," Maggie said, and promptly collapsed to the ground.

Quinn knelt beside her. "Are ye all right, lass?"

Maggie nodded, feeling numb. She dragged herself to her feet, leaning on Quinn. "I need to ask you something, and it's going to sound crazy," she said. "I mean, daft."

His brows darted up and a smile played about his lips. "More daft than what ye have said to me already?"

She nodded again. "More daft. Tell me what year this is."

Quinn frowned. "'Tis the year of our Lord, 1711."

Her eyes fluttered shut, and she felt her body start to sag again. Quinn caught her in his arms, and suddenly she knew he was all that lay between her and insanity.

"Lass, are ye ill?"

Maggie opened her eyes. This was impossible. Absolutely impossible. But she'd seen Rob Roy MacGregor with her own eyes. Now it all made perfect sense—Quinn's clothing and his strange speech—yet it made no sense at all.

"Seventeen eleven," she whispered.

He frowned, and for a moment, she thought she saw real concern in his beautiful green eyes. "Aye," he agreed.

Maggie nodded. "Of course it is," she said. "I knew that."

"We need to ride, lass, if ye are able," Quinn said.

"Sure," she agreed faintly. "Whatever."

Hysteria threatened to overwhelm Maggie as they rode toward the manor house. She was no stranger to panic. During the first months after her parents died, when the reality of it all sank in, she began to suffer from severe anxiety attacks. Luckily, she'd found a therapist who had taught her how to use slow, deep breathing to calm herself.

She used those techniques now, filling her lungs with the moist morning air, letting the scent of wild roses on the breeze waft over her as she slowly released her breath and then inhaled again, and again, until she had stopped shaking.

Okay, this was all still supposition. She had no real proof she had somehow traveled back in time. *Back in time.* She began to laugh and the hysteria threatened her once again, hovering like some kind of ghostly apparition.

"Lass, are ye all right?"

She couldn't speak, but she nodded and that seemed to satisfy Quinn. Maggie slowed her breathing again and tried to focus on something that would help ground her— something else the therapist had taught her.

Maggie closed her eyes and pictured the faces of Ellie and Allie, and the small house they had all grown up in near Austin. She thought about Ellie's dry humor and Allie's matter-of-fact personality, and her friend, Rachel, dying her hair a different color every other week. They were her family, and her family was her foundation. Just thinking about them gave her a more concrete sense of reality, something she was holding on to with everything inside of her.

The horse beneath them continued to rock Maggie gently as she gazed at the beautifully stark countryside now beginning to glow in the morning's light. It looked much the same as it had every morning since she had arrived in Scotland, but not exactly the same: She realized that during the last few days, she'd been so caught up in her "adventure" she hadn't seen the subtle differences in the world around her. For one thing, there were no paved roads. None whatsoever. And no phone lines, or road signs, or modern buildings of any sort. On her bus ride to the site of the cairn, she'd seen such things, even in the Highlands.

And don't forget that you just met Rob Roy MacGregor last night.

She closed her eyes against the proof she didn't want to see. If only she had never come. If only her sisters had never had the crazy idea of sending her on the dig at the cairn.

The cairn.

If she'd traveled back in time, it was logical that no one from the group would have been there, and there would have been no indication of the dig. Perfectly reasonable. She swallowed hard.

Quinn shifted in the saddle behind her, and Maggie realized she had placed a large amount of trust in this man. He'd seemed sincere about Ian and his family, but everything had changed now, and she didn't know what—or who—to trust.

Maggie lifted her hand to her lips, remembering the kiss he'd given her. He had rocked her to the core of her being with that kiss. Was it real, or like the Scottish countryside around her, just a surreal imitation of life as she had once known it to be?

She reined in her overactive libido. Quinn's kisses didn't matter. What mattered was finding a way to get back home again! Her first instincts had been correct—she needed to get back to the cairn. But first, she would make good on her obligations to Quinn. To Ian.

The future wasn't going anywhere.

It was dark by the time they reached the duke's estate. He knew it was too late to make any headway with their plan, but it was the perfect time to sneak into the stables. The lass needed to get a good night's sleep. Her babble about what year it was had unnerved him, as well as the wild look in her eyes.

As he kept Saint to the shadows and tree line on the edge of the property, he pondered how Maggie had begun to get under his skin in such a short time. Why did the lass affect him so? She was nothing to him, nothing but a means to an end. He tightened his jaw. That was all. Still, he sensed he would need to handle her gently.

The thought of handling Maggie gently brought images to mind that sent a rush of heat through his veins. The kiss they had shared had set up a throbbing in his blood, a need that intensified every time he came near her. He didn't think he had imagined that the lass felt something for him in return.

Maggie was still asleep when Quinn finally guided Saint into the stables, situated some distance behind Montrose's home. His friend Bittie would hide them for the night, and at least they would have the warmth of the hay in the loft above the animals. He was taking a big risk, actually hiding in the duke's stables, but the sooner Maggie could begin her work as a servant, the sooner they would learn if Ian was alive.

Bittie didn't ask questions when Quinn helped the strangely dressed woman off the horse and then bundled her up the ladder to the loft. He laid his extra plaid upon the hay, and she collapsed upon it, dead to the world again before he finished lapping it over her. He sent Bittie on an errand, and when the man returned, he carried a flour sack filled with cheese and bread and a bottle of wine, and a bundle of clothes for Maggie.

Quinn sat down beside her, and the desire he felt every time he looked at the lass flared again. She lay on her side, her legs pulled halfway up to her chest, her small hands folded beneath her chin. Lit by a lantern hanging from a nearby post, her face was like porcelain beneath the dark lashes brushing her skin. Her long red hair was pulled back in a loose braid, but one tendril had escaped and curled across her cheek.

As Quinn watched, Maggie brushed it away from her face, and then turned onto her back and lifted both arms above her head, stretching, pulling the soft pink material more tightly across her breasts. The "pajamas" she wore were very thin and lay like silk upon every curve of her body. One of the buttons on the front of her blouse had come undone, exposing the plump curve of one breast.

Suddenly he wondered what she would do if he lifted that soft pink fabric and caressed her with his tongue. She had been yielding beside the campfire. Would she yield again? She opened her eyes without warning and blinked, then smiled lazily. Quinn almost reached for her, but managed to control himself.

"Hungry?" he asked, his voice soft as he brushed his hand lightly across her face. Maggie's eyes widened, and she accepted a mug of wine and the cheese and bread Bittie had found for them. She drank the wine greedily, and as he watched the tilt of her head and the movement of her throat, he knew he wasn't going to be able to sleep beside her this night, no matter if it was the safest place.

"Easy," he cautioned, "ye will have a head in the morning if ye drink too much."

Maggie dragged the back of her hand across her mouth and smiled up at him. "I've had a hard day, Quinn MacIntyre. I deserve a little relaxation, don't I?" She leaned against him and he steeled himself against her warmth.

"Aye," he said. "Here, eat some bread and cheese."

She took the food and devoured it. Her tongue darted out from time to time to catch crumbs of bread, driving him insane with longing, until finally she finished eating and lay back on the hay, full and content.

Ah, lass, he thought, *but I could make ye more content.*

"I'll leave ye to yer sleep," Quinn said, but didn't move.

Maggie pushed up on one elbow, frowning at him. "Where are you sleeping?"

He shrugged. "In the woods likely."

"Don't be silly," she said, and lay back down, patting the hay beside her. "Just stay here."

In another moment, she was asleep. Quinn watched her for a moment, watched as her soft lips opened and closed slightly. Then, his heart pounding, he slid down beside her and gathered her to him, one arm beneath her shoulders, the other curved around her waist. She moved easily, turning toward him, repositioning her head upon his chest, moving one hand to rest there, too. And when she cuddled closer, he almost groaned aloud.

One kiss, he thought. *If I can but touch her lips to mine one more time, that's all I ask.*

He cupped her face with his free hand, stroking her cheek with his thumb. Maggie shifted, her leg rubbing against his erection in her sleep. Quinn swallowed another groan and slowly lowered his mouth to hers, the warmth of their breath mingling as he touched her lips with his.

She stirred, pressing more tightly against him as she opened her mouth and kissed him back. Her hand slipped away from his chest, across his belly, and down to rest upon the hard length of him, and this time he did groan out loud.

Quinn trembled as he deepened the kiss, his tongue darting to collide with hers, his fingers trailing down her neck and over her collarbone to find her right breast and finally, finally, caress the softness there.

Maggie's eyes flew open and she stared into his, but there was no fear mirrored there, only a heat that matched his own. He gazed into the burning blue of her gaze, and suddenly knew that she would not stop him if he continued to seduce her. She was tired and half drunk and half asleep, and vulnerable. He had never been the kind of man who took advantage of a woman.

Reluctantly, he released her. "Go to sleep, lass," he said. "Before we do something we will regret."

Her half-closed eyes opened, full and wide, gazing into his with complete clarity. "Would you regret it?" she whispered, her mouth very close to his.

"No, but—"

"I wouldn't regret it," she said.

Quinn slipped one hand into the wealth of her hair. "No?"

Maggie shook her head, wordlessly, and Quinn lowered his mouth to hers again.

She sighed and leaned against him, and he began trying to remove the curious blouse she wore, still confused by the strange images of crudely drawn cat faces upon the soft cloth. But not confused enough to forget what he was doing. When the blouse parted, he lowered his head and kissed her just where her breasts began to curve, letting the tip of his tongue touch her. Maggie shivered, and he drew in a sharp breath.

Heat coursed through him, making him harder, draining the blood from his face. When he lowered his head and touched his tongue to the sensitive pink nub, Maggie gasped and then moaned aloud as he drew her into his mouth.

She arched against him, and Quinn went a little mad, suckling her, caressing, moving his hands over her body, wanting to please her more than he had any other woman. He moved back to her mouth for a moment and slid his tongue between her lips, possessing her, burning with his need and his intentions, until she trembled in his arms.

Then she was touching him, her hands sliding across his chest and over his shoulders, her nails sharp against the cloth of his shirt.

"Touch me," she whispered.

"Here?" he asked, sliding his hand beneath the strangely stretchy waistband of her soft breeches, diving into the velvet warmth hidden there. Touching her ever so softly.

"Yes," she sighed. Maggie pulled his head back down to hers, kissing him with uninhibited passion as she yielded to him, shifting to give him better access to all that she was. "Especially that," she said against his mouth, arching her hips and gasping as he slipped two fingers inside of her. "Esp-ec-ial-ly there."

He moved to take her breast again, and she cried out as he nibbled and bit her tender skin, and continued to caress her below. The lass clung to him, her breath rapid, precious in its longing, until suddenly he could wait no longer. He released her and sat up. Maggie moaned softly and reached for him, whispering, "Don't go."

"I'm going nowhere, lass," he said, "unless I take ye with me."

With two quick movements, he pulled his shirt and plaid from his body and then returned to her. She had shed the breeches and blouse and lay back on the plaid, completely naked. Quinn covered her body with his own, desperate to feel his flesh against hers, groaning as he stretched atop her and felt the tips of her bare breasts rub against the curling hair of his chest.

He kissed his way up her neck and then back to her breasts again. He felt his control slipping and took one nipple roughly, hoping he hadn't hurt her, smiling against her skin as she cried out in obvious delight.

He pressed his mouth against her ear and murmured gentle endearments, as he revelled in the touch of her skin against his. She was more than ready, more than willing as she lifted her hips, coaxing him.

"Come inside," she whispered, "out of the cold." She pressed her hips upward, parting her legs for him.

Quinn entered her with one thrust, slipping into the fire, losing himself in the slick heat of her body, moving in and out, he hard and thick, she soft and yielding. He filled Maggie again and again, but as sweet as the feel of her body beneath him was, the look in her eyes was sweeter.

Her gaze caressed him, devoured him, enveloped him, and he knew then that her need matched his own. As he moved inside of her, feeling the ecstacy that was Maggie, he watched her watching him. She looked into his eyes in wonder and soundlessly shuddered beneath him as Quinn took all that she gave, and gave all that he had, until at last she cried out, her rapture shaking him to the depths of his soul.

Then he was soaring, plundering Maggie mindlessly, as the world shattered and disappeared, sending him spiraling into sweet oblivion. He collapsed against her, spent and amazed.

Trying to find his breath, Quinn rolled to one side and sprawled flat on his back, his arm thrown across his eyes, his heart pounding. When the stars dancing in his head began to dissipate, he raised up on his elbows to look at her.

She was magnificent. Her auburn hair lay free and flowing over her shoulder, across one bare breast. Her skin gleamed with a fine sheen of perspiration, and in that moment she looked like some otherworldly being, a nymph or faery, or perhaps a selkie captured from the loch, drawn to the shore to give her love to mortal man.

Maggie's arm came down and her eyes flew open, meeting his in startled hesitation. She shivered, and he pulled the plaid around her and then gathered her into his arms, holding her tightly.

"Och, lass, ye are an amazing woman," he whispered against her hair as her arms slipped around his waist. She didn't speak, and concerned, he pulled back a little and looked down.

She was staring at his chest, one hand resting there, her breathing as ragged as his. He tipped her chin upward and she glanced up at him, the blue depths filled with an emotion he couldn't name. "Are ye all right? Did I hurt ye?"

Maggie shook her head and looked away, then leaned her face against his shoulder. "No," she said softly. "And you're the amazing one. I've never—it's never been—" She broke off and kissed his collarbone. "You're amazing," she repeated.

Quinn stroked her hair back from her face and she looked up at him again. How had this happened? How in the space of a few impassioned moments had this woman become so precious to him? He'd bedded many a lass, but he'd never felt like this. Never felt so—protective.

"Quinn—" she began, and stopped.

"What is it, love?" he asked. She gazed at him for a long moment and then bit her lower lip and shook her head. He slipped one hand through her hair and gently pressed her head to his chest again, where she sighed, her breath sending a tremor across his skin. "Dinna fash yerself, darlin'. Ye've had a long day. Go to sleep, now."

Maggie nodded against him, and in another few moments, she was asleep, her breathing regular and even, but Quinn lay awake for another hour, wondering if he had just made the best decision of his life or the worst mistake.

eight

Maggie's eyes flew open. Above her was a large window without panes or screen. Stars twinkled down through what she realized, after squinting a bit, was a kind of hatch. She blinked. It was in the roof, but the question was, the roof of what? Where was she? She felt disoriented, groggy, and then suddenly wide awake.

Oh, damn.

Quinn MacIntyre was molded against her back, softly snoring. He shifted a little in his sleep, and Maggie's eyes widened. She tried to be very still as she looked around.

Her clothes lay haphazardly beside her and she groaned as she felt Quinn's hand splayed across her stomach and knew she was naked beneath the wool plaid draped over and under them. Beneath the plaid something scratchy made her want to shift, too. Apparently they'd spent the night together on a mound of hay.

Spent the night together. Maggie squeezed her eyes shut, fighting the sudden panic flooding over her.

Quinn. Last night. Naked. In her arms. In *her*.

Maggie clutched the plaid and stared up at the window. What in the world had she been thinking? She hadn't been thinking at all. She'd been terrified by the realization that somehow, someway, she had traveled back in time. Even now she felt hysterical laughter threatening to bubble out of her.

Then his amazing touch and his even more amazing mouth had made her forget the whole time-travel phenomenon, and her five years of celibacy had seemed like a hundred and she'd fallen into bed—or rather, the hay— with him without a second thought.

Now she was having second thoughts. And a third, and a fourth.

Maybe if she tried very hard she could convince herself that it had all been a dream. A very impassioned, amazing dream. But no, Quinn was too real, too deliciously warm, and pressed against her, his arm draped across her waist, other appendages pressing elsewhere, and so she might as well face facts. She'd slept with a man she barely knew.

Rachel would be so proud.

Maggie giggled, feeling the hysteria start to build again.

Beside her, Quinn moved. She felt him rise up on one elbow and then his breath was soft against her cheek.

"Lass?" he whispered.

Maggie pretended to be dead to the world, keeping her breathing even. If he knew she was awake he would likely want to pick up where they'd left off, and she had to sort a few things out before that would happen again—if ever.

An imge of the night before flashed through her mind— Quinn leaning close to her, his gaze filled with a gentleness she hadn't expected, Quinn painting a fiery path across her lips, the side of her neck, her throat, and most of all, Quinn joining with her in a way that had touched the very essence of her soul.

Okay, so she could be persuaded again—easily. That's why she had to avoid being in close proximity to him, at least for a little while. She kept breathing, and after a moment, she heard him sit up and release his breath in a long, low sigh. Straw crackled beneath his feet as he stood.

Once she heard him walk away, Maggie opened her eyes the merest slit and was treated to the sight of a naked Quinn with his back to her, the muscles above his taut buttocks tightening as he lifted his arms and slid his shirt over his head. Then he picked up his plaid and she watched until he folded the long piece of cloth and wrapped it around his waist, obscuring the view, and then closed her eyes. He was beautiful.

She tried to slow her breathing back to where it should be. A few minutes later she heard the sound of his boots hitting the rungs of the wooden ladder that led to the loft, and then heard him call out to someone.

Quickly Maggie grabbed her pajama pants and top and shrugged into them, then dropped to her knees again and crawled to the edge of the hayloft to peer down. Quinn was not alone. A large, burly man stood with his back to Maggie, his hands on his hips, as Quinn began to pace back and forth in front of him, speaking intently.

"Do ye have the garb?" Quinn was saying as he dragged one hand through his tangled hair. The bigger man handed him a bundle and shook his head.

"I dinna like this, Quinn. Ye shouldna be takin' such a chance. Let me go and—"

"Ye know they willna let ye inside the house," Quinn said as he took the bundle. He gave the man a smile. "Ye smell of dung, Bittie."

"Aye." The one called Bittie turned to follow Quinn as he moved toward one of the stalls. His face was fleshy and jovial, his eyes a little vague and his speech a little slow.

His voice grew somber. "But I will take a bath, Quinn, if it means ye will no be caught by the duke."

Quinn laughed. "Nay, I wouldna put ye through that kind of sacrifice, not even for my life."

As Maggie watched, Quinn shed his plaid and began to dress. She sighed. Apparently men in the past didn't wear underwear. What a lovely custom. He donned a pair of black breeches and stood for a moment in thought, giving her a chance to take a long look at his broad, well-muscled chest and firm stomach. His upper arms were as big around as grapefruit, and her breath came a little quicker as she remembered the strength in those arms when he held himself above her and stroked in and out and—

Maggie closed her eyes again and rolled to her back, her heart pounding, heat burning into her face. *Get a grip!* she admonished. *You are in a crazy situation. Don't make it crazier by falling for a guy three hundred years older than you!*

"Remember, Bittie," Quinn was saying below, "dinna speak of this to anyone."

Maggie scurried back to the edge to look down at the two men again. Darn it. She'd missed a good two minutes of ogling Quinn before he finished dressing. Now he wore a bright red jacket with gold buttons down the front and a black tricornered hat with a feather jutting from the top. It was some kind of uniform. She frowned.

"Aye, ye can count on me," Bittie said and then paused. "What is it I should not speak of, Quinn?"

Quinn smiled and readjusted his hat. His dark curls tumbled from beneath it, and Maggie remembered that at one point in their lovemaking she had laced her fingers into his hair, expecting roughness, surprised by the softness there. His mouth had been soft, too, gentle, and then roughly passionate, then soft again. She lifted two fingers to her mouth, remembering how it had felt to be so possessed and yet so cherished. Had it been that way for him, too, or was she just imaging such a deep connection?

"Ye must not tell anyone that I am here with the lass. No one must know."

"Oh, aye. I willna tell a soul." He frowned. "But ye dinna want to sleep in the loft every night, do ye, Quinn? T'will be too rough for such a fine lady as that."

Quinn buckled a polished saber around his waist and nodded. "Aye, Bittie," he said, "ye are right about that. Nay, and this is where ye can be of more help to me. As soon as I leave here, take the lass to Ian's cottage."

Maggie rose up a little on her elbows. *Ian had a house?*

"Should I no take her to Mary?" Bittie asked.

"We spoke with Rob last night," Quinn said, his voice hard. "We are not welcome there until we learn what happened to Ian."

"Rob will no stay mad at ye," Bittie said, his gruff voice confident.

"That depends on what I find out about Ian," Quinn said. "But Ian MacGregor has more luck in his little finger than the rest of us poor beggars have in our whole bodies, so I'm bound to believe he's alive. It won't be long before he'll be back charming the lassies."

"Maybe ye'd best not let him close to yer wee lass, eh Quinn?" Bittie said. Maggie leaned over the edge a little farther to try to see Quinn's face, but Bittie was in the way.

"She is not my lass," Quinn said, and Maggie felt her heart sink. "Just a poor girl lost and alone. When I'm through here, I'll get her back to her family."

Bittie glanced up at the loft, and Maggie ducked down, holding her breath until he spoke again. "She's a little thing, ain't she? Kind of helpless, like a kitten."

Maggie frowned. She was not helpless. Just because she'd gotten lost and sort of had a little pity party didn't mean—

"She's small, to be sure," Quinn agreed, interrupting her thought and making her eyes widen. "But *helpless* isna exactly how I'd describe her. She stood up to Rob Roy Mac-Gregor!" He chuckled, and Maggie smiled. "Aye, the lass has spunk!"

Well! This was the first time in her size-twelve life that anyone had called her small! And Quinn thought she was spunky! But he'd also said she wasn't "his" lass. Well, maybe he just didn't want to be presumptuous.

Right.

"The duke keeps those under arrest in what we call the dungeon. It lies back behind the manor house proper," Bittie was saying, and Maggie turned her attention back to the two men. "If Ian is alive, that is where he would be kept. There are guards who will know ye are not one of them, so ye must be careful."

Maggie frowned. *Be careful?* What difference would being careful make if there were guards?

"Thank ye, Bittie. 'Tis a huge favor ye have done me and mine this day. When I get Ian out of Montrose's clutches, ye will be rewarded handsomely."

Maggie's mouth dropped open. What was he planning to do? Just stroll into the dungeon and kill a few guards and take off with his friend slung over his shoulders? *If* he was even still alive? Was the man out of his mind?

"Are you out of your mind?" she shouted before she could stop herself.

Quinn and Bittie turned and looked up at the loft. Maggie lay flat on her stomach, peering over the side at them. She managed a slight smile and a wave.

"Hi. Morning. Did you sleep well?" She hauled herself up from the floor and then glared down at the two men, hands on her hips. "And, oh yeah—are you out of your freaking mind?"

Bittie looked at Quinn. "What did she say?"

"Who knows?" Quinn folded his arms over his chest and shrugged. "Half the time I dinna ken anything she says." He frowned as Maggie climbed down the ladder from the hayloft and then jumped the last few feet before turning to glare at him. She felt at a distinct disadvantage as she stood there in her pale pink pajamas, but she was determined to confront him.

"I said, 'Are you out of your mind?' Are you daft?'"

The men exchanged glances. "Nay," said Quinn. "Why should ye ask such a thing?"

Maggie gestured to his clothing. "Please tell me that you aren't disguising yourself as one of Montrose's guards!"

Quinn smiled at her slowly, sending a trickle of need through her veins. "All right, lass, I willna tell ye." He turned to speak to Bittie again, and Maggie grabbed his arm and jerked him toward her.

"Quinn, listen to me—you can't do this. It's insane. It's suicidal. It's kamikaze!"

He shook his head. "Ye see now, I understood ye until just that wee last bit."

"You know what I'm saying." She lifted her chin. "I thought this was why you brought me along. *I'm* supposed to find out if Ian is alive!"

Bittie shot Quinn an inquisitive look. Quinn kept his gaze steadily on her.

"Could ye leave us for a few moments, Bittie?" he asked.

"Aye, Quinn." The big man headed out of the stables, shaking his head. As soon as he was gone, Maggie turned on Quinn, but the shadow in his eyes made her postpone the lecture she'd quickly planned, and her voice softened.

"Quinn, please don't do this. Let's stick to the plan." She reached out one hand to his arm. He covered her hand with his.

"Maggie, I was wrong to put so much blame upon ye. I dinna wish to place ye in danger. Ye will stay here with Bittie and—"

"No, Quinn," she said, cutting him off. "You can't do this. I won't let you do this."

He cocked one brow at her. "Oh I can't, and ye won't?"

"No." She released a pent-up breath. "Look, just think about it. I'm guessing that you are a wanted man around here, right? That it's likely someone around here would recognize you?"

He shrugged. "It doesna matter. It must be done."

"But why take such a stupid chance? If you're caught nosing around and you're captured, then who's going to help Ian? On the other hand, no one knows me. I can do what you asked me to do in the first place—get a job in Montrose's household and find out about Ian. Then, if"—she swallowed hard—"if he is alive, we can come up with a plan to set him free without getting you or anyone else killed!"

Quinn leaned back against one of the stalls and gazed at her intently, the green flecks in his eyes growing deeper. "I thought ye dinna want to help me, to risk yerself where—what was it ye said—the people with guns were?"

She felt the blush creeping up her neck and looked away. "That was before."

Quinn pushed away from the stall, and suddenly she was in his arms. "Aye, that was before. Before last night. Now I know I canna let ye take such a chance."

Maggie shook her head. "Quinn, I want to do this. It was my fault that Ian was captured and"—she reached up and smoothed the stubble on his jaw—"and I couldn't bear it if anything happened to you."

He took her hand and kissed the palm. "And do ye think I could bear it any better if something were to happen to ye, Maggie mine?"

"There's no danger to me," she said, a little breathless.

"All I have to do is be a scullery maid. Even if I'm caught where I'm not supposed to be, no one is going to suspect I'm helping you. I'd just get, I don't know, my pay docked or something."

Quinn shook his head. "They talk fair strange in the colonies." He gazed into her eyes for a long moment and when he spoke, his voice was tender. "Yer words make sense"—he smiled—"for once. Are ye sure about this?"

She nodded. "Yes, it will be fine."

"I'll agree, on one condition."

"What?"

"If there's even a hint of suspicion cast yer way, ye must leave immediately and come straight back here, to the stables." His fingers bit into her shoulders, and Maggie shivered. What was it about this man that made her feel like a teenager caught in the throes of hormones and first love?

She blinked. Love? She backed away from him and his hands fell back to his sides.

"I agree," she said. "Trust me."

"I do," he said, closing the distance between them again. "With all of my heart."

Maggie laughed, the sound forced. "Quinn, we spent one night together. You don't have to say things like that."

He cupped her face with his hand and tilted her chin upward. "I dinna do anything I dinna want to do."

She pressed her hands against the tailored red jacket he wore and sighed. "I never could resist a man in a uniform."

Then his mouth was on hers, and he picked her up in his arms and she was mindless with need and desire as he carried her into one of the empty stalls. The hay there was clean and fresh, thank goodness, but Maggie had to admit, it probably wouldn't have mattered if hadn't been, that's how crazy she was to feel Quinn's body next to hers again.

They fell into the hay, and once again Quinn made

everything disappear as he stoked the sizzle between them into a blazing fire.

"Hurry up and finish the floor," the cook said. "Jenny will be here soon to prepare the guards' meals."

So far, on her first day spent working at the manor house, Maggie had washed about a million dishes, rinsed them, dried them, put them away, scrubbed the cabinets and the wooden countertops, swept the huge room, and was now scrubbing the floor. Her fingernails were ragged and sore, her back was killing her, and her knees—she couldn't think about her knees, because if she did, she'd start crying, and she was not going to cry. She wouldn't give the evil woman presiding over the kitchen that satisfaction.

As she leaned down on the scrub brush once again, Maggie suddenly realized what the cook had just said. "Jenny will be here soon to prepare the guards' meals." She smiled.

"Jenny?" she asked aloud.

Cook turned and crossed to her, staring down at the floor as if she might whip out some white gloves and start checking for dirt any moment. "Aye. She prepares supper for the men on guard duty."

Maggie looked up at the cook and let her mouth turn down and her gaze shift into pitiful. She had learned a lot in the past few hours. "Och, Cook, ye are no goin' to make me help her, are ye? Not after all I've done the day?" she whined, sitting with her shoulders slumped.

The cook glared at Maggie, her second chin quivering with anger. "I wasna goin' to, but since ye complain so heartily, that's exactly what ye will do! And dinna be giving me any mouth aboot it! Now finish that floor!"

Maggie groaned and started pushing the scrub brush around in a circle, but kept her head down to hide her smile. "Aye, mum," she said.

By the time she finished the floor Maggie was bone weary. The last thing she wanted to do was, well, anything at all. She wanted to soak in a hot tub and drink a tall glass of ice tea and sleep for a hundred years. She smiled grimly. Make that *three* hundred years and she'd be back where she belonged. But if Jenny prepared the meals for the guards, she probably delivered those meals as well.

As she dragged herself up from the floor, a girl with pale blonde hair, who looked about sixteen, rushed into the kitchen, her face twisted with anxiety. She was about Maggie's height, but thin as a rail. She wore a dark skirt and tea-colored blouse, covered with a worn blue bodice. Strangely enough, the girl reminded her of Allie and Ellie when they were young.

As Jenny took an apron from a hook by the door and tied it around her small waist, the girl looked fearfully toward the cook, every muscle in her body and her face taut with strain. The cook grabbed her by the arm and pulled her over to a large basket of potatoes and started lecturing on wasting food and not putting too much in each of the pewter bowls used to serve the guards.

"Mind me now, Jenny," the cook said, shaking a finger in the girl's face, "or I'll throw ye out. I've got this one now"—she jerked her thumb in Maggie's direction—"and I can train her in yer place."

The girl's face went ashen. "Oh, no, mum," she said, her voice frantic. From across the room, Maggie glared at the cook's back. The woman was a monster. The poor girl was shaking. "Dinna dismiss me, mum, please," Jenny begged. "Please!"

"Then earn yer keep!" Cook said, and shoved the girl toward Maggie. "This here is Maggie. She'll be helpin' ye cook the guards' meals from now on. Mind that the two of ye dinna tarry with gossip and such or I'll dismiss ye both! And I'd best not be hearing that either of ye doxies were flirting with Captain Pembroke again, or I'll not only dismiss ye, but I'll box yer ears!"

She turned and lumbered out of the room, leaving Jenny crying in her wake. Maggie immediately crossed to the girl and put her arm around her.

"Please don't worry about what she said. I'm not going to be working here very long, and I won't be taking your place."

Jenny wiped the tears from her face and looked up at Maggie, her blue eyes wide with fear. "Och, dinna be lettin' Cook hear ye say such a thing. She'll dismiss ye outright!"

Maggie smiled and squeezed the girl's frail shoulder, falling back into her brogue. "Then ye will have to keep my secret, eh Jenny?"

"Oh, aye. I dinna wish to cause any trouble for ye."

"I will help ye all I can. By the way," she said, trying to sound casual, "who are they guarding?"

Jenny looked to the right and the left, probably to make sure the cook hadn't returned; after all, the gargoyle had dictated no gossip. " 'Tis just a rumor, but 'tis said that it is the Piper!"

"The Piper?"

"Aye, the notorious highwayman!"

Maggie leaned away from her, relief washing through her. Ian. He was alive.

"They say he will be hanged soon," Jenny said.

Yikes. "Really. Can the duke do that?" Jenny frowned at her, looking confused, and Maggie smiled brightly. "What are we feeding the guards tonight?"

After a few minutes of talking companionably to the girl, Maggie saw Jenny begin to relax; she even smiled once or twice. The kitchen was large, with a wealth of wooden cabinets and countertops polished to a fine sheen. The sink had a hand pump, which Jenny showed her with pride. It was an amazing thing to the girl, having running water right there in the kitchen!

If Maggie had any doubts about being in the past, they would have been resolved as she handled the dishes and pans that were definitely not from the twenty-first, or even the twentieth century. It took about an hour to prepare the meal of boiled potatoes, boiled cabbage, and stringy beef, and by that time, Maggie felt she had made real headway in befriending the shy girl beside her.

"I'm so glad to have yer help, Maggie," Jenny said, as they finished dishing up the meal into the pewter bowls. "We can each carry a tray and finish the job in half the time."

"How many guards are there?" Maggie asked as she began loading her tray.

"Outside the dungeon there are two, Duncan and Charles, and downstairs, where the actual cells are, is another, James—a fine lad."

She smiled softly and Maggie smiled, too, certain that whoever James was, he was special to Jenny. Then the girl's smile faded.

"But be careful if Captain Pembroke is there," she said. "Dinna raise yer eyes to him."

Her voice sounded shaky as she said this last. Maggie glanced over at her as Jenny put bowls and bread and tankards of ale on her own round wooden tray. Maggie had added a bowl of broth she'd skimmed from the top of a kettle of soup the cook had prepared for the staff, as well as ale and bread, for Ian. According to Jenny, prisoners were only fed once a day, at breakfast. Maggie narrowed her eyes. *That* was about to change.

"Ye don't—dinna care for Captain Pembroke, I'm thinkin'," Maggie said, watching Jenny's face. Jenny looked away, her fair complexion flushing red at the comment. "Who is he?"

"He's the captain of the guard," she said. "He is a bad man," she added softly. "He tells everyone that I have—offered myself to him." She looked up, her blue eyes blazing with anger and tears. "'Tis no true—I despise him!" She lifted the corner of her apron to her face and burst into tears.

Maggie set the tray down on the big island counter in the center of the kitchen and took her into her arms. Jenny clung to her. "Has he hurt ye, Jenny?" she whispered. "Has he touched ye?"

The girl stopped crying abruptly and pushed away from her, looking even paler than before. "I shouldna have said anything. Please, dinna say anything to anyone. Captain Pembroke is the duke's kin and if I were heard disparaging him—" She shivered, shaking her head. "Please."

Maggie felt the girl's anguish as if it were her own. That was followed by an anger so deep she thought she would explode. How dare this Pembroke person lay hands on the girl? Had he raped her? She couldn't bring herself to ask, but whatever he had done, it had left Jenny shattered. No wonder she shook when that old battle-axe, the cook, yelled at her.

"I won't say a word," she assured her, then hurried on impulsively. "Let me take the guards their meals tonight," Maggie said, even as her heartbeat quickened. No way was she letting Jenny face that bastard again!

Jenny glanced up at her, a spark of hope in her eyes, but it quickly faded. "Thank ye, Maggie, but if Cook should find out I dinna do my part, she will turn me out. And Captain Pembroke isna always there."

"But—"

"Thank ye," Jenny said, once again calm. "If ye will just help me take the trays down, that will be fine."

The two carried their trays out the back door of the kitchen, and Jenny took the lead, heading for a stone building separate from the manor house. As they grew closer, Maggie saw two tall men standing outside what appeared to be a heavy iron door. The guards greeted Jenny warmly and gave Maggie a curious glance. After speaking with them for a few moments, Jenny led Maggie a few feet away.

"They said that Captain Pembroke is downstairs," Jenny whispered, her voice trembling.

"Let me take the tray down, then," Maggie said hastily.

"Nay." She shook her head. "James is down there tonight. Captain Pembroke knows that we love each other, and he never bothers me in front of him." She jerked her head up, concern in her eyes. "But he might hurt ye, Maggie."

"I'll be fine," Maggie said, putting an extra lilt into her voice, hoping it would give her the confidence she needed to face what lay ahead.

She had never considered herself brave. One of the hardest parts in raising Ellie and Allie had been the parent-teacher conferences. It had taken everything inside of her to deal with an irate English teacher or a disapproving math instructor, and just walking into the conference room had always twisted her stomach into knots. But she had done it, and taken up for her sisters when necessary and agreed with punishment when that was needed.

This was different. This time she wasn't standing between a civilized educator and a wayward teen, but a frightened young woman and a man who would use his power to take advantage of her. Maggie hardened her resolve and tightened her jaw as she followed Jenny back to the small porch where the guards stood in front of the large door.

She kept her eyes down as one of the men stepped forward and unlocked the door. Jenny ushered her inside, and Maggie looked up to find herself in a square, empty room occupied only by a table and four chairs, set in the far right corner. To the left was a door, and when they crossed to it, Maggie stared down into a dark stairwell lit dimly by a sconce, and she swallowed, hard.

"I am goin' with ye, Maggie," Jenny said beside her. "James willna let anything happen to me."

Maggie swallowed hard. "Are you sure?" *You're a coward, Maggie Graham,* she told herself.

"Aye. I am sure."

The two women carried the tray to the bottom of the stairs, where there was an open space about ten feet by ten feet square that contained only a table pushed against the wall next to one of the two doorways that opened off to either side, leading away from the small room. Maggie glanced down the hallway to the left and saw a row of iron doors a few feet apart all the way down the wall. She shivered at the thought of what might lie behind them.

Two men stood in the square entryway, hands on the sidearms at their waists and the swords at their sides. The men looked up as the women stopped a few feet away. Gathering her courage, Maggie stepped forward with the tray and smiled.

"Good evening," she said, faking a confidence she didn't feel. One man was of medium height and looked to be in his midtwenties. He had dark hair and gray eyes that flashed a warning as he moved to take the tray from her hands. *James*, Maggie decided. He set the tray down on a table apparently there for that express purpose.

The other man was a little older, much taller, and as he turned and his razor-sharp eyes pierced her, Maggie's heart began to pound beneath her tightly laced bodice. *Pembroke.* For all intents and purposes, Captain Pembroke looked like a fop. His thigh-length coat and knee-length breeches were made of baby blue satin and a riot of lace and frills ran down the front of the ivory blouse he wore, which matched his silk hose and his tall, chunky-heeled shoes.

His long, curling wig, fashioned from blond hair, framed his long, narrow face, and that, along with his clothing and his own delicate features, served to give the man a deceptively feminine appearance.

Maggie knew better. One glance into those clever, dark eyes was all it took to see the intelligence and masculine cunning behind the pretty clothes. Pembroke was a predator, no doubt about it. He moved to meet Maggie, speaking in a perfect English accent.

"I heard there was a new maid," he said, his gaze raking boldly over her body, "but no one told me how delicious she was. What is your name, girl?"

She dropped a little bob of a curtsey. "Maggie. How do ye do, sir?"

"I do just fine, little one." His voice was sensual, with just a touch of effeminate posturing. Pembroke took a step closer, and with a hand almost hidden by the froth of lace dripping from his sleeve, lifted her chin and ran his thumb across her lower lip.

"Sweet Maggie," he said, his voice languid, "I will have to tell Cook to have you bring me breakfast some morning." He glanced over at Jenny. "And bring little Jenny with you, eh?" He shot James a challenging look. "Can you think of a better way to start the morning, than to lie betwixt two soft and willing doxies like these?" James's jaw tightened perceptibly, but he said nothing.

Maggie flushed angrily as Pembroke laughed and then chucked her under the chin before moving toward the stairwell. He paused at the doorway and looked back at James, his pompous English accent grating on Maggie's nerves. "Don't forget, MacIntosh, that you are in charge. If that Scottish trash, MacGregor, escapes, you will earn his punishment." His gaze shifted to Jenny. "And then who will keep your Jenny warm at night?"

As soon as the odious man left the room, Maggie took the tail of her apron and wiped the coarse cloth across her chin where he had touched her.

"Damn his eyes," James said fiercely before turning his gaze on Jenny. "The two of ye must be verra careful. The captain is known for his ruthlessness." He glanced at Jenny and his face twisted with worry. "Jenny, ye must not ever be alone with him." The girl dropped her gaze to the floor and nodded. He took her hand. "I dinna know what I would do if something happened to ye."

"We'll be careful," Maggie said. She took a deep breath. "I'll look after Jenny." She forced a smile and saw relief flood across his face. No wonder Jenny was smitten. From the way he looked at her, it was obvious he adored the young woman—and was terrified for her. If Pembroke had already violated her in some way, Jenny apparently hadn't shared that event with James.

"Cook said we're supposed to feed the highwayman tonight," Maggie lied. "Where might I be findin' him?"

"Well, thank God they are finally feeding him," James said. " 'Tis inhuman."

"Aye," Maggie said. "There are many inhuman things in this house. One is in the kitchen."

Jenny and James laughed, sharing a warm look. Maggie looked down the corridor and bit her bottom lip. "Are there prisoners in all of those rooms?" she asked.

"Nay, not at the present. Besides the highwayman, we've two more, one who refused to pay rent to the laird and another who was caught reiving the laird's cattle."

"Reiving. You–ye mean he stole them."

"Aye. We'll be hangin' him soon likely," James said, still smiling. "Follow me, lassies."

Maggie's mouth went dry at his words, but she quickly recovered and retrieved the bowl of soup she'd pilfered for Ian, along with a tankard of ale and a crust of bread. She made a mental note to bring food to the other two prisoners the next evening, and then hurried after James and Jenny. James led them down the hallway and stopped in front of one of the

doors to the cells. Taking a ring of keys from his pocket, he
turned it in the lock and swung the heavy door open. Jenny
started to walk into the cell, but Maggie stopped her.

"Let me do this, Jenny." She glanced over at James.
"You—ye can find something to occupy yerself, I warrant."

James glanced at Jenny and then into the cell, obviously
torn between his duty and a chance for a moment alone
with Jenny. "He is shackled to the floor," he said, "but
dinna get too close and ye'll be safe." With that admonition
he grabbed Jenny by the hand and pulled her back into the
hall. Maggie grinned and shut the door securely behind
them, then turned to face the cell.

She looked around the dank stone room and shuddered
as the smells assailed her. Then all of that meant nothing as
a sound made her turn toward what looked at first like a
pile of filthy rags. As she drew nearer she saw the pile of
rags was actually a man, wearing torn and dirty clothes,
lying on a filthy pile of hay in the corner of the room.

Swallowing hard, she hurried toward him, setting the
food and drink on the floor. She bent over his prone figure,
and gagged. His hair was matted and dirty and tangled
across his face. He had a dirty plaid wrapped around him,
and he lay on his side, moaning. The stench coming from
him wasn't from the dirt.

Her heart in her throat, Maggie knelt down beside the
man and gently pushed him onto his back. His hair fell
away from his face and she saw a handsome man in his
midtwenties. The plaid fell back from his chest, and she
caught her breath at the sight of the blood-soaked shirt he
wore beneath and the iron shackles around his bruised
wrists, the chains anchored to the stone floor.

"Ian?" she whispered. "Is it you?" His eyes flickered
open, and Maggie saw the pain in the sky blue depths. *I did
this*, she thought. *This is my fault.*

nine

Ian moaned and his mouth moved, but no words came out. His lips were dry and cracked, and she quickly picked up the mug of ale and brought it to his lips. He drank greedily and she had to take it away, cautioning him to sip more slowly. He obeyed and then relaxed back against the hay and sighed.

"Thank ye, lass," he said, his voice faint.

"Are you Ian MacGregor?" she whispered.

His eyes flew open again, and he tried to smile. "Does my reputation precede me?" he said hoarsely. "Who are ye, lass?"

"Quinn sent me," she said. "To find out if you're all right."

He laughed, and then dissolved into a coughing fit that left his face ashen. His chest rose and fell rapidly for a moment, then he took a deep breath before he spoke.

"All right? Aye, if ye call lying in this pigsty while yer blood slowly ebbs out of ye 'all right.' "

"Your wound—has it been seen to by anyone?"

His face was pale, but he shook his head. "Nay."

She reached toward the dirty plaid and then hesitated. Ian gave her a halfhearted smile, looking at her from beneath long lashes. "I willna bite ye, lass," he said. "And I'd be that grateful if ye'd just look at the wound. It fair stings, it does."

Maggie nodded and pulled the dirty shirt aside. She gasped, horrified. He had been shot in his left shoulder and the wound was swollen and angry, puckered and filled with pus. The smell almost knocked her backward.

" 'Tis bad, eh?" Ian asked. She looked up at him, suddenly aware that her shock must be evident. She tried to smooth the horror from her face, but couldn't. How could the duke leave him in this hole in the condition?

His eyes were closed, and she cautiously laid her hand on his forehead. He was burning up, his skin like parchment. He needed to be in the hospital. Her throat tightened. There were no hospitals in the Highlands of Scotland in the 1700s. He would likely die unless something was done to help him soon.

"I know not who ye are," he said, his voice faint, "and ye speak strangely, but if Quinn did send ye, listen to me, lass." His blue eyes were fervent. "Dinna let him play the hero. I'd rather die here alone than have him here beside me."

"As if I could stop him," Maggie said. "You know how he is."

"Aye," he said, and then laughed weakly. "Indeed I do."

Maggie gazed at him, feeling helpless. She had a first-aid kit in her backpack, but it was in the stable. And antibiotics! Her sinus infection had cleared up on its own and she had a full prescription! But it would be morning before she could sneak the supplies into his cell.

"Let me get your supper," she said, moving away from him to retrieve the tray. She brought the bowl of soup to him, and he managed a few sips before falling back against the filthy hay.

"I am sorry, lass. I have no strength."

Maggie brought the bowl to his lips and slipped one hand behind his neck to give support. "You've got to hang on until Quinn can get you out of here."

Ian smiled wanly. "Hanging is what I'll be doin', lass, if I live long enough."

"Hanging?" Maggie's eyes widened as his meaning hit her. She lost her brogue altogether. "You mean they're going to hang you?"

"Aye, I heard the guards talking."

"When will they—?" She broke off, unable to finish the sentence.

"I dinna know." His face was pale, and Maggie patted his arm reassuringly and brushed a lock of blond hair back from his brow.

"You can't die, Ian," she said. "I don't think Quinn would ever get over it."

Ian's eyes met hers. "Aye, lass. I will try to be strong."

"I'll be back," she whispered, "with bandages and medicine."

She started to leave, but Ian caught her hand and she turned back.

"Dinna let him risk himself," Ian said, "or ye, to save me."

Maggie squeezed his hand and gave him what she hoped was a reassuring smile. "Stay strong," she said, and headed out of the cell. She had to tell Quinn, but if she did, he would risk his life to save Ian's. There had to be some way to save Ian without sacrificing Quinn. She rushed up the stairwell, and Jenny was waiting for her.

"Maggie, is everything all right? Ye took so long I feared—"

"Fine. Everything is fine," she said hurriedly. "But I have to go and do something very important. Can you—

will you tell the cook that I'm ill, if she comes and sees I'm
not here?"

"As if she would care," Jenny said, shaking her head. "If
ye had just given birth, she would expect ye to be down on
yer knees the same night scrubbing."

"Then just tell her you—ye don't know, okay?"

Jenny frowned at her words. "Oh-kay?"

"Is that all right with you—ye?"

Her eyes lit with understanding. "Och, of course. Dinna
worry. I just thank ye for helping me take the meals downstairs." She smiled shyly. "And for the time alone with
James."

"No problem. Thanks, kiddo." Maggie walked away
and then stopped and turned back. She grabbed the girl by
the arm and pulled her into the shadows, deciding to take
a chance. "Listen, I don't want to drag you into this, but if
someone doesn't help the prisoner, he's going to die."

The girl's face paled. Good. She had a conscience.

"Do you think you could talk James into sneaking me
into Ian's cell later tonight?"

Her face turned more ashen. "Oh, dear, I dinna know."

"Would you ask James? I can't let Ian die."

"Ian?" she said softly. "Is that his name?"

"Yes, Ian MacGregor. He's been wrongfully accused of
being a highwayman. Just ask James to help, please?"

"MacGregor?" she whispered. "James is a MacGregor,"
she said, then hastily added, "but dinna tell anyone. He has
changed his name, as all the MacGregors have since the
edict."

Maggie felt more hopeful. Clan loyalty was a biggie in
the Highlands. "Tell James, all right? If I can't help him tonight, maybe tomorrow morning I can sneak in some bandages and things when I bring his breakfast."

Jenny nodded. "James is meeting me after his shift. I
will ask him then."

Maggie wouldn't press her further on the matter. She was asking them to take a terrible chance. "Thanks." On impulse, she hugged the girl tightly before turning away, but Jenny stopped her, one hand on her arm.

"Maggie?" she said.

"Yes?"

"Ye talk strangely sometimes."

Maggie sighed. "I know. I'm from the colonies."

"Ah," Jenny said with a nod, as if that explained everything.

Quinn was getting worried. The kitchen maids were usually done with their chores an hour or so after supper was over. He had told Maggie to meet him in the stables when she finished her first day of work, but now it was growing late.

Bittie had gone to find out what he could, but Quinn had grown impatient and had soon left the stables, wearing an old cloak with the hood pulled over his face. He kept to the shadows and found a place behind a thick clump of bushes where he could watch for her. Montrose's servants and men walked by, attending to the duties that kept a huge household running smoothly, and several women passed by, but no Maggie.

He was ready to draw his sword and storm the kitchen, when a woman, striding too quickly for decorum, her hair half unbound and flying behind her, came rushing down the stone walk nearby.

Quinn reached out and grabbed her arm as she passed him, and she screamed. Cursing his stupidity, he clapped his hand over her mouth and pulled her back into the bushes, holding her tightly, sure any moment someone would drag them both from the hiding place and throw them in irons.

But apparently God was on their side, Quinn thought,

for there was no sound, no outcry from beyond the thick branches scratching his face.

"It's me," he whispered in her ear, having to resist kissing her just below the curve of her jaw where she liked it best. He didn't want to frighten her more. "Dinna scream," he cautioned, and carefully lowered his hand.

A blow caught him in the ribs and he grunted as Maggie whirled and hit him again, a right punch to his stomach.

"What in hell?" he said softly and furiously. "I told ye it was me!"

"I knew it was you!" she said. "At least, after you jerked me against you I knew it was you! I told you never to do that to me again!"

"Keep yer voice down unless ye want me caught and thrown in with Ian."

That seemed to calm her, and to his surprise, she threw herself against him, her arms going around his neck as she pressed her lips against the hollow of his throat and began to cry.

"Maggie, darlin'," he said, "shhh, *alanna*. Ye must be quiet, and we must leave at once."

"I'm sorry. Oh, Quinn, I'm so sorry." She clung to him tightly and sudden understanding washed over him and his hands slid to her arms, pushing her gently away.

"Ian is dead," he said.

The grief hit him and Quinn almost groaned aloud, but he kept his emotions under control as he gripped her arms, feeling that if he let go, he would fall. A muscle in his jaw twitched and he gritted his teeth to keep from crying out his anguish. Ian, his friend—dead now, because of him.

Maggie looked up at him and the moonlight fell upon her tear-streaked face. "Oh, no, Quinn, forgive me, I didn't stop to think—" She lifted her hands to his face, one on either side as she spoke to him. "Ian isn't dead, Quinn. He's alive!"

Quinn closed his eyes and felt the relief down to the hollow of his bones. "Thank the Lord," he said. He straightened and started to move past her. She grabbed his arm.

"Where are you going?"

"To Ian," he said. "I'm getting him out of there."

Her fingers bit into his arm. "Quinn, you can't just go barging into the duke's jail and rescue him! We've got to have a plan!"

He dragged his hand through his hair, shaking his head, unable to think. Ian was alive. There was no way Quinn would walk away and leave him for another minute in Montrose's dungeon.

"Aye, I have a plan." He laid his hand on his sword. "I'll cut down any man who tries to stop me, and I will free my friend." He started forward again, and Maggie slammed her shoulder into his stomach, forcing him to stop.

"Just stop and think, damn you!" she whispered fiercely. "If you go in there now, by yourself, you're just going to get killed—then what good will you be to Ian?"

Quinn drew in a deep, trembling breath. She was right. If he blundered in with no solid plan, he would be risking not only his life, but Ian's as well.

He nodded, and then rested his hands on her shoulders and searched her gaze. "He is alive, but in what condition? Was he truly shot?"

Maggie bit her lower lip and her eyes grew anxious. "He was shot and is very weak. I'm going to sneak in some bandages to him either tonight or in the morning. I hope to be able to cleanse his wound then." She glanced down at her hands, knotted together in front of her. "We need to get him out of there, no doubt about that, but as long as I can continue to help him—"

"Are ye tellin' me the truth?" Quinn demanded, giving her shoulders a slight shake. "Dinna lie to me, Maggie."

Her eyes blazed up at him. "I'm not lying! He's hurt,

and he stinks to high heaven, but he's had some ale and a little soup. I'm trying to find a way to sneak back into his cell tonight and bandage his wound. Tomorrow I'll come back and take care of him again. We'll keep it up until we can figure out a way to rescue him."

"Be careful, lass. Dinna take any rash chances," he said. Her face seemed to sag, and suddenly he remembered she'd been working since early that morning. He unclasped her hands and brought one palm to his lips, only to stop when she winced. "What is it?"

"Nothing," she muttered. Quinn pulled her out from the half shadows into the full moonlight. "Quinn—someone will see you!"

He stared down at the blisters and the caked blood on her hands and then shook his head. "Och, Maggie, what have I done?"

"Hey, a little floor scrubbing never hurt anybody. And you haven't done anything," she said, pulling her hands from his and sliding them up around his neck. "Yet. In fact, I'm starting to feel a little neglected."

He lowered his mouth to hers and gently caressed her lips. She drew away from him slightly. "Please," she whispered, "don't go to Ian now. Wait."

Quinn leaned his head against hers and then straightened and nodded. "All right, lass. I will trust what ye say." Slipping his arm around her waist, he led her to where Saint was tied, back behind the last outbuildings, in a copse of trees.

Maggie leaned against him heavily, and when she stumbled, he picked her up in his arms and carried her the rest of the way. Once there, he lifted her into the saddle and settled behind her. Keeping a sharp eye out, he waited until he was sure there wasn't a soul around, and then nudged Saint into action.

"He's alive, Quinn," she said softly. "I'm so, so glad."

Her voice was heavy with guilt. Poor lass. She still felt responsible, and why shouldn't she? He'd certainly made her feel as if it was all her fault. She'd risked herself not only to find Ian, but to help him.

For the first time in a very long time, Quinn lowered the barrier he kept ever vigilant around his heart. He slipped his arm around Maggie and pulled her back against him, feeling the gentle thud of her heart beneath his fingers as they rode silently together.

Never in her life had Maggie felt so safe, so protected, so *wanted*, as when Quinn climbed into the saddle behind her and wound his arm around her middle.

"Where are we going?" she asked sleepily.

"To Ian's grandmother's cottage. Ye need a good night's sleep in a real bed."

Maggie yawned. Sleep. In a bed. "Hmmm," she said, her eyes sliding shut, "that sounds wonderful. Does she know I'm coming?"

"If she's lookin' down from Heaven, then aye, she knows," he said, a smile in his voice. "She left it to him."

"Funny," she said. "Very funny." She leaned back against him and sighed.

It was all beginning to hit her now—the inexplicable journey through time, her part in Ian's capture, making love to Quinn—and somehow it was all too surreal to believe. She felt as if she had simply been cast in a movie set in 1711 Scotland. She and Quinn were just actors, along with everyone else—Bittie, the slightly dumb sidekick; Jenny, the abused maid; Montrose, the villain; and even Rob Roy MacGregor, historic hero.

As she and Quinn rode across the Highlands, the sun was setting in glorious splendor, the first faint clouds of mist rising across the velvet green hills and a distant loch.

Suddenly she felt as if she were sailing across some parallel universe, some dream world.

But the stark reality remained. Ian lay in a dank and dirty hole of a cell, waiting for rescue. She hadn't told Quinn how ill his friend had become and that he was in danger of being hanged. If she had, she knew nothing would have stopped the passionate highwayman from rushing into the dungeon to free his friend. No, before she told Quinn any more, she had to figure out a plan.

The sun was gone now behind the distant hills, the air growing colder. Even with Quinn's plaid draped around them both, Maggie wished she had put her pajama pants back on beneath her servant's skirt. She rode astride, her bottom once again in Quinn's lap, her legs curved over his as she leaned against his broad chest.

From the moment her back touched him, his presence had burned into her and sent fresh desire and energy coursing through her body. Saint settled into a rhythmic, rocking step, and she tried to relax as the movement pressed her harder against Quinn.

Her legs were bare above the black stockings Bittie had provided, and from time to time Quinn's hand holding the reins would lightly rest against her thigh. Maggie tingled with tiny electric shock waves that permeated the fabric and made her long for him to touch her bare skin. When his free hand moved to slide her skirt upward, she trembled with a desire she tried desperately to hide. Quinn apparently sensed her need, and he stroked his hand up her bare leg to her hip, hesitated, and then moved back over her skirt to skim his way over her waist, her ribs, to her breast.

There he caressed her soft flesh, making her sigh and press back harder against him. He moved his chin against her neck, raking her unbound hair out of the way, and the roughness of the stubble on his face sent a rush of fire through her veins just before she felt the warmth of his mouth against her neck.

His tongue darted out and flicked against her earlobe, traced a path downward to her shoulder, where he bit her gently. Maggie sighed and then moaned aloud as he pulled the edge of her blouse from her shoulders and slipped his hand beneath the fabric. His fingers slid over the top of one bare breast and moved downward across the sensitive nipple, now taut with desire. With each touch of his callused hand, fire burned against her skin as desperate need pooled between her legs, making her press downward against the saddle.

Maggie found her breath and heartbeat moving into the same rhythm as Quinn teased the curve of her jaw with his mouth and her body with his touch. He moved his hand away from her breast and she almost cried out aloud, but then she felt him drawing up the long skirt again, this time sliding his hand beneath the soft material to find the part of her that needed his touch the most. She hadn't had a chance to wash her single pair of panties yet, and that day she had gone without, feeling a little daring and wicked as she did her chores. She was dissolving into liquid heat, her breath coming in short gasps of pleasure, when all at once he stopped touching her. A little moan of protest escaped from her, then she realized he had knotted the horse's reins in front of her and looped them around the saddle horn. Maggie leaned back against Quinn, her chest rising and falling rapidly with expectation.

Now Quinn's fingers brushed up her thigh and to the softness between her legs, and she gasped as he found her there, naked and ready. He stroked her with a gentle passion, and in seconds she arched back and cried out as the shudder of her release rocked through her.

She felt Quinn lifting her and turning her to face him. Her legs were hooked over his thighs, and she looked up into his passion-filled eyes. He had pulled Saint to a stop beneath the moon rising high above them, the pony standing at the peak of one of the lower hills.

Maggie shivered, realizing they were on display for anyone passing by to see, but there was no one around in the still, unnatural twilight, and she was too far gone to even care. She leaned forward and wound her hands around his neck, her voice soft with passion.

"Do you really think you can make love to me on top of a horse, Quinn MacIntyre, and do me justice?"

"That all depends," he said, as he let his mouth skim across her bare shoulder. "Do ye trust me?" She hesitated, and he moved his lips to brush her ear. "Remember, I willna let ye fall."

"Yes," she whispered, "I trust you."

Quinn slid both hands into her hair, cradling her face as he lowered his mouth to hers. She met him halfway and climbed into his lap, clinging to him with her legs as she pressed herself down against him.

Beneath his kilt he was hard and ready, and as he devoured her mouth, her breast, the shivery spot behind her ear, she began to rub herself against him. When she could bear it no more, she lifted his plaid and found him bare beneath the coarse cloth, long and rigid and all for her.

Maggie lifted her lust-blurred eyes to Quinn's as she reached down and touched him, reveling in his sharp intake of breath and the way his green eyes slid half shut as he gazed back. She was desperate to feel him inside of her, and using his broad shoulders for purchase, she lifted herself above him and lowered her body, gasping as he filled her. Her pulse pounded as she slid back down to him, his arms around her, supporting her.

Her blouse was pulled below her breasts, but she didn't feel exposed. She felt strong and beautiful and somehow more powerful than she ever had in her life.

This time she was in control, and her legs and arms trembled as she lifted herself up again and then down, taking him inside of her, over and over again. His fingers bit into her back and Quinn trembled as she moved harder and faster atop him, up and down, the sensation sending throbbing waves of pleasure cascading through her as her knees pressed against his rock-hard thighs.

Maggie's breath came faster and then Quinn reached between them and touched her and she shattered into the night, into the moonlight, cradled in his arms. Now Quinn was in charge as he gathered her against him, and it was his power that drove into her, his need that surged thick and hard into the softness that he plundered, raided, stole. Maggie had no time to wonder or think as her desire quickened anew and he took what he wanted, again and again.

She found Quinn's mouth, devoured it, claimed it, even as he claimed her with every touch, every move, until the heat began to rise inside of her, burning brighter and hotter than before, and his hands were on her hips, his fingers strong and rough as he lifted her over the hard length of him again and again. Maggie felt the heady build of passion raise her higher and higher until she was mindless with need and the world disappeared around them, leaving only the fire where their bodies met and filled one another, stroke by amazing stroke. She cried out as she reached the sky, and then toppled over that exquisite precipice and Quinn caught her, shuddering in her arms, clutching her to him, keeping her safe even as he fell, too, whispering her name.

Saint started walking again, slowly, rocking them both into the soft oblivion that came after the storm.

What seemed like a thousand years later, Maggie roused enough to look up at him. "I'm glad I trusted you," she said, smiling up at him, feeling a little shy.

He chuckled. "Aye, lass, so am I."

She sighed and closed her eyes. Her stomach growled suddenly. I hope there's going to be a real supper at this cottage" she said. Quinn laughed. "Ye have a healthy appetite for such a little woman," he said.

Maggie curled herself against him, her arms around his waist, her face pressed to his chest. Maggie could hear his heart pounding beneath her own as she held him, never wanting to let him go.

"Just for some delicacies," she murmured, and closed her eyes.

Maggie woke before dawn to find she was alone. Quinn had told her he would rise early and build a fire and then take care of some neglected things around the cottage. As she lay back against the soft feather pillow, she was glad to have a few moments to herself, some silence in which to think. Staring at the weathered beams in the ceiling, Maggie reevaluated her situation. She was trapped in the past with a hunky stranger who made incredible love to her. Which would be great, if she knew she could go home again, because after a few days in 1711—in spite of her love of history and her growing affection for Quinn—she was pretty sure she didn't want to stay here. And what would happen to Allie and Ellie if she couldn't get back? A wave of panic rushed through her and she took several deep breaths, releasing each one slowly until the anxiety passed.

It was her fault Ian had been captured, and she couldn't leave until he was safe. But as soon as he was—

As soon as he was, what? Could she so easily leave Quinn and go back to her old life? Her old *lonely* life? And what if she *couldn't* get back? Then what?

Stop, stop, stop, Maggie commanded. *You'll find a way back. One thing at a time.*

Rising up on one elbow, she glanced around the room. Last night she'd been asleep when they got to the cottage, and she had only a vague recollection of Quinn depositing her in the bed and crawling in beside her. It was a plain room with rough-hewn walls and little in the way of decoration. But the bed was comfortable and had a worn coverlet stuffed with feathers.

"Quinn?" she called softly.

The door to the rest of the cottage was open, and she could see a fire flickering in the stone fireplace in the other room. It was dim and cold in the bedroom and Maggie shivered and snuggled down under the heavy coverlet. Thick wooden shutters latched across the only window in the room to keep out the chilly night air, always a losing battle in the Highlands.

She wasn't used to sleeping naked, but she didn't want to get out of bed to look for her pajamas. Clothing was unnecessary when snuggled up against Quinn's warmth. Maggie frowned. So why wasn't he here keeping her warm? He couldn't be taking a shower.

Speaking of bathrooms, she could do with some time in a real lavatory. Maybe the manor house had something better than a bush and a log. She'd have to ask Jenny. Were there hot baths in 1711? So far all she'd had was a sponge bath in an ice-cold stream.

As Maggie pondered her hygiene problems, a faint light filtered through the crack where the shutters came together. The sun must be rising. She could see a candle on the table beside the bed, and dragging her backpack up on the bed, she rummaged inside it until she found a small lighter. Ellie had promised she would need a lighter sooner or later, and now she blessed her sister as she flicked the flame to life and lit the candle. The soft light chased away the shadows, and she looked around at her room.

Something white lay across the end of the bed and she

reached for it, shivering as the cold air touched her bare skin. It was a nightgown! Quinn must have left it for her, but she'd been too sleepy when they first arrived.

Maggie pulled the gown over her head and found it was softer than she'd imagined something homespun in the Highlands could ever be. The garment was warm and cozy, with a soft little ruffle tucked around the high neck and the edge of the long, billowy sleeves that fell over her hands. She bundled back under the covers to stay warm.

Now she was wide awake. Where was Quinn, and why wasn't he here inside—oops–*be*side her?

As if in answer to her thought, she heard a stealthy movement, like wood being drawn across wood, and realized the outside door to the cottage was opening. Fear rushed through her all at once. What if it wasn't Quinn? Quickly she sat up, blew out the candle, stuffed her contraband items into her pack, and burrowed back under the thick coverlet.

When the shadowy figure came into the room she breathed a sigh of relief. Though he moved silently across the room, she could hear him breathing and knew it was Quinn. Maggie watched his dark shadow as he walked to the window and stood there for a long moment, then something rattled, and the shutter opened a few inches.

The pale light of morning gave a softness to the usual rugged lines of Quinn's face. His eyes were somber and filled with melancholy as he looked out the window, and Maggie felt a tug on her heart. Then she realized what he was wearing.

The vampire outlaw had returned.

"Please tell me you haven't been doing what I think you've been doing," Maggie said.

Quinn jerked his head toward her, the vulnerability in his face disappearing. "I'm sorry I woke ye, lass. Go back to sleep." He turned his face back toward the dawn.

"Right." Maggie thought for a moment and then threw the covers back, shivering as her feet hit the floor and the cold air slipped underneath the warm gown she wore. She crossed to his side and laid one hand on his arm. "I sort of remember this outfit," she said, smoothing the billowing sleeves of the black shirt he wore. "A guy who saved my life was wearing one just like it."

Quinn closed his eyes and without turning put his arm around her and drew her to him. Maggie slid her arms around his waist and leaned against him.

"Quinn, where have you been?" she asked softly. He looked down at her, and Maggie felt the familiar rush begin as he lifted his hand to brush a tangled lock of hair back from her face.

"I think ye know where I've been," he said.

"Robbing the rich and giving to the poor?" she quipped, wondering if he'd ever heard of Robin Hood.

Apparently he had, for he smiled in understanding. "Aye, that's the way of it."

"So you *are* a highwayman."

He raised both brows. "Was there any doubt of it? Here now, lass, get back in bed before ye catch a chill." Quinn pulled back the covers, and Maggie scrambled gratefully under the warm quilt.

"So who did you rob?"

"Bittie told me that Killearn, Montrose's man, was on the way back to the manor house with the duke's rent money. I waylaid him on the road and took everything he had." He gestured to a bundle on the floor.

"But why?" Maggie looked up at him. "Why would you risk being caught just when you found out that Ian is alive?"

Quinn's jaw tightened and he folded his arms over his chest. "Because if I'm going to get Ian out alive, I'm going to have to have help. I dinna know if I can count on the MacGregors, and so I may have to hire men to help me."

Maggie shook her head. "Quinn, you can't possibly think you can hire enough men to overpower all of the guards in Montrose's household?"

"If I have enough money, aye, I can." He stripped the black shirt from his back and flung it to the floor, and before she even knew what she was doing, Maggie was on her feet again, beside him. He closed his eyes and shivered as she slid her arms around his waist, then turned toward her, pulling her close.

"Quinn, you aren't thinking straight," she said, the heat of his body warming her, making her long for him to make love to her again. She tugged him toward the bed. "Come to bed and sleep for a little while." Maggie sank into the mattress and pulled Quinn down beside her.

"Maggie mine," he whispered, moving her long hair back from her shoulder as he pressed his mouth against her neck, "I need ye."

Maggie shivered, and this time not because of the cold. He lifted his head, and his breath warmed her lips just before he tightened his arms around her waist and lifted her against him to ravage her mouth. His urgency sent a new thrill of desire rippling through her, just before fear and regret and common sense broke through the passion. She pulled away, breathless.

"Maybe we shouldn't do this anymore," she said, and then looked around to see who could have said something that stupid.

ten

Apparently *she* had.

His hands grew still on her waist. "What? What do ye mean?"

What *did* she mean?

Quinn must have taken her silence for more rejection, because his voice turned deeper. "Do I not please ye? Dinna think ye can make me believe that. Ye moaned so loudly last night I feared ye would wake poor Grandmother Mim in her grave."

"Quinn . . ."

He lifted one hand to her face, sliding his fingers over her cheekbone and into her hair, combing the tangles gently. "What's troublin' ye, Maggie mine?"

Maggie closed her eyes and leaned against him, feeling the dark curly hair on his hard, bare chest brush against her face. "Quinn, this has all happened too fast. I mean, we've only known each other a few days, and—I'm scared."

"Scared?" He held her tighter, his breath warm against

her hair. "Darlin', why should ye be afraid? I willna let any harm come to ye."

"I can't stay with you, not forever."

Maggie looked up at him, her heart pounding beneath her ribs. He looked confused.

"Forever, is it?" He shook his head, the confusion changing to something darker, hotter, and dangerous. "Och, lass, do ye not know that there is no forever? There is today only. Tomorrow we might not even exist."

"That's what I'm worried about," she said faintly. "I'm—uh—I'm not from around here, you know? I have to go back home once we save Ian."

His green eyes grew lazy as he laid her down upon the bed and stretched out beside her. "Och, lass," he whispered against her ear, "dinna think of that now. Think only of this—" Maggie drew in a sharp breath as he caressed her breast through the nightgown, his fingers stroking her body tenderly.

"Hmm, yes, that's—really—nice"—Maggie drew in a deep breath—"but, but—" She pushed his hand firmly away and sat up, dragging her hair back from her face. "Look. You're amazing in bed and—"

"Thank ye," he said, his voice smug.

Maggie rolled her eyes. "And I feel, I mean, I'm really not into casual sex. When I make love to a man, I have to at least feel like the relationship is going somewhere."

Quinn pulled her back down on the bed. "It is going somewhere, lass," he said as he slipped his hands around her waist again and slid his body against hers. She shivered and tried to keep her thoughts straight. This was crazy. He was a man from the past. She had to go back to her own time. She couldn't leave her sisters on their own, not even for great sex.

She smiled as he turned her face to his and began

nibbling at the corner of her mouth. She knew how to get through to him, turn him off, and protect her own heart all at the same time.

"Here's the thing," she said, sliding her hands up his chest to cradle his head between her hands, lowering her voice to a husky whisper. "I love you, Quinn."

What better way to get him to run like a scared rabbit for Ben Lomond, than to start talking the *L* word? Great idea. Nip this in the bud now before somebody—like her—got hurt.

Her heart began to pound as if to say "Too late!" and Maggie suddenly realized she didn't want him to run.

He didn't. Quinn didn't move. Just for an instant, then he was out of the bed and standing in front of the open window, like a beautiful, naked stone statue staring down at her as the soft morning light streamed in through the window and lit his body from behind. Then he turned his face toward the rising sun, and a soft, slow smile gradually tilted the corners of the mouth she so loved to kiss.

"Ye love me," he said, looking for all the world as if Maggie had crowned him king of Scotland. He glanced back at her, and the softness in his eyes made Maggie realize something even worse.

Her words were true. She loved Quinn.

But no way was she going to let him know that. She'd just laugh and act like she was teasing him. Maggie swallowed as he continued to beam at her. How could she take the light out of those beautiful green eyes?

"Well, maybe I was overstating—I mean, we've only known each other, what, a couple of days? That's just silly! I think that all in all—" She shook her head and sighed. It was no use.

Maggie slid out of bed and walked back into his arms. It was too late anyway. She'd never been good at hiding her feelings. Her love for him had to be shining in her eyes. It had to be, for suddenly she realized she didn't just love Quinn, she adored him, she idolized him. He was her hero, and she wanted him more than any man she'd ever known or had ever imagined in the most delicious fantasies of her mind.

"Okay," she said, "look, I know this is dumb. Dumb of me to think and dumb of me to admit. Maybe I'm sort of mesmerized by the spectacular sex we've had, but—" she broke off, feeling stupid as Quinn smiled at her, his eyes amused, but something tender there, too.

"Och, lass, ye dinna love me."

Wait a minute. Maggie frowned. "Yes, I do."

He shook his head and slid his hands over her shoulders. "Ye love the way I make ye feel," he said, "just as I love making ye feel that way. It is easy to confuse the two."

Great. He was going to talk her out of being in love with him. Fat chance, buddy.

Maggie took a step back, and his hands fell to his sides. "I am not confused. I don't give my love easily, Quinn. I'm not some teenybopper with a crush on her favorite TV star. I love you!"

Quinn frowned. "I have no idea what ye just said."

"Forget it," she said, turning away from him as her heart began to ache. "I take it all back."

His warm hand closed around her arm and he spun her into his arms again, immediately bending her backward as he lowered her to the bed. "Dinna take it all back, just dinna take it all so seriously," he murmured as he slid into bed beside her.

Maggie folded her arms over her chest. If Quinn Don't-Take-It-Seriously MacIntyre thought he was getting laid after that, he had another think coming!

Raising up on one elbow, he gazed down at her, his mouth quirking up in amusement.

"I'm not in the mood," she told him.

He laughed softly and began to nibble the side of her neck.

"I mean it, Quinn."

"I know ye do, lass." He unwound her arms from her chest and began to caress her breasts, sliding rough fingers over the material, making her nipples harden and tingle.

"Do you really think I'm this easy?" she asked, trying to keep the anger in her voice, but oh, he did make her feel so good.

"Nay, Maggie mine," he said, sliding her nightgown up around her waist as he positioned himself between her legs. "I think ye are the sweetest lass I have ever lain with in my life, but ye are far from easy. In fact, I would say ye're a bit difficult sometimes."

"I am not!" she said, staring up at the ceiling.

"Nay, ye are not. I was trying to make a jest."

Then she met his eyes and sucked in her breath. Quinn held himself above her, hands pressed into the bed on either side of her shoulders, his gaze warm and affectionate and very, very sexy.

She wanted to tell him that sexy looks were not going to make everything all right, that if they were going to continue to make love, he needed to be in love with her. But he was busy pulling her nightgown up higher and she hated to interrupt him.

"What do you think you're—"

Quinn took one taut nipple in his mouth, and Maggie gasped and arched against him.

"Don't you think Rob Roy has already heard that Ian is alive?" Maggie asked as the two rode toward Loch Lomond. It was just after dawn, and the grass and heather across the hills were bright with dew. *Diamonds on amethyst,* Maggie thought, distracted as Quinn remained silent.

After her startling pronouncement of undying love, Maggie had spent the next two days, while scrubbing the kitchen floor, kicking herself metaphorically black-and-blue. Quinn had continued to act as he always had, so apparently her confession had neither scared him away nor endeared her to him. To punish him just a little for being such a smug—*man*—Maggie had spent the last two nights in Jenny's room, pleading the need to rise early to take care of Ian before Pembroke made his morning rounds. Quinn had just shrugged and said for her to do whatever would ensure Ian's health and well-being. The jerk.

She'd spent those rather sleepless nights beside Jenny trying to figure out one, how to keep from falling even more in love with Quinn than she already had, and two, how to make Quinn see that he needed to handle the problem of Ian's escape with brains, not brawn. So far, she'd come up empty on both.

But when Bittie told her that Quinn was going to talk to Rob Roy, Maggie had bribed the cook with a trial-sized bottle of cologne from the bottom of her backpack to give her a day off. She wanted to be with Quinn when he talked to Rob Roy again. When he'd picked her up that morning, a mile from the manor, the happiness in Quinn's eyes made her heart fill with longing.

"Perhaps he has heard Ian is alive," Quinn said as Saint ambled across the dew-bright grass beneath his feet, "but I told him I would return when I knew where we stood, and so return I must."

Maggie frowned and ran over her knowledge of Scottish history and Rob Roy MacGregor. Yes, 1711 was right before Rob Roy had been declared an outlaw. At this point, he was still trying to raise money to pay back the Duke of Montrose. He had borrowed one thousand pounds from Montrose to finance a herd of cattle, but before he could give the man his profits, the money had been stolen from Rob.

Now Montrose was threatening to put Rob Roy in the Glasgow Tolbooth, the local prison. Would they take Ian there? It would be impossible to break him out of that well-guarded fortress.

"He's just afraid it will hurt his negotiations with Montrose," she told Quinn, pushing the thought of Ian to the back of her mind. "If he can repay the duke the money he owes him, he might be willing then to take a bigger risk for Ian."

"How do ye know about that?" he asked. "I dinna tell ye."

Oops. "Uh, I heard a rumor about it at the manor."

"Aye, no doubt the gossips have spread it far and wide by now. But Ian is part of Rob's clan. He shouldn't refuse to aid him." He fell silent again.

Thankfully, Ian was slowly getting better. There had been plenty of the broad spectrum antibiotics, which Maggie had been forgetting to take, for Ian, and the medicine, along with fresh, daily dressings on his wound, and hot food, had made for a marked improvement.

"Are you worried about what Rob Roy will say?" she asked, as Saint started downhill next to a babbling brook that ran down to the glen below, and they began to ride beside the dark waters of Loch Lomond.

"Nay, I am not worried," he said grimly, "for I fear I already know."

When they arrived at the outlaw's house in Craigrostan, Rob's wife, Mary, met them at the door, shook her red head, and *tsked* under her breath before taking Maggie inside while the men stayed outside to talk. Maggie would have rather stayed with Quinn, but she didn't want to be rude.

"So," Mary said in her low, melodic voice, after ushering Maggie inside and offering her a wash at a wooden bowl full of water sitting on a table in the corner. "How long have ye been with our Quinn and when will the wedding day be?"

Maggie took the towel the petite woman handed her. She smiled hesitantly and blotted her wet face. "Oh, I only met him a few days ago. We're just, er, friends." *With benefits*, she thought, fighting back a smile.

"Och, friends, is it?" She gave Maggie a knowing look as she crossed to the stone fireplace and lifted the lid from a pot hanging over the flames. A savory smell swept through the cabinlike dwelling.

"That smells wonderful," Maggie said, racking her brain for a subject that would steer them away to more neutral ground. "Do you have children, Mary?"

"Oh, aye," she said, taking a ladle from a wooden table nearby and dipping it into the pot to stir. "I've two sons and pray to have another before another year passes." She glanced up. "And what about ye and Quinn? Any bairns in the makin'?"

Maggie just laughed and tried to think of an excuse to run out the door. She turned and looked out the open window beside her. Over a dozen men had gathered, and Quinn stood in the middle of the group. Maggie could tell that he was not a happy camper.

"What's going on out there?" she asked, glancing back at Mary. The woman moved to stand beside her and then cursed eloquently under her breath before running to the door.

"I told that man not to do this, but does he ever listen to me?" She jerked open the door and stormed out, with Maggie close on her heels.

Rob had started off amiably enough, listening to Quinn's report on Ian, but as they had talked, more people had arrived, first one by one and then in small groups. As the men began to cluster around him, a low murmur began.

The door to the cottage opened, and he saw Mary

MacGregor hurrying toward them, with Maggie in tow. Before the women reached the fire, upward of thirty men had gathered. Most gave him dark looks as he concluded his story.

"And so, Ian is alive, and I need yer help, the help of the clan, to set him free."

Rob's dark eyes met his levelly. "Do ye now?" he said.

"Aye." He glanced around at the other men. "If ye are willing."

"Willing to put our necks in the noose by walking into Montrose's keep and trying to waltz out with one of his prisoners under our arms?" one of the men called out.

"Perhaps we can sneak the lad out under our plaids," another said. Laughter greeted that remark, and Quinn turned on the speaker, but Mary MacGregor spoke first.

"Whist, now," she said, "'tis no time to be jesting, with a man's life at stake." She shot Rob Roy a pointed look.

"Aye, Mary," Rob agreed, "but I wonder"—he turned to Quinn—"were ye concerned with that possibility, Quinn MacIntyre, when ye took Ian into this recklessness with ye?"

Rob's voice cut through the laughter and everyone grew quiet.

Quinn felt a muscle in his jaw begin to twitch. "Ian knew the risks. Ye talk as if he were a wee bairn instead of a man."

"Did either of ye consider the risks, I wonder," Rob said, one booted foot propped on a stone. He wore his customary kilt of blue and gray plaid, with a fairly grimy shirt beneath and a leather jacket atop it. He leaned his elbow against his thigh, a long clay pipe in his hand.

"Did ye or Ian think of anything save yer own foolish selves?"

Quinn took a deep breath and released it, fighting for

control. It would do no good to lose his temper now. "We stole from Montrose, our sworn enemy. We gave away as much wealth as we kept."

"And brought more of the duke's anger down upon our heads!" Rob said sharply, lowering his foot to the ground and straightening. " 'Tis one thing to reive his cattle or take the paltry sums he collects from his tenants, but when ye begin raiding his supplies and stealing from his aristocratic friends, that is when ye will bring the wrath not only of the duke down upon us, but the Crown itself!"

The voices of the crowd rang out in loud agreement. Quinn shook his head, a sense of betrayal sweeping over him. He had expected Rob to balk, but had hoped otherwise.

"How can ye turn yer back on yer own kin?" Quinn demanded. "Ye would protect Montrose, when the man is in the process of putting ye to the horn?"

Rob shook his head, his ruddy face bright in the firelight. " 'Tis exactly why I canna conscience this wild plan of yers. Ye know the position I am in right now. Until I pay back the money that was stolen from me, I willna bring Montrose's anger further upon us."

"I welcome other ideas," Quinn said stiffly.

"And I have none to give ye."

"And yet ye can stand there and rebuke me." Quinn shook his head in disgust. The crowd of men began to mutter and murmur again.

Maggie had crossed to Quinn's side, but she did not touch him. He was grateful, both for her presence and her restraint. She stood beside him, slightly behind his shoulder, as a good Scot's wife should, showing support by her disapproving silence. *Wife?* He frowned at the thought.

"Whist!" Rob Roy cried out. The crowd grew quiet and silence stretched across the people waiting. "I will think upon it," Rob Roy finally said. "But I make ye no promises. First I will want to hear a new plan—one that willna sacrifice the whole of our clan!"

"Robert," Mary said, fire in her eyes as she strode toward her husband, "what are ye saying? That ye will leave Ian MacGregor, yer own kith and kin, in Montrose's dungeon to rot?"

"Stay out of this, woman," he cautioned.

" 'Tis all right, Mary," Quinn said, unable to keep the quiet bitterness from his voice. "I will rescue Ian, and I will do it without the help of the MacGregors." He turned and took Maggie by the arm, letting her know it was time to go.

"Robert!" Mary cried again, and then, seeing no response from her husband except a glower, crossed to Quinn and Maggie. "Ye can stay the night, Quinn MacIntyre," she said. "Ye and the lass, and give my husband and these lads time to come to their senses."

"Nay, Mary, though I thank ye for yer kindness. We have a place to stay." He put his arm around Maggie and guided her toward Saint, grazing near the cottage.

She was unusually quiet as they walked, but regained her voice when they reached the horse. "Quinn, are you sure we shouldn't stay the night? Maybe in the morning—"

"Nay. His mind is made up, and so is mine."

He lifted her up on Saint's back and they rode away, she in front of him, Quinn holding himself so stiffly she thought he might crack. After a long while, she spoke again.

"You Scots are a stubborn, hardheaded lot, aren't you?" she said.

"Aye," he said, his temper flaring, "and if ye want to stay behind with that lot, just say the word, woman, and I will take ye back!"

"No," she said, her soft hair caressing the edge of his

taut jaw as she leaned back against him. "I'm exactly where I want to be."

"Now, there's a smile to light up the mornin'. Come here, missy, and give me a kiss."

Maggie's rigid smile grew more taut as she deftly avoided the groping hand and puckered lips of another one of the duke's male guests. For the last week and a half she'd been the serving maid for Montrose and his aristocratic friends, promoted after the duke saw her on her hands and knees scrubbing the hall.

She'd made the mistake of thinking he was Lavery, the upstairs butler, and had smiled up at him. Montrose had immediately ordered that she be moved from the backbreaking tasks she'd been assigned to the more prestigious position of serving maid.

And all because she had good teeth.

Well, maybe that was being a little too modest. The truth was, the women in this age led such hard lives that their faces, as well as their bodies, began to sag and wrinkle all too early. Maggie didn't believe she was a beauty by any means, but when matched against some of the leather-skinned girls working in the manor, she knew she was Miss Universe in comparison.

While the other girls envied her, and some groused about her being promoted when she'd been there for so short a time, Maggie wished she could be back scrubbing the floors. Dodging the hands of the aristocrats had made her a nervous wreck. Most of the men were likely just out for a squeeze or a quick grab, but there was one who truly frightened her—Phillip Pembroke, captain of the guards.

The man dogged her steps it seemed, was always where she was working, never actually touching her, but making such innuendoes that her face stayed scarlet in his presence. Once he had backed her into a corner, his hands behind his back, bringing his face nearer and nearer to hers. Maggie hadn't known what to do. To scream or hit him would be to lose her position and perhaps be thrown into the gaol with Ian. Finally, Pembroke had laughed and moved away from her without a second glance, making his way back to his quarters.

She truly hated him.

But she was there for a purpose, and so, as she put bowl after bowl of soup in front of the bewigged gentlemen sitting at the duke's long table in the formal dining room, and put up with their pinches and crude remarks, she listened for news about Ian. Despite her new position, she still cared for the wounded man, late at night when Pembroke had retired for the evening. Ever since James had learned Ian was a MacGregor, he'd helped Maggie in any way he could.

Luckily, Ian was a natural-born actor and had managed to feign near death any time Pembroke visited him, which wasn't often. The stench of the dungeon offended the captain's sensibilities, James had told her.

She placed another bowl of soup on the table and glanced around.

She and Jenny had done a beautiful job of decorating the room for this dinner party. The long table that seated twenty people was covered in heavy white linen, with fine china at each setting and silverware set atop heavy cream-colored cloth napkins. Down the center of the table, every few feet, were elaborate golden candlesticks.

The Duke of Montrose, James Graham, sat at the end of the table in a large, thronelike chair, while the others sat on either side in smaller versions of his carved monstrosity. He had probably once been a handsome man, but now his face had become craggy and thin, his bushy gray eyebrows dominating his face.

He insisted on wearing elaborate white wigs that reached almost to his waist and was purported to be quite vain about his footwear, which was said to come quarterly from Italy. Tonight the coat he wore was a dark burgundy brocade, and his cravat and shirt were of the finest silk.

"I say, Montrose," said a stout Englishman as Maggie moved to set his soup in front of him, "I hear the Lady Covington will be attending your soirée at week's end?"

The man was an earl, Jenny had told her, and rich as, well, a lord. He, like most of the other men—and tonight's party was all men—wore clothing similar to the duke's. Only one man stood out tonight in his choice of clothing, and Maggie tried not to look at him.

"Aye," Montrose said. "She should be arriving at sunset on Friday, no doubt in her usual traveling clothes—a silken gown and her best diamonds." The men laughed at his jest, and Maggie slowed in her serving of soup. Jenny served as well, tonight, on the opposite side of the table. She had the misfortune to have to serve Pembroke.

Normally a mere captain of the guards wouldn't be invited to sup with the gentry, but he was also the duke's sister's nephew, or so Jenny had told Maggie. Tonight he wore a coat of deep rose pink velvet. His shirt, cravat, and all the frothy lace down his front and at his wrists were also pale pink. He reminded Maggie of a grown-up Little Lord Fauntleroy—until she looked into his hard, evil eyes.

"'Tis said," Pembroke said, lifting his crystal wine glass to let it sparkle in the light of the candles ringing the dining hall, "that once Lady Covington took a lover, and when he unclothed her, he found that her undergarments were studded with gems."

His languid gaze slid to Maggie's as he brought the glass to his lips. She quickly lowered her eyes and went about her duties.

"Her mother is from Rome," said another foppish young man.

"Well, then, that explains it," said another. "No Englishwoman would be so outlandish."

"No Englishwoman would take off her clothes in front of her lover!" another chimed in, and all the men laughed again.

Maggie continued around the table, serving and nodding and evading hands and avoiding Pembroke's side.

"What about that scalawag highwayman ye were having trouble with?" asked the man at the duke's left hand. "Have ye caught him yet?"

"Aye, we caught him," Montrose said.

"But I heard ye had another attack not long ago," the same man said. "And that yer rents were stolen from Killearn."

Maggie didn't know anything about the tall, older man speaking, except that she'd never seen him at one of the Duke's dinners before. He was the most conservatively dressed of the lot, though his wig was just as white and just as long as the one Montrose sported. "That was of no consequence," Montrose said. "Killearn exaggerates. A drunken encounter, no more."

"So he came away with his wallet intact?" the same man asked.

Montrose glared at the man. "Do I put my nose into yer business, Argyll?" he said sharply. "Keep yer comments to yerself and eat yer soup."

Argyll. Maggie refilled a water glass. Of course, Campbell and Graham, bitter enemies in this time period. Argyll bowed his head in the duke's direction and then turned with satisfaction to his soup.

"They called him the Piper, did they not?" asked another.

"Aye, the Piper," Pembroke put in, sliding a look toward

the duke. "I caught him personally, and the bastard is now rotting in my gaol." He bowed toward Montrose. "Beg pardon, in His Grace's gaol."

Surely the magistrate will have something to say about it," Argyll said. "Will the outlaw not be bound in the Tolbooth in Glasgow?"

"That is between myself and the magistrate," the duke said loudly.

"I heard he was shot," Argyll said.

"Aye," Pembroke agreed. "A nasty wound. I daresay he may not last the week."

"Is he being treated by a doctor?" Argyll asked.

"Here, girl!" Montrose waved at Maggie, and she hurried to his side. "Take this slop away and tell the cook to send out some real food."

Maggie dropped him a curtsey and almost ran from the room, anxious to be back before he revealed anything about Ian's fate. When she got back with a platter of roast beef, the men were laughing again. She would ask Jenny later if she had missed anything important.

"So, will ye send a guard for Lady Covington?" Argyll asked, after the laughter died down.

Montrose shrugged as he dug into the plate of roast beef Maggie had deposited in front of him. "Aye, to be on the safe side, I suppose I'll send a few of my lads to meet her when she reaches Glasgow."

"If the highwayman is well and truly captured in yer gaol, why go to the expense?" Argyll insisted, cutting into his meat delicately with knife and fork.

The duke glared at him, but his mouth was full. Pembroke picked up the question smoothly, his icy gaze leveled at Argyll.

"Because there are more outlaws in the hills than the one I have in my custody, my lord." He lifted his wineglass toward Maggie. "But soon that will not be the case."

As Maggie hurried to refill Pembroke's glass, her heart began to pound. Quinn would want to know about this Lady Covington. Even if she told him that there would be guards with the carriage, she knew it wouldn't stop him from robbing a rich English lady wearing a fortune in jewels.

Well then, she thought, *I just can't tell him.* She lifted her chin, dodged another grasping hand, and headed back to the kitchen for more gravy.

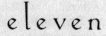

eleven

Quinn picked up his mug of ale and took a drink. Bittie slugged down his second since they'd entered the pub in the village of Drymen, as silent as his friend except for the smack of his lips as he lifted a roasted turkey leg from his plate and took a big bite.

The stone building was an oddity in a village made up largely of small houses topped by thatched roofs and a kirk on a nearby hillside. The Clachan Inn, as it was called, with its high ceiling and large fireplace, had a large common room and was the gathering place for Scottish men from all walks of life. As a result, it was a noisy, boisterous place, where it was as likely for a song to break out as a fight.

Quinn was in no mood for either, and he'd been glad to see that a table in a far corner of the pub was empty when he and Bittie entered. He wanted to speak privately with his friend and enjoy a drink without any trouble.

He'd been enjoying a drink a little too often lately, he realized. Ever since Maggie had told him that she loved him and then promptly began avoiding him. What had the lass been thinking, to bare her heart to him after only knowing him for mere days?

She didn't love him. That had become evident when she started sleeping with Jenny instead of him! After the wonderful night they had spent together at the cottage, he'd thought t'was only the beginning of a beautiful love affair. But the next day she had told him she was going to stay at the manor and share Jenny's bed. It was enough to drive any man to drink. He lifted his ale and took another swallow, just to prove his point.

"So how did ye come by this information about Lady Covington?" Quinn asked Bittie as the man devoured a large turkey leg. "I thought the servants in the house wouldna have anything to do with ye."

"Aye," he said around the bite of meat, "ever since Cook found out I was lovin' both her and the laundry woman, she willna let any of the household servants speak to me." He didn't seem to disturbed by his banishment, and Quinn pressed his point.

"Then how did ye find out?"

Bittie looked uncomfortable for a moment.

"Out with it, lad," Quinn said mildly.

"My niece, Jenny, works in the kitchen, but I dinna tell ye because I dinna want her involved in this. Her mother gave her into my care."

"Ye could have told me. I wouldn't have put a lass in danger." Quinn frowned, knowing he was doing exactly that in letting Maggie work in the manor.

Bittie looked vastly relieved. "Thank ye. She usually keeps to herself, but today, Jenny let it slip," he said, "about Lady Covington. She overheard it during the duke's dinner party last night."

Quinn shook his head. "I dinna understand then, how Maggie failed to hear the same news. She must have known."

Bittie tore off another piece of meat, and Quinn looked away. Dining with Bittie was enough to make him lose his appetite. He was glad he had decided just to drink his supper.

"Oh, aye, she knew," the man said. "The duke announced the matter loudly, and Maggie was serving. Jenny told me."

Quinn shot him a sharp look. "Why would Maggie not send me word?"

Bittie shook his head. "Och, who can say, laddie? She's a woman, and there's no knowing the mind of one. Ye should know that by now."

"Aye," Quinn said shortly, "but I think I understand this one. She doesna want me taking the risk again, and so thinks to circumvent me by holding back the information."

He stopped the serving maid and ordered a whiskey before draining the ale in his mug as the anger burned through him.

First she had removed herself from his bed, and now she thought to muddle about in his business. Ian's life depended on his ability to get enough shillings together to hire a small army, and the only way that would be possible was by turning highwayman again. Her interference could cost Ian's life.

His drink came, and he and Bittie sat in silence again, both lost in thought. Quinn resisted the urge to throw the full shot of liquor to the back of his throat. He would need his wits about him in order to pull off a one-man robbery. Bittie had warned him that Montrose was sending guards, but even that news had not disuaded him.

Maggie was staying at the manor house again that night, which was fortunate, for now he wouldn't have to make up a story about why he wouldn't be at the cottage. He stared down into his whiskey. Though her absence from his bed made his own plans simpler to carry out, he was still frustrated by her decision. Surely the lass missed

the soft mattress at the cottage. Jenny's bed was hard and
narrow, Maggie had said. Surely she remembered the
late-night supper they had together before she left; remembered feeding one another trifles of bread and meat,
licking the juices from each other's fingers. Surely she
missed his arms around her at night, missed the warmth,
the passion, the—

Quinn stopped himself, aghast. Had he really been
about to say "the love"?

He sipped his drink and considered his situation. He
didn't love the lass. He cared about her, aye, he wasn't a
knave. But love—that was something that had died inside
of him long ago.

But he did miss Maggie. Missed her warm, soft body,
her lush, sweet lips, her bonny blue eyes, her laughter, her
quick wit, her—nay, nay, he backtracked, panicking a
little—he only cared about her body.

He took a deep, ragged breath. How her eyes had
flashed with a bit of fire when Rob Roy had denied them
his help. Aye, she would make a fine Scottish wife.

Quinn set his whiskey glass down and straightened. No,
she wouldn't.

But there wasn't a reason in the world the lass should be
lying on a cold stone floor instead of in his arms. Quinn
picked up his glass again and took a long swallow. After
tonight, that was definitely going to change.

"So, how are ye today, laddie?" Maggie spooned another
bit of broth into Ian's mouth as she asked the question.

She suspected he was perfectly able to feed himself, but
liked the attention. And in truth, he was still quite weak, in
spite of his improvement.

"I am doin' much better, thanks to ye," he said softly,
watching her from beneath his lashes, his blue eyes almost

cobalt in the dim light of the cell. His wound was still healing nicely thanks to the antibiotics and antibiotic ointment.

"I'm glad." Maggie stirred the soup, distracted by her own thoughts. Today was the day Lady Covington was due to arrive. She could hardly do her work for worry of the coming night. That very morning she learned that Jenny had told Bittie the news of the countess a few days before, and that Bittie had told Quinn.

Quinn had stayed away from the manor last night, so she had no idea if he planned to rob the woman or not. She had grilled Bittie, trying to find out, but the taciturn man had played dumb. But knowing Quinn, there was little doubt as to what he would do.

"Just the new hay alone is enough to raise a man's spirits in this dreadful place," Ian said, "not to mention the absence of the shackles." Maggie turned back to him, once again smiling at one of the handsomest men she'd ever met. But he wasn't Quinn. She bit back a sigh. Her nights just hadn't been the same since she started staying at the manor, and when he hadn't shown up the night before as he usually did, she'd realized, once again, that although Quinn cared about her, he obviously wasn't in love with her.

"You can thank James. He's taking a big risk," she murmured.

"Aye, but t'was at your bidding," Ian said, his gaze warm. "Ever since he told Pembroke I might have the pox, the captain hasna been to my cell to gloat."

Maggie frowned. She hoped Ian wasn't mistaking her kindness for something more. The first week she'd given him sponge baths until she realized that he was enjoying them way too much. Now she just provided a cloth and a basin of water.

"I can never repay yer kindness, Maggie," he said, "but I'd like to try. Perhaps when all of this is over, ye and I could share a loaf of bread, a jug of wine—"

"'And thou beside me, singing in the wilderness'?" Maggie interrupted, and then laughed at the shocked look on his face. "I didn't know the Scots read the works of an obscure Persian poet," she added.

He looked at her, startled. "The poetry of Omar Khayyam is filled with music and wonder. My father presented me with a book of his quatrains a few months before he disinherited me. But how in the world do ye know of such things?"

Maggie laughed. "Why are you so surprised that I've read the *Rubaiyat*?" she teased.

He shook his head, his voice incredulous. "I'm surprised ye can read at all!" he said. "To think, a woman reading."

Maggie widened her eyes and then just as quickly narrowed them. Of course, in this day and age, women didn't read. It was silly to want to "educate" the man as to what women were capable of, but she still wanted to with all of her heart.

"Imagine," she said dryly, "that a woman could actually have the intelligence required for such a thing!"

Ian nodded, oblivious to her sarcasm. "Aye, 'tis strange to say the least. But ye dinna answer me." He tilted his handsome face to one side. He reminded her of Brad Pitt in *Legends of the Fall*, with his long blond hair, sky blue eyes, and pretty boy looks. Cute. Not Quinn, but still, very cute.

She frowned. "Answer what?"

"About the wine and supper, after I'm out of this wretched place."

"I don't think Quinn would like that," she said as she lifted another spoonful of broth to his mouth. "At least, I hope he wouldn't."

"Oh, ho! I thought so!" Ian cried, jostling her hand. The soup splattered all over Maggie's face and the front of her blouse.

"Hey!"

"Sorry, lass. Ye and Quinn are lovers, aren't ye?" He grinned at her and then lifted one hand to his head and fell back against the hay.

She rushed to his side. "Are you all right?"

"Aye," he said, a little breathless. "And that glad to know that the lad has finally succumbed to a woman's charms."

Maggie blushed. "Well, I doubt it was the first time."

Ian shook his head. "Nay, but ye are exactly the kind of lass he's been needin'."

"And what kind of lass is that?" she asked, genuinely interested, and determined to get more food into him. She helped him sit up again and fed him more soup, then handed him a piece of bread.

He took it and bit off a small piece, chewing thoughtfully as he answered her. "A lass who will make him realize there is more to life than revenge. A gentle lass who will make a home for him, where he can, at last, lay down his sword and rest."

Maggie looked at Ian with new respect. "And you think I'm that lass?"

He nodded. "Aye. No doubt about it. So do me a favor and name yer firstborn after me." He swallowed the small piece of bread, and she saw the light fade from his eyes. "Even though he will be a MacIntyre, I'll still feel that a little part of me has lived on."

"Ian," Maggie said softly, as she covered his hand with hers, "Quinn is going to get you out of here. You believe that, don't you?"

She saw the dart of anguish in his eyes before he quickly looked away. "Oh, aye, lass," he said, the jester back again. "Quinn will come ridin' to my rescue any day now, I have no doubt aboot it. With bells in his stallion's mane and a feather in his cap."

He turned his gaze back to her, and the levity left his voice. "That is what I fear. I meant what I said before, lass. I dinna want Quinn making some grand, heroic sacrifice to save me. I knew there was risk in what we were doing, and I was willin' to take it. Will ye tell Quinn that for me?" His tawny brows knit together as he watched for her response.

"Yes," she said softly. "I'll tell him. But you know as well as I do that it won't make a bit of difference. Quinn is determined to get you out of here. No matter what the cost."

"Aye, lass," he said, "but bear in mind, when dealing with a hardheaded lad like Quinn, sometimes ye must fight fire with fire."

Maggie stared at him for a moment and then grinned. "Ian MacGregor, you are brilliant."

The handsome man nodded. "Well, of course I am," he said.

She gave him a quick hug and then hurried out of the cell, determined to light a torch that would stop Quinn MacIntyre from getting himself killed.

The elements were against him.

Quinn stood beside Saint, the two hidden behind a cluster of gigantic stones thrusting out of the stark Scottish hillside. On any given day in the Highlands there would be a goodly amount of rain, but this day there had been only a fine mist in the morning. The sun was still beaming down, for the nights of summer were growing shorter. There was neither cover of storm, nor cover of night to hide him this time.

Bittie had given him the route the carriage would travel, and now Quinn lay in wait on a hillside not too far from the village of Drymen. Sitting loosely in Saint's saddle, he dragged one hand through his ragged hair, scraping it back from his face before tying a black kerchief over his head.

He checked the load in his pistol, put it back in the holster at his side, and squinted at the setting sun.

Though the evening was clear, it brought to mind another time he had waited like this, readying himself, making soft jests with Ian. The night he met Maggie.

Ah, sweet Maggie. It had been only a short time since she stumbled into his path, but she had changed his life dramatically. Over the last year or so, he had grown used to being alone, just as he had grown used to the need for revenge. Maggie had changed that. Now, when the darkness inside his soul came roaring to the surface, there she was, her innocent face shining up at him like an angel's, chasing away the shadows.

Her admission of love had truly come as no surprise. After their first day together—no, in truth, after their first night of lovemaking—her gaze had been filled with adoration. Lord knew he had not treated her well in the beginning, but somehow, it was as though she had seen through the darkness inside of him and found there was still a spark of something better. Somehow, she had reached past the careful wall he had built around his emotions and touched a heart he'd thought long dead.

Saint moved restlessly beneath him. Now, as Quinn sat breathing the soft Highland air, he knew his anger over Maggie's decision to sleep at the manor had been but a ruse of his own mind. He was not angry—he was lonely. Every minute of every day that they were apart was painful. And now there was no doubt about it—Maggie was not just another woman to be bedded and enjoyed and then bid goodbye. She was important to his life.

Quinn ran one hand over the stubble on his face and pondered that for a moment. How had the lass come to mean so much to him? A feeling stirred inside him, one he feared very much might be some emotion deeper than mere affection. And with that feeling came a revelation.

He was changing. Now he felt, just a little bit, like the Quinn who had once planned to be a piper, the Quinn who had laughed and enjoyed his life. The Quinn he'd thought dead and buried after Montrose murdered his family. Where once revenge against Montrose had been his only concern, now he thought more and more of what it would be like to settle down, to have a family, to return to the joys of his music.

Every time he thought of such a future, Maggie was at the center of those fanciful dreams. The lass had brought him back to life with her laughter and her fire, with her looks of adoration and her cutting wit. He loved her. There, it was as simple as that. He loved her.

His heart leapt up for a brief moment, and then quickly crashed down. There was no way to have a peaceful life with Maggie. It was mere fancy to think it could happen. Life in the Highlands was hard, the Scottish clans always at war with England and one another. There was no peace. And he had his own war to fight, his own score to settle, against Montrose.

Saint threw back his head and whinnied softly. Quinn jerked back to attention at the sound of carriage wheels approaching. From an inside pocket of his cloak he took his mask and pulled it on. As the carriage came into sight, Quinn put his heels to Saint's side and sent his horse down the steep hillside as he had so many times before, with Ian by his side. Only this time, when Quinn rode across the flatland below, directly into the path of the oncoming carriage, and the driver pulled back on the reins to stop the four charging horses, four armed guards immediately surrounded him.

"Throw down your pistol and sword!" the leader of the guards shouted.

His accent was not Scottish. He wore a long, dark blue coat and knee breeches, cut simply enough, but with a froth of lace at his throat and his wrists, he was anything but the usual captain of the guards—and yet, he was obviously in charge. A golden blond wig curled halfway to his waist beneath a dark blue tricornered hat, which sported several feathers and a sprig of heather.

The man wore expensive leather gloves and even more expensive boots that came to his knees. Quinn ran a calculating eye over his foe and was not encouraged. His face was dissipated, the face of a man who has seen too much, done too much, but doesn't regret a moment of his debauchery. "Throw your weapon to the ground!" the captain cried. "Or I will cut you down where you stand!"

Quinn struggled for a moment with the order, wanting to pull his pistol and fire, draw his sword and fight, but common sense prevailed, and he dropped both to the ground.

"Get off your horse," the man commanded. Quinn began to dismount, but before he even got one foot out of the stirrup, all hell broke loose.

The sound of bagpipes seemed to fly over their heads, and then something crashed in front of the horses yoked to the carriage, panicking them and making them rear up on their hind legs. It was a small object that looked like some kind of animal—apparently in pain—but it was also the impossible source of the pipe music! Two of the guards moved to calm the horses, while another ran to see what was making the racket. The leader kept his pistol on Quinn.

"What the hell is it, Malcolm?" he cried.

"I dinna know, Captain Pembroke!" the man shouted back, keeping a wide berth as he walked around the small, flailing creature that lay on its side, its legs moving back and forth as the sound of bagpipes—and drums—echoed loudly around them. "Ye had best come and take a look!"

Pembroke. Maggie had told him of the cold-hearted captain of the guards and he had been worried until she assured him that the man never bothered her.

The captain turned his head, and Quinn saw his chance. He dug his heels into Saint and charged toward his captor. The captain threw himself sideways to the ground, his pistol flying in the opposite direction. Quinn was about to make his getaway when he drew his horse up short at the sight of a masked figure on horseback directly in front of him.

The rider was short and slight, dressed all in black, his coat thigh length. He had a pistol in each hand. He aimed one of the guns at the guards and the other at Pembroke on the ground.

"Throw down!" the mysterious rider growled. He rode his horse around Quinn and Saint so that he had a clear shot at the captain of the guard. As they passed him, Quinn blinked.

The horse wore a mask. A black mask with two eyeholes tied around its face just like the one the rider wore.

A smile curved Quinn's mouth as the rider's slight stature suddenly made sense.

Damn the spunk of the lass! What did she think she was doing?

The captain of the guard cursed and stumbled to his feet. His gun was already several feet away from him, and he drew his sword and tossed it aside, too, motioning to his men to do the same.

Quinn dismounted, never taking his gaze from Pembroke. Maggie had told him the man was some distant relative of Montrose, and was known for his absolute ruthlessness. As the dark, furious eyes of the other man followed him, Quinn knew the rumors were true. Aye, those were the eyes of a serpent. He wouldn't be turning his back on this one. A chill rushed over him at the thought of Maggie being anywhere close to such a man.

Quinn retrieved his weapons and kicked the guards' into a pile, and then turned his pistol toward Pembroke.

"Now, my friend, 'tis our show," Quinn said. "I want the four of ye to lie facedown on the ground, and not a word out of any of ye."

With a muttered oath, Pembroke motioned to the other three guards, and soon the four lay prostate on the ground, even as the strange object nearby continued to whirl and whine. As soon as Quinn had the four tied, he would see exactly what in the world was making the commotion.

But what to tie them with?

"Here!" The rider threw something toward him. He looked down. A bundle lay at his feet.

Quinn picked it up and saw it was a dozen or more short, twisted lengths of rope. "Thank ye," he said. "'Tis lucky for me ye showed up when ye did, since ye came so well prepared."

The rider didn't answer, and Quinn knelt down beside Pembroke and tied his hands and feet, making sure the bonds were very tight before moving on to the next man. When he finished, all four guards were trussed up like suckling pigs, with their faces in the dirt. But before Quinn could rise, he felt the barrel of a gun in his back.

"Now ye," the rider growled from behind him. "On yer knees."

Quinn smiled and turned. "I thought we were on the same side," he said, obeying her command.

A strand of auburn hair had escaped the confines of the black kerchief on her head, and the wind blew it against her face. Maggie tucked it back and scowled.

"I have plans for ye," she said roughly.

"What kind of plans?"

She leaned down and whispered in his ear, "Naked plans." Maggie straightened and glared at the four men watching her, her voice deepening again. "But aye, I did agree to help ye with this venture, so get up, laddie."

Pembroke stared at Maggie, his dark eyes narrowed, his

gaze calculating. Quinn stood and moved quickly in front
of her. If the man managed to recognize Maggie, it would
make her employment at the manor too dangerous to continue. She had to keep taking care of Ian until Quinn could
expedite his friend's escape. Maggie should have realized
this could happen, that not only was she risking herself, but
Ian, in what she no doubt considered a grand lark.

With a glance at Pembroke to make sure he was secure,
Quinn grabbed the pint-sized thief by the arm and half
dragged her a good twenty feet from the trussed-up men on
the ground before releasing her and glaring down into defi-
ant blue eyes.

"What the bloody hell do ye think ye're doin'?" he demanded, his voice hushed and stern. "Are ye out of yer
mind?"

twelve

Maggie shrugged. "Must be, I'm in love with you, aren't I?" she whispered back.

"Get back on yer horse, and go to the cottage," he ordered under his breath. "This is rank foolishness."

"Oh, it's foolish if *I* do it, but bold and brave if *you* do?" she said, her chin lifted, hands on her hips.

"Aye." Quinn said, his anger rising. "A woman has no place in such things. Go to the cottage." He folded his arms over his chest and waited for her answer. She was generally a sensible lass. She would do as he said.

"Oh, bite me," Maggie said, and walked toward the carriage.

He followed her, prepared to throw her on the back of her horse and tie her there if need be. She stopped in her stride and bent down to pick something up from the ground. The strange object she had thrown as a diversion had finally stopped its racket and movement, and Quinn moved quickly to her side to see what had distracted everyone and allowed one man—woman—to take control of a group of armed men. It might be something to keep in mind for his future raids upon the duke.

"What the hell is that?" he murmured, as she smoothed her hand over what appeared to be some kind of animal, green and furry, about the size of a small fox.

She held the object up, patted its smooth head, and smiled. "It's Nessie."

"Nessie?"

"You know. Loch Ness, all that stuff."

Quinn shook his head. "Ye mean, the monster of Loch Ness?" The legend of the Loch Ness creature was one that his own mother had told him about when he was a lad. He cocked his head and examined the object.

It did look like the beast of the stories his mother had told him—it had a long, curved neck, a long tail, and short, heavy legs. He didn't remember his mother ever saying the monster had green fur, but in every other way it was a miniature version of the legendary beast. He shook his head. Where had she gotten such a thing?

"It's a replica," she said, as she saw his obvious confusion. "You know, a smaller image of the real thing. A toy, actually. Watch what it can do." She pressed a button hidden in its green side and the four stout legs started moving, even as the loud wail of a bagpipe began once again.

"That's bagpipe music," Quinn said, unable to believe what he was hearing.

"Yep."

"That's impossible." He took the creature out of her hands and turned it over and over. " 'Tis not a bagpipe. There is no mouthpiece, no bladder, no—"

"It's not a bagpipe. It's a toy." She shoved it into the bag at her waist, muffling the sounds somewhat, and glanced behind him. "I'll explain later. Right now, I think we'd better get back to the business at hand."

Before he could stop her, she strode toward the carriage and jerked the door open, speaking in a deep, harsh voice. "Out of the carriage!" There was silence from inside the vehicle. "I said—" She stuck her head into the interior and then turned toward Quinn, her face pale. "There's no one inside."

Quinn moved immediately to her side. " 'Tis a trap," he said. "There may be more guards coming."

"You can count on that, my good man," Pembroke said from his prone position. "A dozen or so." Quinn and Maggie turned toward him, and his dark eyes were liquid with promised retribution. "They will catch the two of you, and then you and your friend, Ian MacGregor, will all dance at the end of a rope."

"Get on yer horse," Quinn told Maggie, and without question she spun around and ran to the little mare. He followed her and held the horse's bridle as she mounted awkwardly with the pistol still in her hand.

Quinn stood at the head of the mare, staring at the mask the animal wore. He pointed to the mask and raised both brows at Maggie.

Maggie shrugged. "Bittie lent her to me and she needed a disguise, too." She turned toward the tied men and gave them a salute with one black-gloved hand. "Okay, boys," she said in a loud, gruff voice. "It's been fun, but we must away."

Quinn frowned at her. "We must away?" She shrugged again, tossing him a brilliant smile that rocked him for a moment. He shook his head to refocus his mind and hurried over to his own horse. "Just stay close to me."

Thunder echoed in the distance, and Maggie turned in the direction it came from and sighed. "Oh, great. I cannot tell you how sick and tired I am of getting soaking wet."

Quinn's dark brows pressed together as Saint danced to

one side. "That isn't thunder," he said, whirling his horse and heading into the hills. "Come on, lass!"

As Saint began to climb, Quinn looked to make sure Maggie was behind him. Aye, she was crouched over her mare's neck, a full length behind. Her long red hair had come undone beneath the black kerchief on her head and flew behind her like a ruddy piece of the wind.

Poor lass, he thought, as they plunged on. *She must be fair terrified.* Maggie fell farther behind as they went over a particularly craggy spot, and Quinn glanced back to make sure she was all right. He blinked, and then he grinned.

Maggie was smiling from ear to ear, her blue eyes bright and sparkling with life. What a woman! Where any other lass would have been frightened and barely hanging on for dear life, she was actually enjoying their adventure!

He laughed, but then realized what this could mean. Likely the lass would want to join him on every gambit he undertook!

There was no time to consider this new problem. He had led their pursuers on a ragged chase across the Highlands, with several clever turns and hidden trails that would take better men than they to find. Quinn felt almost sure they had lost the villains. He gave Saint his head as the horse picked his way down a rough, rocky patch.

Below, Quinn could see the beginning of the forest, and sanctuary. He slowed, waiting for Maggie to catch up, and began to plan how he would keep her from joining him on his rides. With any other woman it would be easy, but with this lass, the very thing he told her not to do, that was what she would attempt.

Short of tying her up every time he went raiding, he couldn't think of any way to force her to do as he asked.

The more he pondered the problem, the more he realized that if he wanted to keep Maggie safe, there was only one answer.

He had to give up his plans for revenge.

Maggie couldn't believe she had actually taken part in a heist and then ridden hell for leather across the Highlands at Quinn's side! As her horse, which she had privately rechristened "Thunder," had galloped beside Saint, she'd felt a giddiness unlike anything she'd ever experienced.

She'd always been the most cautious of souls. Forever in the back of her mind was the fear that something would happen to her, and then what would happen to her sisters? She'd been determined that the twins would not have to go through any more trauma in their young lives.

Ahead, Quinn slowed and led her into a deep, dark forest. As she followed, Maggie suddenly realized that during the years she'd cared for the twins, she had developed more than a motherly personality—she had practically taken on the attitude of a *grand*mother! She had dressed sedately, driven sedately, lived sedately—until now.

Her heartbeat quickened. Now she felt as if she could do anything!

The adrenaline surged through her veins and Maggie laughed out loud, feeling wild and free—just before her horse stepped in a hole and sent her flying straight toward a rock twenty feet tall.

Maggie missed the rock. Although she rolled for several feet when she hit the ground, when she finally came to a stop there wasn't any major part of her body that screamed it was broken, though she did hurt all over. In spite of the aches and bruises she would have tomorrow, she still felt more alive than she ever had in her life.

"Maggie!" There was horror in Quinn's voice as he leaned over her.

Maggie flung her arms around his neck and pulled him down to her, finding his mouth through the shadows, possessing it even as she felt his bewilderment and then the quickening of passion as his arms tightened around her.

Suddenly her blood was on fire, and she shoved Quinn to his back and shed her breeches, yanking them over her feet and off before straddling his hips and finding his lips again. He was hard as a rock beneath her and made short work of her shirt, pulling it over her head, molding his hands over her breasts as he broke their kiss and lifted his mouth to her bare skin.

Maggie had never felt so glorious, so strong, so brilliant. So capable of anything. She jerked Quinn's black breeches down and slid over his marvelously rigid flesh, the evidence that he felt the same furious passion as she.

There was no time for soft caresses or gentle touches—it took only seconds for Quinn to understand her need, lifting her up and then letting her slide down, impaling herself upon him, watching her ride him as she had ridden her pony across the Highlands, wild with abandon and freedom.

His hands curved around her waist, and with his help, Maggie rose and fell upon his shaft, again and again, feeling the pulsating throb build and grow within her, sending her higher and higher, closer and closer to the incredible pleasure only Quinn could give. Just when she thought she had reached the clouds, his mouth closed around her nipple and sent her into space. She closed her eyes and moaned, arching back as his arms tightened around her. Then he rolled her to her back and began to move inside of her, hot and hard, taking her all the way to Jupiter, breathless, mindless. Then he grew still.

Maggie's eyes flew open even as she moaned her protest. She was filled with him, completely and utterly, and Jupiter was nice, but she had really wanted to go all the way to Pluto. She urged him on, pressing up against him, her hands in his hair.

But Quinn slid his hands up her body to cradle her face between them, and his green eyes glittered into hers as an amazing smile lit his face. She drew in a sharp breath as their gazes fused, and she grew still as well.

"Maggie," he said softly, "do ye remember when ye said that ye loved me?"

Her voice was a whisper. "Yes," she said, her heart fluttering like a hummingbird inside her chest.

"Och, lass, forgive me for not knowing then what I know now."

"What?" she asked, afraid to hope.

"That I love ye more than the sky and the moon and the stars. Ye are my heart, sweet Maggie." He kissed her softly.

Then everything changed, just like that. Maggie stared up at him in wonder as slowly, gently, Quinn began to truly make love to her. As he stroked her body below, with each shattering thrust, Maggie felt him claim her, possess her, love her, tell her wordlessly that she belonged to him, and he to her. And as their bodies collided and she soared upward into the stratosphere he created, Maggie felt the last little bit of fear inside of her crumble and disappear.

With a cry of surrender, she let herself love Quinn MacIntyre with every fiber of her soul. When Quinn shuddered and cried out, too, and then looked into her eyes, Maggie knew he had surrendered as well. He loved her.

She came back to earth slowly, drifting in his arms, spent, magnificent in her exhaustion. Now there was no going back. She was Quinn's. He was hers. Forever.

Maggie woke with the dawn, her head on Quinn's chest, her legs tangled in the plaid he'd thrown across the two of them after making love for the—she'd lost count of how many times. The man was a stallion. As she lay in his arms half awake, the realization that she was naked, on the ground, in Scotland, beside a *highwayman,* made her smile.

In Maggie's wildest dreams she'd never imagined such a thing happening to her. Though she ached in every part of her body from the night spent on the hard ground—*and other hard things,* she thought smugly—it didn't matter. Nothing mattered now but Quinn and what they felt for each other.

Immediately, guilty images of Ellie and Allie filled her mind, but she pushed them away. There were things to be figured out, okay, she knew that. But right now she was wrapped in afterglow and, like Scarlett O'Hara, would think about her sisters and Rachel and her life back in Texas tomorrow.

Maggie sat up and stretched her arms over her head, relishing the feel of her long hair as it brushed against her bare back. The cold morning air was refreshing, making every molecule in her body sit up and take notice. Suddenly she was filled with a joy so wonderful that she couldn't help it—she laughed out loud.

"I have bedded a faery," Quinn said, his voice rough from sleep. "I can only pray she will nae fly away from me."

Maggie glanced over her shoulder and almost melted. Quinn lay on his side, watching her, his dark hair tousled against a jaw that was shadowed by morning stubble. She had seen him shave a few times, once at a stream, once in the stables; watched the wicked blade of a dagger as he scraped it across his face and throat. She should have told him not to bother, that she loved his rough beard. Now she wanted to rake her face against his, just to feel the burn. His eyes were gray green this morning, like a stormy sea, but there was nothing storm tossed about the emotion she saw mirrored there. He loved her. She hugged the knowledge tightly to herself.

"Good morning," she said.

"Good morning, Maggie mine," he said. He reached up and ran one finger down her bare arm, and she licked her lips. His eyes darted to her mouth and his voice grew deeper. "Did ye sleep well?"

"Aye," she murmured, lying down again beside him. "Like a newborn babe." She grinned. "Who slept on rocks."

He slipped his arms around her waist and pulled her on top of him, leg to leg, belly to belly, other parts to other parts. Her mouth hovered above his as she gazed into his eyes.

"Perhaps I make a better mattress for a faery princess," he said. "In fact, perhaps her ladyship would like to try bouncing on the mattress."

Maggie laughed and kissed him, her heartbeat automatically kicking up a notch at the touch of his lips. "Maybe I just would," she said, her voice sounding silky and sexy to her ears. Amazing what being loved would do for a girl.

"Of course," he murmured, as he leaned up and began nuzzling her neck, "ye are never going to do such a foolish thing again."

Maggie was half lost in his touch, but still cognizant enough for his words to sink in. "Hmm? What foolish thing? Bouncing on your, er, mattress?"

"Dressing like an outlaw and placing yerself in danger." He slid his hand up her side to capture one breast.

She stopped his hand before things could get any hotter.

"Wait a minute," she said, sitting up and straddling his hips. "I saved your butt, laddie. You were the one in danger, and if you think that I'm not going to"—Quinn twisted his wrist beneath her hand and broke free—"that I'm not going to"—he gently pulled her arm behind her, making her arch her back as he ran his tongue between her breasts—"going to—"

What was she not going to do?

Quinn pulled her down to him and his mouth closed over her right nipple.

"Not going to—not—no, no, no . . ." She melted into the fire that was Quinn's mouth until he finally paused and spoke.

"Ah, Maggie," Quinn said, "have I told ye that making love to ye is like drowning in pleasure?" His voice was soft as he moved his mouth to her ear and began licking the tender spot below her earlobe, but somehow Maggie found the strength to pull away from him. "Ye dinna want to make love to me again?" he asked, confusion in his voice.

"Oh, aye, laddie," she said. She pushed him back to the ground and bent her head to slowly kiss a path down his chest to his navel, letting the tip of her tongue touch him after every kiss. She raised her head slightly, while her hands kept busy smoothing the dark curls clustered in the middle of his chest. "I want to make love to you, but first we need to get something straight between us." Quinn grinned unabashed as she blushed. "Something *else*," she said.

"All right, lass, what do ye need me to say?"

She smiled. He was going to be cooperative after all. "You have to tell me that you won't go on any more moonlit escapades unless I go with you."

"Lass, dinna be silly. Of course I willna let ye do that. It is too dangerous."

"Okay, well, that's a shame, because I would really like to do this." She moved up his chest again and bit his right nipple gently. His hands slid around her waist and tightened there. "And this"—she laved the left nipple and bit it, too, even as she pressed her hips down against the hard length of him—"or this—"

She slid back down to his navel, painted it with her tongue, and then kissed her way downward as Quinn's fingers clutched the top of her head. She stopped just short of her destination, and he moaned in frustration.

"What are ye tryin' to do to me, girl?" he cried.

Maggie sat up, and attempted to ignore the jolt that shot through her as she did.

"It's too, too bad," she said, hoping he didn't hear the tremble in her voice. "There are a lot of other fun things that I wish I could do"—she leaned down and kissed him on the mouth, letting her tongue trace his lips—"that I would do *right now*,"—she pressed her hips into his—"but if you're going to be a chauvinist pig and tell me I can't ride with you on your little jaunts, I guess from now on we'll just have to be friends."

"This is blackmail of the most evil kind," Quinn said, his fingers sliding over her hips and biting into her flesh. She shivered, but fought back, determined not to succumb to his touch without getting what she wanted first.

"Blackmail? Hey, the Scots invented blackmail, didn't they? Isn't that when a reiver promises not to steal a rich man's cattle in return for payment?"

"Aye," Quinn said and then caught his breath as Maggie wiggled again on top of him. "Ye are killin' me."

"So, you should understand this perfectly," she said as she clamped her legs more tightly around his now shifting hips. "Stop that. And really, if you think about it, you win both ways. I'll help you rob from the rich and give to Ian, *and* you'll get great sex. I don't see a downside here for you, laddie."

Quinn lifted his head to say something else, but she dipped her own head down to the very sexy little indention just below his belly button and licked him there, just once. He let his head fall back to the ground.

"No, dammit, I willna risk ye! Ye mean too much to me."

"Well, there is *one* way we can compromise," she said.

"Tell me," he groaned as she licked him once again.

"Simple. You don't put yourself at risk either. That means you don't play highwayman anymore. We'll find another way to get Ian out."

There was a long silence, then an equally long sigh. "Ye win," he said. "May the saints forgive me—ye win!"

"I thought so," Maggie said, and then set about assuring him that he had truly made the right decision.

Maggie was dreaming.

In her dream, there was a voice, a deep, dark voice. It was cursing. And with every curse, there was a sound.

Click.

Click.

Then the voice: "What the hell?"

After a few more curses, and a few more clicks, there came the sound of a bagpipe being murdered.

She opened her eyes to darkness, and a single beam of light dancing across the ceiling, keeping time with the moaning bagpipe until the noise finally stopped. Then she realized—she wasn't dreaming.

"Quinn?"

Maggie sat up and rubbed her eyes, trying to adjust them to the dark room. She was in Ian's cottage, with Quinn. But where was he? And what were all these sounds and lights and—she went suddenly still.

"Where in the world did ye get all of those strange things?" Quinn asked from the floor at the end of her bed. The dancing light rose and shone upon her breasts beneath the thin gown she wore, one at a time. "And how does this work? How does it contain the fire that makes it shine?"

Oh, boy. Quinn had been looking through her backpack.

"Excuse me," she said, "but that is my property, and it is private!"

He moved the light of the small flashlight over her breasts again, then down to the apex at her thighs.

"Private? Take off yer gown, lass, and I will show ye private." He moved the light up to her face and Maggie shadowed her eyes, wishing she had something to throw at him.

"Put it back!" she ordered, then gasped as Quinn was suddenly beside her. "Don't do that!"

"Sorry," he said mildly, clicking the light off and on. He lay back on the bed and directed the light at the ceiling again.

"You're going to wear out the battery," she said. "Now turn it off and come back to bed!"

"Battery?" Quinn sat up and pulled her down beside him. "All right, lass, what are these things?" He lifted her backpack from his shoulder and poured the contents out on the bed.

Maggie stared down glumly at an empty box of Band-Aids, the end of a roll of gauze, adhesive tape, hair barrettes, rubber bands, safety pins, antibiotic ointment, matches, a lighter, a pair of tiny scissors, a huge package of bubble gum, and two chocolate bars. She'd eaten the other two. For a moment it was as if she was back in her own time, at Fado's Pub, celebrating her birthday with her sisters and Rachel.

"And what in the name of heaven—" Quinn pulled out a length of foil squares attached to one another. "What are these?"

Maggie grabbed the condoms out of his hands and threw them back into the backpack, then started gathering up the rest of her things as she glared at him. "Those are mine, just like everything else in that bag, and I will thank you to keep your nose—and your mitts—out of it!"

"Mitts?" He frowned at her, the humor in his voice disappearing. "I have no mitts. What are ye getting so upset about? I just wanted to know where these remarkable inventions came from."

Maggie stuffed the candy bars into the pack, changed her mind, and took them both out, tossing Quinn one and tearing the wrapper off of the other.

"Well, it's none of your business, okay? Just stay out of my things!"

His dark brows clashed together over suddenly cold green eyes. Quinn stood slowly, his shoulders taut with anger as he tossed the candy back to her. She didn't try to catch it, but let it fall to the floor.

"Quinn—" she began, feeling miserable.

"Dinna fash yerself," he said, "I will most certainly 'stay out of yer things.'" He crossed to the door and went out of the room, slamming the door behind him.

"Well, that went well," Maggie said, and began to plot how she could get Quinn to forgive her, without answering his questions about the stuff in her pack.

For the next few days Maggie worked at the manor house, made sure Ian was well fed and not abused, and made mad, passionate love to Quinn every night. He had gotten over their fight, and had insisted that she stay with him at the cottage again, instead of in Jenny's room. He missed her, he said, and Maggie's heart had soared at his words. They never spoke of her "things" again. Every night after her workday was over, he met her in the stables. Sometimes they slept there; other nights they waited till dark and then slipped away on their ponies, back to the cottage.

She'd worked hard at avoiding Pembroke since the night she'd appeared as a diminutive highwayman, though she couldn't imagine that he would have recognized her beneath her disguise. She realized now that it had been foolish of her to take such a risk when she was still needed at the manor, but at the time, it had seemed the only way to keep Quinn from being killed or captured.

On the fourth day after her mad escapade, Maggie trudged slowly up the stairs from Ian's cell, resenting eighteenth-century servantdom, and her boss, the cook, in particular. The woman was evil, that's all there was to it. She hadn't liked the way Maggie had mopped the floor the night before, and had made her do it again. Now her back felt like it was about to break.

Halfway up the steps she realized she'd left the supper tray behind. She paused, so tired she could have stretched out on the steps where she stood and fallen asleep.

"Later," she mumbled aloud. "The tray can wait."

She turned to go up the stairs once more, when her way was suddenly blocked by the looming shadow of a man.

"Duncan?" she called, thinking it was one of the guards on duty. Maybe he would go and get the tray for her. The guards were all fairly smitten with her and Jenny and did anything they asked of them.

The man moved down another of the dark steps, and the light from a lantern hanging from a hook on the wall suddenly illuminated his face. Maggie felt the blood drain from her face. Pembroke.

Not thinking, she took a step back and almost fell. The captain of the guards was at her side in a second, one arm under her elbow, the other around her waist.

"Careful, my dear," he said, his smooth voice sending a chill down her spine as she looked up into his dark, hungry eyes. His fingers tightened around her waist, and he pressed her back against the wall as she glared up at him, her heart pounding.

"Okay," Maggie said, "I'm fine now, just fine. Let me pass, please!"

At her words, something flickered in his gaze and his mouth curved up in a cruel smile. A sudden wave of real panic swept over her as Maggie realized she was alone and unprotected. James was at the end of the corridor, beginning his nightly check of the prisoners. Jenny was in the kitchen. Not that either one of them could do a thing to help. They were servants, and just like her, at the mercy of their employers—and this man.

Pembroke must have seen her sudden fear, for he chuckled, and suddenly Maggie gasped for breath as he grabbed her around the throat, his fingers biting into her neck. He leaned against her and she could feel his erection through the soft cloth of his breeches. Terror raced through her veins and her hands came up flat against his chest, weakly trying to push him away.

Pembroke had her at a distinct disadvantage, staggered on the stairs as they were, but when his grip on her neck finally relaxed and she could breathe easier, she thought he was going to let her go. Instead, he slid his hand down to squeeze her breast so hard she cried out.

"So, it was you," he said, his voice casual, contemplative. "I knew I recognized that curious pattern of speech, though you did do well in your imitation of a lad's voice. It was your delectable little body, however, that gave you away, though in truth, I did not put it all completely together until now. What is this 'oh-kay' that you speak of?"

Maggie drew in a sharp breath. He knew. He knew she had been the one beneath the highwayman's mask. She began to struggle in earnest then, and his hands tightened around her arms as he slammed her back. Her head hit the stone wall and she saw stars in the blackness that flooded her vision. Tears ran down her cheeks, and she opened her mouth to scream.

Pembroke quickly leaned down and thrust his tongue roughly between Maggie's lips, effectively cutting off her

cry and making her choke and gag. When he broke off his
assault, his breathing was ragged, the look in his eyes terrifying.

"You see," he said, "I have waited for the right time to
taste your wares, and after seeing you in action the other
night, I do believe now is the perfect moment."

"I don't know what you're talking about," she whispered, frozen with fear.

"Your little performance with the highwayman," he
said, lifting her skirt with one hand and then slipping his
hand beneath.

Maggie grabbed his wrist and struggled to keep him
from touching her.

"I'll tell—"

"Who?" He dropped her skirt and jerked away from her.
Grabbing both of her wrists, he slammed them against the
wall on either side of her head, and then pressed his hips
against hers and began a slow grinding movement. "Who
will you tell? Your precious Piper? Good. I look forward to
telling him how wet and willing you were for me when I
took you."

"I'll tell the duke!" she cried.

He laughed loudly at that. "As if Montrose cares what I
do to a serving wench. Besides, all I have to do is let His
Grace know that you aided the highwayman, and you will
be hanged with that piece of trash below."

Revulsion filled her as Pembroke moved her right wrist
over her left so that he could hold them both in one hand,
freeing the other to allow him to unbutton his breeches.
Maggie began to fight him again and almost retched as he
pressed his now bare flesh between her legs.

"Now," he ordered, "spread your legs, my little whore."

"No!" She spat in his face and then stared in horror at
what she'd done.

Pembroke released her, stepped back slightly, and

reached inside his coat, drawing out a lace handkerchief. Maggie saw this was her chance, but she couldn't move. She was paralyzed with fear. The man wiped the drop of spittle away carefully and then, without warning, drew back his fist and punched her in the face.

Maggie cried out and fell to her knees. The momentum of the blow sent her rolling down the steps until she lay in a heap at the bottom of the stairs. She looked up through the pain and saw James running toward her. Maggie stretched her hand out to him.

"Help me!" she moaned. James made a move toward her, when Pembroke's sharp command stopped him in his tracks.

"Leave us!"

Maggie pushed herself up on one hand and saw Pembroke walking slowly down the steps, buttoning his breeches. She looked back at James, and their eyes met for half a second, then without a word, he turned and headed up the stairs.

Good. It was good he was leaving. His life would be forfeit if he defied his captain. But damn, she'd hoped for an instant that he would draw his sword and run the bastard through.

The entire right side of Maggie's head throbbed, and she lifted her hand to her face. He'd caught her across her right cheekbone, and when she brought her hand away, blood dripped from her fingers. The faceted rings he wore on almost every finger must have cut her.

"Get up."

Maggie's heart thudded beneath her chest like a hammer. He was going to beat her and rape her, and when Quinn heard of it, he would seek Pembroke out and kill him. And then Quinn would be hanged for murdering one of Montrose's kin.

No.

Pembroke stopped a few feet away and watched her struggle to her feet, amusement curving his lips. His smug smile sent a wave of strength through Maggie. She straightened her shoulders. She was not going to give up without a fight. *C'mon, Maggie,* she thought, *for once in your life, be brave!*

"Does it make you feel like more of a man to think you can physically overpower me?" she asked, forcing strength into her voice.

He gazed down at her, his handsome features ugly now that she knew the depth of his depravity. "I do hope you will at least put up the semblance of a fight," he said. "It is so boring when the wenches simply lie there unmoving. That little maid you befriended, what is her name?" He tapped his chin thoughtfully. "Ah, Jenny. Yes, Jenny is a perfect example. She lay beneath me like a limp rag."

Blinding rage filled Maggie and chased away the fear. "And speaking of limp rags—can you say erectile dysfunction? I knew the moment I felt your flaccid bit of flesh between my legs that I was in no real danger."

A terrible fury flared up in his dark gaze, and she took a step back and hit the stone wall again. There was no place to go.

Okay, Maggie, her inner voice chided, *I said be brave, not stupid.*

"You will regret those words, my dear Maggie," he said, and lifted his hand to strike her again.

"Not as much as you will," she promised, and with every ounce of strength she had left, Maggie slammed her knee up, aiming for his groin. Pembroke saw her intent at the last moment and managed to move just enough in that second to deflect the impact slightly. He still went down, though, and trembling, Maggie turned and ran—straight into a broad, familiar chest. A strong arm caught her and held her tightly.

"Quinn," she whispered, clinging to him. Then she looked up into his face and he looked down into hers. Too late she remembered the blood on her cheek, the swelled evidence of Pembroke's violence. A new wave of fear danced down her spine as his jaw tightened and the anger in his green eyes shifted into cold, murderous rage.

"Ah, I presume this is your companion from the other night?" Pembroke said, his voice flat. "However, you must excuse us, my dear man, for this is a private party."

"Stay here, lass," Quinn said, setting her away from him. It was then she saw he had his sword in his hand. Maggie threw herself back against him.

"No, Quinn," she begged. "Please. Let's run. We can make it to the horses."

"Aye, run," Pembroke agreed, drawing his own sword from the scabbard at his side. "Like all MacIntyres and MacGregors are wont to do." Maggie drew in a quick breath, and the man laughed. "Oh, aye, I know who your lover is, sweet Maggie. I have my spies, even in Rob Roy's camp."

Quinn pushed her back with his left hand and half turned. "I willna run," he told her under his breath. "But ye will. Ride to the place I first found ye, and once I have ended the life of this vermin, I will join ye there."

Maggie shook her head wordlessly as he advanced upon Pembroke.

Quinn had not been worried when Maggie was late coming to the stables to meet him. She was often delayed by her duties after supper. He hated that she still had to work so hard in her guise of servant and was determined to end her servitude soon.

As he had waited for her to arrive, Quinn was going over his latest plan for freeing Ian as he lay upon the hay in the loft. His mind had wandered to thoughts of a cottage where he and Maggie could find happiness together, somewhere far from Montrose's holdings, perhaps Ireland, or even France, when someone came in through the side door of the stable below and slammed it. The terrified outburst that followed sent him quickly to his feet.

"Bittie! Bittie, where are ye?" a man's voice cried out. "'Tis Pembroke, he's attacking Maggie! I dinna know what to do!"

Quinn had grabbed the scabbard and belt holding his sword and reached for a rope hanging from the rafters. Swinging down to land directly in front of the man, he recognized the guard helping Maggie care for Ian.

"Take me to him," he'd said grimly, buckling his sword around his waist.

Now as he faced Pembroke, Quinn tightened his grip on the hilt of the blade and prepared to kill the man who had dared touch his love.

"Quinn," Maggie pleaded, "I'm all right. If you kill him, Montrose will hunt you down."

"Do not worry, my little doxy," Pembroke said, brandishing his sword in front of him. "For in a matter of moments this outlaw's life will be at an end, effectively putting your fears to rest once and for all."

"T'will be hard to do once ye are skewered on the end of my blade," Quinn told him, and slashed his sword in an arc downward toward Pembroke's neck. The man parried with his weapon, and for a moment, Quinn had no thoughts other than exacting a quick dance to one side and a rapid series of feints and thrusts that kept him alive. Pembroke was fast, and if he was not careful, the blackguard's predictions would come true. That could not happen, for if it did, Maggie would be left at his mercy.

"Go on, Maggie," he said over one shoulder. "Do as I say and leave me to deal with this bit of refuse."

"No," she said. "We're in this together."

"By all the saints," Quinn said, raising his blade to stop a downward cut from Pembroke as he spoke, "will ye no listen to me, woman? I canna think while ye are in danger!"

"And I can't leave while you're risking your life," she countered.

"Shall I ring for tea to accompany this sweet interlude?" Pembroke asked, and then lunged forward, slashing his blade sideways.

The tip of the sword sliced across Quinn's chest, and Maggie screamed. Quinn stumbled back, the cut burning as blood began soaking through the rough linen shirt he wore. Pembroke lowered his sword and made a small bow.

"First blood is mine," he said.

"Aye, but last blood shall be mine." Quinn attacked, laying a rapid succession of blows upon his enemy that kept the man from retaliating. Maggie had grown silent, and Quinn was thankful. Perhaps she had fled after all. He prayed that she had.

He forced Pembroke backward toward the wall behind the man; relentlessly he bore down upon him, steel clanging in rhythm until they were almost chest to chest, their blades sliding practically hilt to hilt as Quinn glared into his assailant's face only inches from his own.

"Do you truly imagine that you can beat me, MacIntyre?" Pembroke asked, amusement in his eyes. "I have studied at the finest schools in the world."

"And I am fighting for the woman I love," Quinn said.

"The whore, you mean."

Quinn's left hand was free and he had Pembroke's throat before the man knew what had hit him. Pembroke's sword fell to the floor as he gagged and choked, and Quinn discarded his own. So murderous was the rage within him that he wanted to kill the vile predator with his own hands.

"Ye will never speak so of any woman again," he promised, as his right hand joined his left.

The pain sliced into him without warning, sharp and deep. He staggered backward and stared down at his chest. A small dagger—a *skean dhu*—buried to the hilt, protruded from just below his sternum. The handle was fashioned from carved bone, some part of his mind realized. Then Pembroke stepped forward and pulled the blade out.

"Ironic, wouldn't you say, that the great highwayman, the Piper, would be brought down by his own countryman's pathetic little weapon?"

Quinn gasped as blood gushed from the wound, eating up the stains already soaked into his shirt. Maggie screamed from somewhere behind him, and he sank to his knees and then fell forward. The side of his face struck the stone floor, adding new pain that laced through his head. He reached out blindly with one hand, groping for Pembroke's leg, determined to bring him down. His fingers brushed against a boot, but the man lifted his foot and kicked him in the head. Quinn rolled to his back, away from the next blow. Then Pembroke laughed, and Maggie was crying out something— and the last thing Quinn heard before oblivion claimed him was the clang of a bell, not bright and sharp, but dull, hollow.

Och, Maggie, he thought sorrowfully. *Why did ye not run?* And then he knew no more.

Maggie stood staring down at Pembroke and Quinn. The heavy pewter tray dropped from her nerveless fingers to clang against the stone floor. Pembroke lay unconscious, and she stepped over him to reach Quinn. Luckily, the supper tray on the small table nearby had been within easy reach. When the captain had stabbed Quinn, Maggie grabbed the heavy rectangle and slammed it into the back of Pembroke's head.

Quinn moaned, and Maggie hurried to his side. He had one hand pressed to his chest as if to catch the blood flowing from the wound. Quickly she shed the cotton petticoat she wore under her skirt and began ripping it into long strips. Wadding a few together, she pressed them into Quinn's chest and then wrapped the longest strips around him, pushing him to one side and then the other to get the bandage around him. They had to get out of there, but first she had to stanch the wound, get the bleeding under control.

Maggie held both hands on top of the thick padding and pressed down slightly, keeping pressure on the bandage as she crouched beside him, her gaze darting from Quinn to the stairway to Pembroke and back again to Quinn. If only James had not turned tail and run. If only Bittie or Jenny would come and help her. How could she lift Quinn? How could she even get him up the stairs, let alone away from the manor?

Footsteps sounded on the stairway. Maggie reached across Quinn's body with one hand, the other still applying pressure, and picked up his discarded sword. She wasn't going to let them take Quinn without a fight. Her heart pounded as boots thudded against stone, her breath catching in her throat as the first man came into view.

James. With several guards behind him. He stopped at the last step and cursed under his breath.

"Move out of the way, lass," he said.

"No!" Maggie shook her head fiercely and lifted the sword. It was heavy, and she could barely keep it level as she pointed it at the guard. "Pembroke attacked me, as you well know. Quinn was only defending my honor."

"Aye," James said, "'twas I who ran to the stable and told him. Now step aside and let me and my cousins carry him to the stable. Bittie can ready a wagon, and we'll take him to safety."

"Your cousins?" Maggie's mouth fell open as six husky young men, two in guard uniforms, the other four in clothes common to servants, hurried to her side.

He stepped closer and laid one hand on her shoulder. "Come, lass. We must hurry, for by the looks of it, Pembroke may have dealt him a deathblow if we dinna get him the help he needs. There is a healer nearby, true to our clan."

Maggie turned back to Quinn and stared, aghast, at the bandage beneath her fingers. It was soaked through with his blood. Her heartbeat began to thud in her ears like the roar of the ocean, and for a moment, she thought she might faint. She drew in a deep breath.

"He's not going to make it, is he?" she whispered and looked up to meet James's gaze squarely.

He shook his head. "'Twould take a miracle, I fear."

Maggie stood, shoulders back, chin lifted. "Pick him up. I know just where to find one."

thirteen

It looked the same. For a moment, Maggie hesitated as she gazed up at the place where her adventure had begun. Above the ancient cairn the stars glimmered brightly, and the moonlight painted a path up to the top of the craggy hill.

Maggie directed the men toward the cairn and hurried after them, cursing the thin leather shoes she wore and the skirts that slowed her as they carried Quinn on a makeshift stretcher to the top. Once there she drew in a deep breath and turned her face into the wind.

She had dreamed of coming to Scotland all of her life. Even as a child, she'd been fascinated with movies and books about the Highlands. To think that not only had she made it, she had actually journeyed to Scotland's past, had lived some of its history, and had found her soul mate.

It had been a grand adventure.

She refused to let it end like this.

"I dinna understand," James said from beside her as his cousins began pulling stones from the entryway of the cairn. "I'm as devout as the next man, but at least with the healer the man would have a fighting chance."

Maggie shivered as she stared at the mound. There was something about the structure now that felt almost sinister, but this was Quinn's best and possibly only chance. She'd told James that the cairn was a holy place, and she intended to pray all night until God healed him. She smiled without humor. It wasn't a lie. She would pray that she and Quinn would be taken back to her time, where there were modern hospitals and doctors and clean hands.

"Aye," she told him. "I'm sure. This is what Quinn would want, I promise."

"But why do ye want us to replace the stones, once ye are inside?" His dark brows knit together plaintively. "Ye dinna plan to die with him, do ye, Maggie? To seal yerself inside?"

The men had finished opening the doorway and were taking Quinn in. Maggie followed after them, James behind her. She stuck her head through the opening.

"Over there," she told James's cousins. "No, that's too far, back a bit. Yes, that's perfect." She nodded and then turned back to James to answer his question. "No, of course not," she told him honestly. "Trust me, James, I know what I'm doing."

"'Tis fair strange to me," he said. He looked around warily and then shot her a sharp look. "Ye wouldna be a practicer of the black arts, would ye, lass?"

Maggie moved to let the men exit the cairn, and then entered, ducking through the opening as she paused to smile back at James. "No, James, I'm not a witch. Give Jenny my love. Tell her, if I don't see her again, that I will always remember her kindness." She reached out and squeezed his hand. "As I will yours."

James shook his head, looking worried, but squeezed her hand in return and then went outside and started instructing the men on replacing the stones. Maggie moved to crouch beside Quinn and watched them block out the pale moonlight streaming through the doorway. As soon as they were finished, she closed her eyes for a moment. When she opened them again, she drew in a quick breath. Bright, silvery moonlight poured through the dozens of holes in the ceiling and painted a familiar pattern on the floor around them: three intertwined spirals.

"Quinn," she whispered as she knelt beside him, "get up, my love."

His eyes flickered open, and she saw death in the shadowed depths. "I canna, sweet Maggie," he whispered back, "for I am mortally wounded."

"No," Maggie said firmly. She cradled his face between her hands, her gaze never leaving his. "No, you are not. I have come across space and time to find you, and I'm not losing you now."

Quinn lifted one hand to her face. "I love ye, Maggie mine," he said, "but I never understand half of what ye say." His hand fell back to his side once more as he gazed blearily around at the cairn. "Where are we?"

"In the cairn. Remember? The place I wanted you to take me, when we first met?" If she could just get him on his feet, he could lean against her. She slid one arm underneath his shoulders and shoved him forward into a sitting position. Maggie heard his sharp intake of breath and felt his body shudder beneath her hands.

"Oh, love, I'm sorry, but you've got to get up. You've got to come with me."

"All right, lass," he said, his words slurred, "if it means that much to ye, help me to my feet."

Maggie helped him to his knees, and he leaned against her heavily as he staggered to his feet and then almost fell. She pressed her hand against his chest and felt once again his lifeblood trickling away.

"Walk with me, Quinn," she commanded urgently. "Say the words with me. Follow forward—take a step, love—follow back—a few more, hurry now—ages lost—just four more now—ages found."

Quinn cried out and sagged against her, his weight bringing her down with him to the cold, stone floor.

"Quinn!" Her shout echoed through the cairn as Maggie struggled to hold him while the sudden surge of power swirled around them, tried to keep him from being swept away from her into the black unknown. But the flood of energy was too intense, and Maggie screamed as Quinn was wrenched from her side and every star in the galaxy exploded inside her mind.

"Quinn, please eat something."

Quinn lifted his head from his hands and turned toward Maggie. She sat beside him on the comfortable bed where they'd spent their nights together ever since he'd returned from a place called a hospital. There he'd been prodded and poked and given medicine in a tube that had rendered him unconscious in order that the physician could sew up his wound. Maggie had told the mob of people who surrounded him when she took him to the "ER" that he had been "mugged." He had remained in the clean, orderly building after his surgery for a week, after which time he was pronounced well enough to return home.

Return home.

In the hospital he'd had a fever, Maggie told him later, and he'd remembered little about it until he woke up, in a strange bed with Maggie, and she told him they had traveled through time to the year 2008. She had saved his life by bringing him to what she called a "modern hospital."

He hadn't believed her at first, but after being brought to this large, fancy house—'twas not a cottage no matter what

Maggie said—and seeing the marvels she had shown him, he'd had little choice but to accept her words.

For the next week, Quinn had tried to adjust to his new surroundings. Maggie was eager to help. She'd taken him into the bathing room and demonstrated all of the wondrous things there—the clean, bright, bathing tub and the sink with running water, the hot shower, the toilet that flushed away the body's refuse with the touch of a handle—he shook his head at the thought of such amazing luxury. The first night back from the hospital, she had helped him take a shower, and had even gotten in with him. He'd been too stunned to even take advantage of the situation.

Instead, he had let her scrub him with a bar of sweet-smelling soap and wash his hair with scented liquid from a bottle. After she finished, she led him out of the glass-encased cubicle and toweled him dry as if he were a child. He'd crawled back into bed and slept like one dead.

It was morning now, and once again Maggie was trying to convince him to eat the breakfast she had prepared for him. He wasn't sure what day it was. He didn't even know how long he'd been sitting on the side of the bed after he awakened. Quinn glanced at the tray of food on the bed beside him. Eggs and bread and some kind of meat. A meal fit for a king, or at least a duke. He hated to disappoint her, but he had no appetite.

"I'm not hungry, lass," he said.

"Then talk to me," she begged, not for the first time. "Tell me what you're thinking."

Quinn couldn't meet her eyes. He took a deep, steadying breath. "I'm thinking I have lost my mind."

She took his hand between both of hers, her voice warm. "No, no, you haven't. I know exactly how you feel, love. At least, I think I do. It's all a shock. And the travel itself—it's terrible. I thought you were being wrenched away from me—that you would be lost in time forever!" Quinn's fingers tightened against hers.

"Aye," he said, feeling some comfort from her words. "I feared the same thing."

"I know this is all hard to accept, but it's real. We *have* traveled through time." She glanced toward the door and lowered her voice. "Just remember that for now, it's our secret. People would think we've gone crazy if we told them the truth."

Quinn fought back a groan. How could it be possible? But how could he deny his own eyes? Of course, now everything about Maggie made sense—why she spoke so strangely, the odd things she carried in her leather bag, even the "Nessie" she had used to distract Pembroke and his men.

"Would you like to come downstairs?" she asked softly. "The girls have been anxious to talk to you."

He looked at her aghast. He had met her sisters that week and they were bonny lasses, but the last thing he wanted right now was to interact with people in the twenty-first century. What would he say? He would be a barbarian next to such creatures. "I'm sorry, I canna—not yet. But go and visit with yer family. I'll be fine."

"No, I don't think so. I'll just stay here with you." She slid her arm through his and leaned on his shoulder. "Maybe we could take a nap together."

She rubbed the side of her face against his arm like a cat, and Quinn knew what kind of "nap" she meant. There was nothing he wanted more than to lose himself in Maggie's love and in her body, but he couldn't. He had to think. Had to figure this out.

"Perhaps later," he said.

Maggie looked up at him and pouted, her lower lip stuck out dramatically. He laughed for the first time since—since he had come to this place.

"Fine then," she said, and flounced off the bed to bend over a large white sack on the floor. "I went into the village and bought you something to wear." She pulled something out of the sack. "It's called a jogging suit," she said, tossing two green pieces of clothing into his lap. He felt the material—slightly heavy and soft to the touch. "I also bought you some jeans and shirts."

"What is jogging?" he asked, curious in spite of his melancholy. "What are jeans?"

"Jogging is like running," she said.

He nodded. "Ah. In case we must run from the authorities, aye?"

"No, it's uh—in this day and age, people run to exercise, or for fun."

"Why?"

She frowned. "You know, that is a very good question. And jeans are a kind of breeches made from a very tough kind of material."

"Thank ye," he said, forcing himself to look her in the eye and smile. "I will put it all on later, but right now, I'm going to lie back down."

"Are you in pain?" she asked anxiously. Her blue eyes mirrored her concern, and Quinn reached up to brush that recalcitrant strand of auburn hair back from her face. She'd worried and fussed over him like a mother hen ever since his surgery.

"Aye," he said, "a bit. I just need to rest. Dinna fash yerself."

"Easier said than done," Maggie said softly. "Would you please eat something?"

Quinn picked up the tray and handed it back to her. "I'll just stretch out a wee bit longer," he said. "I'll eat later, I promise."

He could see she wasn't happy about that, but she took

the tray and moved toward the door. "Are you sure you'll be all right until I come back up?"

Quinn frowned at her. "I am no a bairn," he said, unable to keep the irritation from his voice. Maggie grinned and then stuck out her tongue before she turned and sashayed to the door. She paused and looked over her shoulder. "No, but you're just as cranky as one."

Quinn smiled as she closed the door behind her, realizing just how close they really were. She didn't waste time or energy berating him for his rudeness. She understood and was giving him time to deal with what had happened.

As soon as she was gone, Quinn felt a kind of panic sweep over him.

When they had stumbled out of the cairn, a man called Alex had been there and had greeted Maggie like a long-lost friend. Alex seemed to be in charge of things at the cairn.

Quinn was so ill from his wound that the whole thing now seemed like a dream. Alex, along with another man, had lifted Quinn between them and whisked him down the hillside. At the bottom he had been placed in—surely an aberration of his fevered brain—a huge insect. It was bright red and had large windows in it, front, back and on the sides, and four fat wheels, two on either side.

Maggie climbed in beside him and the insect began to move before Quinn finally realized it was not an insect, but a kind of carriage. A carriage without horses.

Maggie had sat with his head cradled in her lap, and the entire trip was something of a blur. He had a sense of great speed, as if he rode a fast stallion, but he himself was called upon to do nothing, simply lie and doze as his blood continued to seep away.

After his release from the hospital he and Maggie had ridden home in a similar vehicle, this one a dark green.

Maggie had operated the carriage, and he envied the ease with which she managed the huge piece of steel.

Home.

Quinn glanced around at the room in which he lay. Maggie's home was almost as fine as the duke's, though smaller, and the room he'd been given was luxurious. The four-poster bed was large and covered with a deep green coverlet and a pile of pillows of all sizes and colors. The polished wood floor gleamed, and part of it was covered by an ornate rug woven in soft shades of deep green, rose, and cream, which complimented the cream-colored walls.

The most amazing thing was how clean it was. It was the cleanest room he had ever seen in his life, and the brightest. Two large windows opposite the bed let in an amazing amount of sunlight, enough to lighten the heart of any melancholy man, but there was also a light in the ceiling and two lamps, one on either side of the bed.

When Maggie flipped a switch near the doorway, the light in the ceiling came on. The lamps were operated with a switch at the bottom of each. There was no flame, no candle inside. He had asked Maggie hesitantly if it was a kind of magic. She had laughed and said yes, a magic called electricity. Then she explained it, and he had shaken his head.

He closed his eyes. The stitches across his chest ached, but he ignored them and tried to think. Oh-kay, as Maggie would say, somehow he had journeyed through time to the future, leaving all that he knew behind in his own time, 1711. Everything, including Ian.

Quinn opened his eyes. He had to go back. He had to save Ian. There was no time to sit and dwell upon what had happened. He had to find a way to get back to where he belonged!

His heart constricted at the thought of leaving Maggie, and truth be told, he wouldn't mind staying in her world for a while. It seemed quite peaceful, and filled with miraculous things. But he could not. He had to return and save Ian from certain death.

He began to plan. In the cairn, before they traveled through time, Maggie had been saying words, like a chant. It seemed reasonable to suppose that the words had something to do with their amazing journey.

He'd have to ask her, but then he'd have to tell her that he wasn't going to stay with her; he would have to tell her good-bye, perhaps forever.

Maggie was so happy to be back home with Quinn that she could scarcely contain herself. Once he was in stable condition at the hospital, she'd known that God had granted her most fervent prayer—that the man she loved would return with her to her time, where the two of them would live happily every after.

Her sisters and Rachel had been so glad to see her it was almost more than she could stand. They'd been so afraid they had lost her forever. Maggie hated the fear she'd seen in their eyes as they all hugged her tightly the night she returned. They were terrified she might disappear again. Like their mother and father had. She took a deep, shuddering breath and then hurried down the stairs, anxious all over again to see her family.

Maggie paused at the doorway and gazed at her friend and her sisters where they sat. Rachel's long hair was currently the color of a ripe apricot with bright purple streaks throughout, and Maggie felt comforted just by the sight of it. Rachel's eclectic style extended from the top of her crazy hair to her short red skirt and a baggy purple T-shirt that said "I Love Nessie."

Allie was still slim and serene in her usual classic attire, a pale cream-colored blouse tucked into pale blue slacks, complimenting her shoulder-length blonde hair and making her blue eyes look like the sky on a summer day in Texas.

Ellie was still curvy in her usual black, this time a short lace dress that looked vintage. Her short, spiky hair had been freshly dyed black, and her blue eyes stood out as much as Allie's, thanks to the carefully applied black eyeliner surround them.

Maggie smiled. How had she ever imagined she could make it without Rachel and the twins? Another thought chased quickly after that. How could she have ever imagined she could make it without Quinn? And would she be able to keep him? That was the real question.

"So, how has everyone been?" Maggie asked as she strolled into the room and sat down in a green, rose, and cream calico-covered chair in the living room. It was a nice room, quaint and old-fashioned. Allie and Ellie sat on an overstuffed, dark green sofa. Rachel sat next to them in a chair identical to the one Maggie sat in.

All three of them stared at her in disbelief.

"How has everyone been?" Ellie said, shaking her head.

"How has everyone been?" Allie echoed, shaking her head in an exact copy of her twin's.

Rachel took it to the next level. "How has everyone *been*?" She said, rising up out of her chair, her eyes wide with incredulity.

Maggie quickly waved her back into her seat. "Okay, okay, I know you've all been worried sick! Please believe me that I didn't do it on purpose! I came back as soon as I, er, got my memory back." Part of the convoluted story she'd told them included a complete, though temporary, loss of memory.

Rachel glanced at the twins. "Notice she doesn't say she was anxious to get back to *us*."

"Yeah, like you would have been either," Ellie said, lifting one dyed black brow at her honorary aunt. "If that Scottish hunk had found you."

"Don't be ridiculous." Maggie smoothed her hands down the legs of her jeans. It was so great to have her own clothes back again. The soft green T-shirt and jeans made her feel more like her old self than she had in a long time. "I came back as soon as I remembered who I was."

"You said that already. And tell us again, how exactly it was that you wandered off from the dig camp," Rachel demanded.

Maggie sighed and rolled her eyes. "I've told you this at least three times. I went out walking in the moonlight, um, just thinking, and I, er, tripped and rolled down the other side of the hill. I must have hit my head. When I came to, I couldn't remember anything and started wandering away from the camp." She'd given the story over and over in the days since she and Quinn had ended up back in her time. "After a day of wandering, I ran into a, uh, shepherd, Quinn, and he took care of me until I started getting my memory back. Now, will you please stop interrogating me?"

"Hmmm," Ellie said, "you know, I never would have pegged Quinn for a shepherd. Weightlifter maybe."

"Where does this guy live?" Allie asked.

"In the Highlands," Maggie said vaguely. "You know, in one of those little cottages."

"What's the address?" Allie asked persistently.

"How did he get stabbed, again?" Ellie asked.

Maggie rolled her eyes. "I told you, we ended up in Drymen at the pub, and when we left, someone ran up, grabbed my bag and stabbed Quinn."

"But you still have your bag," Allie said.

"Uh, he dropped it when a guy ran out of the pub—because I screamed."

"And," Allie went on, as if Maggie hadn't spoken, "no one who was at the pub that night remembers seeing either of you."

Maggie frowned. "What did you do, hire Scotland Yard?"

"You don't hire Scotland Yard," Ellie said, "they're the police."

"Let's just say that I have my ways," Allie said mysteriously.

"Okay, girls, let's get to the heart of the matter—the guy. He took care of you, huh?" Rachel's smile was lascivious, and Maggie frowned at her. "I just bet he did. Wanna elaborate?"

Maggie laughed to cover her embarrassment. "There's nothing to elaborate about," she lied. "He was a perfect gentleman."

Rachel snorted. "Sure he was."

"Let's cut to the chase," Allie said. "The problem is, Maggie, we don't believe you." Her sister smiled at her, her picture perfect face calm and complacent. Many a man had taken one look at Allie's blonde beauty and jumped to the wrong conclusion—that she was dumb. Expecting a vague intellect and at best a penchant for fashion, most were shocked when she opened her mouth and proved them wrong.

While Maggie was used to her bluntness, she knew she had to keep the facade in place. She stared back at her sister, lifting her chin as if she'd been terribly insulted. "I beg your pardon?"

"You heard her. We don't believe you," Ellie said, flopping back against a pillow on the sofa. "So why don't you tell us the truth instead?"

Maggie started to deny the accusation, but as she gazed around at the faces she loved, she smiled. "You guys don't know how glad I am to see you," she said softly. "You just don't know how glad."

The three women looked at one another and then, almost in unison, jumped up and surrounded her, folding her into their arms, crying wet, sloppy tears all over her.

"We were so *worr*-ied," Ellie cried, unmindful that her black eyeliner was running down her face as she sat down on the arm of the calico chair and put her arm around Maggie, hugging her tightly.

"You were gone so long, Maggie! We thought you were—!" Allie didn't finish the sentence, but sank down on the floor at her sister's feet and laid her head in Maggie's lap.

Rachel stood behind Maggie, her arms wrapped loosely around her neck, sobbing along with the sisters, and then all at once gave a little groan and straightened. She circled around in front of Maggie and put her hands on her hips, staring down at her sternly.

"And then you show up with this cockamamie story about having amnesia." She cocked her head to one side. "Come on, Mags, we know you didn't let us all worry while you played footsie with your honey up there, but your story is just a little too hard to believe."

Allie and Ellie were both on their knees now, their heads resting in her lap. Maggie stroked their hair, so very different, back from their faces, so much alike.

"Look," she said, "you guys are just going to have to trust me."

Allie wiped the tears from her face and stared up at her. "Why? If your story is true, why do we have to trust you? What do you mean?"

Maggie sighed. She'd been through the worst and the best times in her life with these three women. There was no reason to think they couldn't take the truth of what had happened to her. Her only fear was that they would think she was nuts.

"Okay," she said hesitantly, "there's more to the story. But if I tell you, you'll think I should be locked up in the loony bin."

Allie and Ellie sat back on their heels and blinked as they looked up at her in confusion.

"Try us," Rachel said, her eyes narrow, her stance like a drill sergeant's.

Maggie drew in a deep breath. "Sit down. All of you." When they were all seated again, she took another deep breath and then began.

"It all started one night when I couldn't sleep . . ."

They didn't believe her.

The three women stared at her, their mouths open, their eyes huge in their faces. Then they all jumped to their feet and began talking all at once, asking questions that she tried to answer, each growing more and more upset, until Maggie had finally called a halt.

When they had all finally calmed down and were sitting again, their faces twisted into similar shades of terror, Maggie knew what she had to do. She smiled.

"Gotcha."

Another stunned silence was followed by near hysterical laughter.

"Well!" Rachel said. "You certainly paid us back for every trick we've ever pulled on you! I'm impressed."

Maggie laughed, even as she felt a sudden sadness flood over her. If Quinn returned to his own time, she wouldn't even be able to talk to her sisters and Rachel about him. About the real Quinn.

"Yep," she said aloud. "I thought it was finally time I taught you all a lesson. I'm not a time traveler. I bumped my head, lost my memory, met Quinn. You can believe it or not." Her bravado sounded weak, even to her.

"You okay, kid?" Rachel asked, one hand on her shoulder.

Maggie raised her brows. "Hey, you're the one who fell for it. I'm fine." She jumped up and headed toward the kitchen. "You know what? I'm starving. In the past, all we had was porridge. What's in the fridge?"

The three converged on her, still giggling, and bustled her into the kitchen. They warmed up leftover roast beef, and she smiled and ate the sandwich Allie made her, and then ate a huge bowl of ice cream.

The girls decided they should play Scrabble—a longtime family favorite—and Maggie didn't have the heart to say no. It was two o'clock in the afternoon before she finally yawned and said she'd had enough. Just being downstairs for a few hours had made her miss Quinn terribly. What would she do if he decided to return to the past?

"Allie is still the reigning champion," she announced, "and I need a nap."

"Someday I am going to beat you," Ellie said to her sister. "I don't get it. How can you still beat me at Scrabble?"

Allie smiled, not gloating over her victory at all. "It's about the way you think. That's why I'm good at math and you suck. That's why I can play chess and you can't."

Ellie frowned. "Are you calling me dumb?"

Her sister looked shocked. "Of course not! You're one of the smartest people I know! And so am I, we just have different kinds of smarts."

"Okay, girls, I'm out of here," Maggie announced.

They all looked up in alarm, and Maggie stared down at them. "I'm going upstairs," she explained.

She felt bad for making them panic, so she kept talking. "Quinn's probably sprawled across the whole bed, and I won't be able to move him."

"I bet you can make him scoot over," Rachel said, her voice slightly evil. "If you can't, I've got a few moves you can use."

"Shhh," Maggie warned, "children in the house." It was an old joke between them and soon they were hugging and making plans for later.

After ten minutes more, she finally escaped up the stairs, feeling a little depressed. She'd really thought they might believe her.

When she opened the door to the bedroom, the small lamp on the bedside table was on. Quinn lay under the covers of the bed, his eyes closed. The sight of him lying there made tears come to Maggie's eyes. She'd come so close to losing him. The terrifying thing was she knew she was *still* in danger of losing him. He hadn't said anything yet, but she knew he was worried about Ian. And she understood. She was worried, too.

Maggie moved quickly to the bed and slid in beside him, lying on top of the covers.

"Quinn," she whispered, "are you okay?"

He opened his eyes, and that familiar green hit her. But there was distance in his gaze and she stilled beside him.

"What is it?" she said. "What's wrong?"

"Why did ye not tell me that ye were—are—a time traveler?" Quinn asked.

Maggie shook her head. "It's pretty obvious, isn't it?"

"Nay, I dinna see that it is."

"Well, you'd have thought I was crazy."

Quinn looked away. "Ye dinna give me any credit for being a thinking man, do ye?"

Maggie opened her mouth, shut it, and opened it again. "What do you mean?"

He rose and walked around the room, slapping the top his fist with the other hand. "I mean, ye think I am stupid."

"I do not think you're stupid," she said, outraged. She jumped off the bed and grabbed him by one arm as he paced by. "I think you're one of the smartest people I've ever known!"

"But ye dinna trust me to believe ye, even though I love ye." His green eyes held hers in a steady gaze and Maggie finally groaned and sank back down on the bed, her chin in her hands.

"Please don't do this," she begged, tugging him down beside her. "And try to understand. I just didn't know how to tell you."

Quinn nodded. "And what if I had not been stabbed by Pembroke?" he asked.

She blinked at him. "What do you mean?"

He stared straight ahead. "What were yer plans? When had ye intended to return to yer time—without me? And what am I now? An unwanted tagalong that ye had to bring to yer time to save his life?"

Maggie bounced off the bed and turned to face him, hands on her hips. "Is that what you really think? That I brought you here to save you, not because I want to spend the rest of my life with you?"

He shrugged and she picked up a pillow and threw it at him. It bounced off his head harmlessly and he continued to stare at her.

She began to pace angrily around the room, her auburn hair flying out behind her. "If you only knew what I went through—how I agonized over telling you—like the time you went through my backpack and found all my stuff! I wanted to tell you then, but I didn't think—" She broke off and looked away.

Quinn stood, his face like granite, his arms folded over his chest. "Ye didn't think that I could—what do the people in your time say—?" His fingers flexed against his upper arms as he frowned. "Oh, aye—ye dinna think I could handle it."

"That's not all you won't be handling," Maggie muttered as she folded her arms over her chest and met his eyes glare for glare.

"I heard that," he said, his voice harsh. "And while we're on the subject of handling it, I dinna like the way you handled Ian in such a familiar way," he said.

"What?" Maggie cried. "What are you talking about? Ian is my friend."

"Aye, a friend who wants to have"—he frowned as if searching for the right word—"benefits."

Her mouth dropped open. "Quinn MacIntyre! You should be ashamed for even thinking such a thing—about me and about your best friend! What is the matter with you?"

Quinn looked away, but not before she caught a flicker of sadness in his eyes.

Maggie stared at him for a long moment and then drew in a deep breath and smiled. "Okay, now I know what's going on." She strode across the room and punched him in the arm.

"Damn, but ye pack a punch for such a wee lass! What was that for?"

"You deserve worse. How dare you try and make me mad, make me think you're some kind of jealous jerk, just so you can return to your own time and save Ian? What kind of woman do you think I am?"

Quinn sighed and shook his head. "The kind that is too smart for me."

"Damn you, Quinn." Maggie folded her arms across her chest. "Did you really think that would work? That I'd fall out of love with you because you acted like an idiot for five minutes?"

He ran one hand through his tousled dark hair. "I must

go back to my own time. I dinna want ye to be hurt if I dinna return—if I canna return."

Her mouth went dry. "What do you mean? Of course you can return."

Quinn gave her wistful smile. "I'm no going back in time to have a tea party, lass. I'm going back to fight a devil, and save a man I love as dearly as I loved my own brother."

"I know," Maggie whispered, moving to his side and sliding her arms around his waist. "But at least let me have the hope that you'll come back to me," she said. "At least let me have that."

Quinn gathered her into his arms and held her close, his breath warm upon her hair. "Aye, all right then, lass, I'll no take that away from ye."

She snuggled against his chest, careful not to touch his stitches. "Let's go into town tomorrow. There's so much I want to show you and—"

"Aye," he cut her off. "We'll go to town." He turned toward her slightly and brushed his mouth across hers. His chin was scratchy with stubble, and a little thrill ran through her blood. "Tomorrow."

"So do you want to go to Edinburgh? I think we should probably start with Drymen and ease you into things. We can—"

"Shhh," Quinn said. "Tomorrow. He settled his mouth over hers. She felt his warm tongue slip inside to dance with hers and closed her eyes as his hand slid down to caress her breast. Suddenly, tomorrow seemed fine.

"Are you naked under there?" she asked weakly.

"Come and find out," he offered.

With a sigh she pulled the covers back and found to her extreme satisfaction that her suspicions had been correct. She quickly set about shedding her own clothes and then slipped in beside him.

"But there's one thing I really need to tell you—"

He kissed her again and made it very, very hard to focus on the decision she had made a few minutes earlier. As she'd stood in the kitchen talking to her sisters, Ellie had mentioned the great library the little town had, and Maggie had suddenly realized she and Quinn could look up Ian MacGregor's name in history books, and even talk to clan historians and the like. Maybe they'd find out someone else had rescued Ian. Maybe Quinn didn't have to go back.

"Tomorrow," he whispered again. Then Quinn began to paint hot, lush kisses down the side of her neck, and her questions and fears faded into liquid heat and didn't matter. All that mattered was Quinn loving her, right now, this minute.

The future would take care of itself.

And perhaps the past as well. Maggie closed her eyes and began to hope.

fourteen

Quinn stood outside the cottage, his back against the house as he gazed at the surrounding countryside. In his mind, this place was in no way a "cottage," but practically a manor house. Maggie had told him it was a "rental," that Rachel and the girls had leased the place when they came to Scotland to look for her.

Across the narrow roadway that ran up to the house, a doe and her fawn grazed languidly, unfazed by the human watching them. But he wasn't watching them, not really. Instead, Quinn's thoughts were wandering back to the many times he'd stood behind Ian's grandmother's cottage and watched just such a doe and a fawn—three hundred years in the past. He shook his head and closed his eyes, leaning his head back until it touched the stone behind him.

The actual land of Scotland had remained remarkably the same, except for the modern introduction of roads to carry the two-eyed monstrous carriages. Everything else had changed. Remarkably changed.

He still had many questions to ask Maggie. Questions

he hadn't been able to force himself to ask the night before. Questions about how he could return to his own time. Once he had her in his arms again, his heart had ached. How could he leave her?

They made love, but for the first time ever he could not lose himself in their passion, could not disconnect his thoughts. When he had brought Maggie to her release and found his, he had held her tightly in his arms, knowing he was going to lose her, knowing his honor demanded he return and save his friend.

He must have been wearier than he realized, for when he awoke, it was morning again. Maggie had risen early and gone somewhere with her sisters. She'd left him a note saying she would return soon and they would do something "fun." He had put on the soft "jogging" clothing again and taken a walk while he waited for her. When he returned, she still had not returned, so he waited outside, anxious to see her.

His mouth quirked up only slightly as he thought about her note. *Fun.* She had explained the concept to him once before. In his time, he was not sure the word existed.

"Penny for your thoughts. Sorry, I meant, a shilling? A pound? I always get Scottish and English money mixed up."

Quinn turned, and there she was just a few feet away, his Maggie, smiling at him, her blue eyes filled with the concern that had been there ever since they had arrived in her time.

"Och," he said, "my thoughts are worth far less, and I refuse to take advantage of yer innocence."

Maggie moved easily into his arms. "After what you did to me last night, I don't know how you can ever think me innocent again." Her smile faded a bit. "Quinn, we need to talk."

"I thought we were going to do something 'fun,'" he

said, wiggling his eyebrows, hoping to bring back her smile.

She did smile, but the gesture was feeble at best. "We will," she said, "but first—"

He nodded. "Aye. We need to talk. Shall we go for a walk?"

"I was thinking we'd go for a drive. There are some things I want to show you."

A drive. In that crazy horseless carriage. Quinn swallowed hard and then berated himself. He was a man, a Scottish warrior; surely he could overcome his fear of this foolish vehicle.

"Fine," he said, forcing his own smile.

She backed away from him and held out her hand. "Then come with me, laddie. I have a surprise for you."

Quinn was thrilled when Maggie took him to a quaint little bookstore in Drymen filled with books on Scotland, followed by a trip to the local library. The bookstore had colorful books filled with what Maggie called *photographs* of Scotland. He was so mesmerized by them that she finally bought one just to get him out of the shop. At the library they poured over books on Scottish history, and used something called a com-poo-ter and the In-Ter-Net—which Maggie said she would not, under any circumstance, try to explain to him—looking for a mention of Ian MacGregor's untimely death.

Maggie did explain during the drive to the library that if there wasn't a mention of his death in these places of record, or if there *was* a record of Ian living on to a ripe old age, it would mean Ian had not been killed by the duke, and there would be no need for Quinn to go back to the past.

Unless he wanted to go back.

Maggie always added that last in her impassioned

diatribes, but he knew how much she wanted him to stay. Could he? As he sat in the library and gazed at book after book filled with more of what Maggie called *photos*, he had gained more respect for her time, and more curiosity. And though he had some problems at first deciphering the type and the spelling of these modern books, by the afternoon he had begun to adapt.

In spite of all the wonders he was beginning to experience, did he want to turn his back on his own time—and Ian—and stay with Maggie?

"Find anything?" Maggie whispered, sliding next to him on the curved sofa, her finger marking a place in the book she held.

Quinn shook his head, discouraged. So far he'd found no record whatsoever of Ian MacGregor, son of Owen MacGregor, grandson of Angus MacGregor, aside from a brief mention that he had attended MacCrimmons School of Piping.

"Nay."

She sighed. "Me either. But I found a bunch of books that were written by different clan historians, full of legends and little-known historical facts, so I'm going to check them out and read them back at the cottage. You hungry?"

Quinn stood and stretched his arms over his head. "Aye." He lowered his arms and glanced down at her. She looked tired. "Come, lass, let's go back to the cottage. We can read in bed."

Maggie shot him a knowing look. "Right. That'll happen."

He sat back down, for once not taking her up on her teasing innuendo. "I did find out something important," he said.

"You did?" She sat down beside him, her blue eyes hopeful.

"I found out that Scotland and her clans finally find peace."

She nodded. "So how do you feel, knowing Scotland is finally at peace?"

He frowned thoughtfully. "I am not sure. Relieved. Gladdened. Wondering if I go back, after I save Ian, what I will do with the rest of my life, now that I know all of our fighting and struggling is pointless." He hadn't meant to say those last words, but he was tired, and his defenses low. "We are still absorbed by almighty England. The United Kingdom." Quinn laughed shortly. "Every Scotsman's biggest fear."

Maggie sat up, her back rigid. "All that fighting and struggling is what led to Scotland's peace, and yes, they became part of the United Kingdom, but they still retained a great deal of their sovereignty. But if you go back, there is also a lot of senselessness ahead, too." She sighed. "Jacobites. Culloden. The clearances. It ends well, but getting there—"

"We get there. I suppose that is the important part." He rubbed the back of his neck with one hand. "I am tired of whispering. Is there a place near here, outdoors, where we can sit and talk?" Maggie stood and tugged on the hem of the loose-fitting blouse she wore, called a T-shirt. It had a picture of a huge lizardlike monster on it and the words "I Love Nessie." The twenty-first century was vastly confusing.

"Sure," she said. "Just give me the books you want to check out, and I'll lead you to it." He handed her one book on Scottish history, still reading the book he held. "Just one?"

Quinn looked up from the book—a fascinating tome on the ancient Celts. He had just gotten to the section on how the Picts had painted their faces and engraved tattoos into their bodies to symbolize spiritual beliefs, or to gear up for war. He pointed to a huge stack on the floor, and Maggie grinned.

"I fear t'will be too extravagant," he said. "Do ye have the coin for such things?"

"Don't worry. This isn't a bookstore, it's a library," she said. "You can borrow as many books as you like, and just as long as you return them, they're free."

"Free?" He stared at her, feeling an unfamiliar surge of joy. Quinn loved books. Loved the feel of them, loved reading them. At the bookstore, when Maggie wasn't looking, he'd wandered over to the music department and flipped through books on the history of different instruments, books on making instruments, books on musical theory, books on bagpipes, and wished he had the coin with which to buy them.

"Aye, laddie," she said, putting on a brogue. "Free. As in 'They will never take—our freedom!' " She lifted her arms above her head and shook them as Quinn stared. She lowered her arms and shrugged. "You'll get it when I show you *Braveheart*. Maybe we could rent it tonight."

"Er, that's grand," he said, without a clue as to what she was talking about. He had more important things on his mind. "Do they have a section on music?"

"Oh, boy, I'm never going to get you out of here, am I?"

He smiled. "Och, lass, I'm a man with a love for knowledge. For instance, I'm verra interested in finding out what color yer bindings are today."

Maggie laughed. One night after Quinn's release from the hospital she had come to bed modeling a hot pink bra and panties. Quinn had loved the frilly things, but insisted on calling her bras her "bindings."

"Okay, ten more minutes, and then if we go home soon, I might let you find out if I'm wearing black or green today," she teased.

Exactly ten minutes later, he watched as the librarian slid each book across a metal plate and then handed it to him. She was down to the last two books when she stopped and glanced up, the expression in her brown eyes changing from bored to interested as she really looked at him for the first time.

"Is this yer book, too?" she asked, turning the book toward him. "The *Kama Sutra*?"

Maggie's mouth dropped open, and Quinn truly blushed, perhaps for the first time in his life.

"Er, aye, I thought it looked, er, interesting."

"Verra interesting," the woman said, lowering her lashes and gazing up at him through them. "And this one?" She held up the last book. "*How to Please a Woman in One Hundred Different Ways*?" Her gaze swept over him, and he sensed, rather than saw, Maggie stiffen beside him.

"Aye," he said.

"We're sort of in a hurry," Maggie said pointedly. "So if you don't mind . . ."

"Och, I dinna mind at all," the librarian said. She reached into her conservative blouse and pulled out a card. She handed it to Quinn. "I'm Elizabeth. Give me a call sometime. We'll do"—she paused—"lunch."

Quinn frowned and took the card, then encircled her wrist with his hand. Maggie blinked as he cradled her hand between his, staring down at it as if he'd never seen one before.

"What is this marking?" he asked.

Maggie moved closer and saw the librarian had a word tattooed around her wrist.

"A tattoo, luv," she said. "Where have ye been living? Under a rock?"

"Something like that," he murmured. "Is it permanent?"

Maggie peered down at the woman's wrist. The word was *Gordon*.

The librarian made a face. "Unfortunately. It was supposed to be a symbol of my undying love for my boyfriend. He left before the ink was dry, so to speak." She batted her lashes at him. "So that means I am available. *Very* available."

Maggie's eyes narrowed, and Quinn grabbed her by the arm before she could launch herself across the countertop. He thanked the librarian and then pushed Maggie in the general direction of the door, while he gathered up the stack of books that temporarily belonged to him.

"Damn!" he said once they were outside. "Are all the lassies in your time that bold?"

She walked very quickly, keeping her eyes straight ahead. "Just the skanks and hos," she said, her disgust obvious.

"Ah, Maggie, she canna hold a candle to ye." His arms were full of books, so he bumped her with his hip. She glanced up at him and smiled, bringing sunlight back into his day.

"Ready to go home and read?" she asked.

"Aye. And perhaps have a cuddle?"

Maggie put her arm around his waist and pushed him toward the horseless carriage. "Aye, laddie. Perhaps."

Back at the cottage, they spent the evening with Maggie's sisters and Rachel, and she'd watched as Quinn charmed the three women with his smile and wit and humor. *He does belong here,* the little voice in her head kept saying. *He does!*

When they finally went to bed, very late, Maggie emerged from the bathroom to find Quinn sitting up in bed waiting for her, looking so amazingly sexy that she had to force herself not to pounce on him.

"I need to tell ye something, lass," Quinn said softly.

"All right," she said tentatively, sitting down on the far side of the bed. She feared she knew what he wanted to tell her. Her heart pounded hard in her chest, reminding her how easily it could be broken.

He patted a spot beside him. "Come here, lass."

Maggie hesitated, but he cocked his dark head toward her, and she sighed and slid across the bed to snuggle next to him, her head on his shoulder. "Okay, go ahead. Talk."

"Verra well then. Here it is." He took a deep breath. "Ye know that I must return. Every day that goes by makes me tremble with fear over what Pembroke may be doing to Ian."

"I know, Quinn," Maggie said faintly. "I was just hoping we'd find something in one of these books to prove that Ian made it without your help. But why would you want to stay here anyway? I understand that your life is in the past. I really do." She slid him a furtive glance. Quinn's ruggedly handsome face split with a smile that lit his eyes from within.

"Och, darling." He hugged her tightly against him. Maggie threw her arms around his waist and clung to him. "I do want to stay with ye. I find this century quite amazing, along with ye yerself. I must go back to save Ian, but that doesna mean that I must remain there. What is to stop me from returning to ye through the magic spirals?"

Maggie turned in his arms and climbed into his lap. She took his face between her hands and kissed him as tears of relief slid down her face.

"Oh, Quinn," she said, and he folded her into his arms.

Much later, when Quinn was asleep, Maggie got up and turned on the standing lamp beside the pale green over-stuffed chair in the corner of the room. She moved her stack of library books beside it, and began to search through them for any mention of Ian MacGregor.

While Quinn's decision to come back to her was wonderful, she was still filled with fear. What if he got killed trying to save Ian? What if he got put in prison? What if the spirals took him to *another time*? She shuddered at the memory of the two times she'd traveled through time, how she'd felt as though her mind and body were being wrenched apart. What if he couldn't come back?

There were too many "what ifs," all of which could be avoided if they could just find out Ian's fate. Two hours later, when the books failed to yield any information, Maggie got on the Internet. By dawn, she was exhausted and ready to admit that it might take a lot longer than she'd expected to dig up any history about Ian. And in spite of having access to a time travel "device," time was of the essence.

Her head throbbed as she crawled back in bed with Quinn and snuggled up against him. He turned in his sleep and welcomed her into his arms, but even in the warmth of their bed, with her head on Quinn's shoulder, Maggie couldn't stop thinking.

She believed that God was a logical deity, and in spite of the deaths of her parents, she believed that everything happened for a reason. It was inconceivable that she had been allowed to travel back in time to meet Quinn, only to be separated from him forever. She couldn't believe it. She wouldn't.

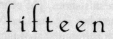

fifteen

"I'm thinking about staying in Scotland."

Maggie watched Rachel's face, anxious to see her reaction to this news. She knew her friend had to return to the States soon, and the girls as well, but she wasn't going anywhere. Her decision felt selfish in the extreme.

The girls survived without me for a month, she thought. *They can make it a little bit longer.* It was a radical thought.

She and Quinn had gone into the village that morning together, but when it was time to go home, Quinn wanted to stay a bit longer. Maggie had dropped him off at the library and told him she'd pick him up there later, then headed back to the cottage to join Rachel for some long overdue girlfriend time. The twins had driven into Edinburgh to meet some friends.

Now the two women sat on the flowered couch in the cottage "parlor." Rachel had her legs stretched out on the couch, her feet almost touching Maggie where she sat at the other end. Her friend hadn't changed a bit since Maggie had been gone—except for her hair color. Today she wore a bright red dress with yellow leggings underneath and purple tennis shoes. The effect was a little dazzling. Rachel pulled her legs up and wrapped her arms around her knees as she smiled at Maggie.

"So you think this thing with you and Quinn is going to work out, huh?" Rachel asked.

Maggie looked around at the beautiful room, and the perfect kitchen leading off of it, and really saw it for the first time. This was a nice place. A really nice place. As in an *expensive place*. How had they paid the rent? For over a month? She had a sneaking suspicion she knew how.

"Yes, I think Quinn and I are going to, er, work out," she said vaguely. "Uh, by the way, Rach, you didn't dip into the old trust fund did you, to finance this little trip for you and the girls?"

"Um, I've been meaning to talk to you about that," Rachel said, her voice hesitant. "You know, when you went missing, the girls were frantic."

"Ra-chel," Maggie said, drawing out her name, "you know our agreement."

"But this was an emergency, Mags, and you've always said if it was an emergency, that was different." Her friend's eyes softened as she gazed at her. "I was so terrified. I thought I'd lost you forever."

"I know," Maggie said, feeling a pang of guilt. "I feel terrible that I put you all through so much *and* cost you so much money. You know I'll pay you back."

"Maggie, please, for once let me do this." She hurried on before Maggie could answer. "I wanted to do it. And I want to continue to pay for you and the girls to stay here as long as you want. It's important to me." She smiled a very vulnerable smile, and it touched Maggie's heart to the core. "You're my family."

Maggie smiled. "I love you, Rach."

Rachel leaned back and visibly relaxed. "Okay, now!

While the girls are out—tell me everything about Quinn, especially the 'in bed' parts, and don't you dare leave out one little detail!"

"Rachel!" Maggie said, pretending outrage, laughing at the eagerness on Rachel's face. It was so good to be back.

"Hey," Rachel reminded her, "I'm not getting laid anytime soon so I have to live vicariously. "So, is he great in bed? Is he really, really great?"

Maggie leaned her head back on the sofa and smiled. "Oh, Rach, *great* doesn't even begin to describe him."

Quinn's arm hurt like the devil, but he didn't regret his decision. This would show Maggie just how serious he was about returning to her once he had rescued Ian. He had gone into the library when Maggie dropped him off, but as soon as she drove away, he had hurried out to do his real errand.

Mission accomplished. He'd heard that phrase on the amazing and magical tell-e-vision the night before. Strange, new world in which he had landed. Maggie had said she would pick him up at the library at six o'clock, and he had returned to the stone building, planning to do more research, but found he couldn't wait. He was anxious to see her, to see the look on her face. He could walk back to the cottage. It was only a matter of five miles or so.

Having made up his mind, Quinn strode from the history section toward the door, then paused at the front desk and stared at the telephone sitting there.

Maggie had explained what a "phone" was and had given him the number of the cottage on a small piece of paper that he had tucked into the new "wallet" she'd bought him. He frowned. He felt like a kept man. If he could make it back to Maggie's time, after saving Ian, what would he do to earn a living?

He had the sudden mental picture of riding a horse beside the horseless carriages, calling out for them to pull over so that he could rob them. Being a highwayman was obviously not a choice in the twenty-first century.

"Yes?" said a staid-looking librarian behind the desk. The flirtatious woman who had given him her number the last time wasn't there, and Quinn felt vastly relieved.

He hesitated, and then took the plunge.

"May I use yer telly-phone?" he asked.

"For a local call?" she asked.

Quinn gave her a confident smile, though he felt anything but. "Yes," he said, having no idea what she meant or to what he was agreeing.

She handed him the part of the phone Maggie had called the "receiver." "I'll dial it for you," she said in a precise accent that was only faintly Scottish.

Quinn hurriedly dug the wallet Maggie had given him out of the back pocket of his jeans. He gave the woman the piece of paper that had the number of the cottage written on it and watched in fascination as she pressed the numerical buttons. It seemed simple enough, but how in the world did it work? He held the receiver to his ear and was rewarded by the sound of a distant ringing. The ring sounded three times and then there was a click, and Maggie's voice.

"Hello," she said.

"Maggie mine," he said, his voice hoarse with affection and pride. "It's me, Quinn."

"Quinn?" she asked, her voice filled with shock.

"Aye," he said. "I thought I would"—what was it they called using this thing? A call? Yes, that was it—"I'd give ye a call." He rocked back on his heels in satisfaction.

Her soft laughter came to him over the earpiece. "You never cease to amaze me," she said. "Where are you?"

"At the library. Could ye come now and join me for an

early supper?" *That she'll have to pay for,* he reminded himself silently. Surely if he came back to her time, he could find some kind of employment. He was a hard worker. He would find his place.

"Sure," she agreed. "And this is perfect, because it just so happens, I have a big surprise for you waiting back in town."

"'Tis quite a coincidence," he said, "because I have one for ye, too. I'll meet ye outside the library."

"Great! I'll be there in fifteen minutes."

There was another click, and Quinn realized the call had ended. He handed the receiver back to the woman behind the counter and, feeling strangely smug, headed outside.

True to her word, Maggie picked him up in fifteen minutes. He was getting used to riding in the horseless carriage, and in fact, was starting to enjoy it. He might even learn to drive one someday. *If* he was able to return.

"I saw that friend of yours, Alex, when I was walking in town, and we had an interesting discussion," he told her as they drove down the main street of Drymen.

"What did he have to say?" Maggie asked.

He told her how Alex planned to shut down the cairn for a few days to go to Edinburgh and pick up a scientist friend. "He says the cairn is emitting a curious 'energy.'"

Maggie laughed. "No kidding."

"We are invited to meet his friend, when he returns to the cairn next week."

"Just like a real couple," Maggie said wistfully. "You know, you are adapting amazingly well."

Quinn cleared his throat. "Ye know, lass, this would be my opportunity to go back, while Alex is not in the way."

"I know," she said, the words a sigh, and then fell silent.

"I have something to show ye," he said after a few moments, "when ye stop this contraption."

Maggie glanced over at him, and there was a twinkle in her eyes. "Is it what you showed me last night, because if it is, I'll pull over right now."

He smiled. "Nay, 'tis something new. A surprise."

"Hmm, sounds mysterious." She pulled the carriage up in front of a row of tiny shops.

"What's this?" he asked.

"*Your* surprise. We'll have to walk down to the right shop. It's at the end." She shifted in her seat. "But first, show me *my* surprise."

"Aye, let's get out where we have more room."

"Oh, a *big* surprise," she said, her voice teasing. "I thought you said it wasn't what you showed me last night."

Quinn chuckled as he opened his door. "I swear, lass, ye get more wanton by the minute."

"Thank you. It's all your fault."

Circling quickly around the carriage, he opened her door before she could, and offered his hand for support.

"Thank you, my good fellow," she said, in a snotty, aristocratic voice, "now throw yourself down over yon water puddle and let me walk across your back."

"How about this instead?" He picked her up, one arm under her legs, the other around her waist, and spun her in a circle. She squealed and laughed until he put her down on the strange stone surface that was not stone, called a "sidewalk."

"Now *that* was fun." Maggie whirled around, her dress billowing out like a flower's petals.

Her garment was white, with tiny red dots scattered across it, made from a lineninsh material. The full skirt of the dress hit her just above the knees. It would be considered quite scandalous in his time, but after what Quinn had seen in the village that day, he realized she was dressed very modestly. She looked beautiful. What if he couldn't return? He swallowed hard and dismissed the thought. He *would* return.

"Okay," she said, coming to a stop. "Give me my surprise."

"First a word of explanation."

Maggie raised both brows. "All right."

"I had been reading a book about the ancient Celts," he told her, as he took off his new jacket and laid it over his right arm, "and learned many had inscribed themselves with symbols of significance. When I saw the name tattoo on that young woman's wrist yesterday, it gave me an idea."

She frowned. "Quinn, please tell me that you didn't—"

With a wide grin, he pushed up the left sleeve of his new T-shirt. There, in all of its reddened glory, adorning his bicep, was his new tattoo.

The triskele.

Maggies's mouth dropped open. "Quinn . . ." she said faintly. "When—? What—?"

His smile widened. He'd really surprised her!

One corner of her mouth quirked up just a little, then looking a little dazed, she dropped her gaze to his arm and gingerly ran one finger around the skin outside the reddened tattoo.

"It—It's amazing," she said. "But why the spirals?"

Quinn slipped his arms around her waist and without hesitation she slid her hands up his chest and around his neck, as he gazed down into her blue, blue eyes.

"This is what brought ye to me, and this is what will bring me back to ye. When I get back to me own time, I will see this symbol every day, and every day I will be reminded that ye are here, waiting for me to return."

The quirk disappeared, and tears glistened in Maggie's eyes. "Oh, Quinn," she whispered, and pulled his head down to hers, kissing him in a way that made him know she understood completely. When they separated, he leaned his head against hers. "Has anyone ever told you," she said, "that you are an amazing man?"

"Just forty or fifty women," he said.

She laughed, moving away, keeping his hand. "I love the tatoo, especially if it helps bring you back to me. Now it's your turn." She pulled him forward.

He drew back in feigned horror. "Ye dinna get a tattoo, too, did ye?"

"Not yet, but give me time."

Quinn frowned as he thought about it. "I dinna think so."

"Why not?"

"I dinna like the idea of yer sweet skin being ravaged like that." He winced. "Ye know, it *stings* to have this done. I dinna want anything to ever hurt ye, lass."

Maggie's gaze softened. "I love you," she said.

"And I love ye, Maggie mine."

Wearing a satisfied smile, she led him down the sidewalk a short distance until she stopped in front of one of the tiny houses and opened its red door. Quinn walked in first, and stopped short, staring around at the small shop. Every bit of space on the walls and countertops in the square room was covered with bagpipes of every size and description. There were Northumbrian smallpipes, border pipes, Uilleann pipes, and—

He reached out and lightly touched the velvet bag covering of a large set of pipes. When he spoke, his voice was hushed, reverent. "*Piob-mhor,*" he whispered.

"What?" Maggie asked.

"The Grrrrr–eat Pipe," said a short man from behind the counter, in a brogue so thick, Quinn wondered for a moment if it was real. The man's face was wizened and wrinkled, and to Quinn, he looked like a gnome in one of the books he and Maggie had checked out of the library. "'Tis tha' most traditional set of pipes," the man added. "And tha' one is quite auld. From the late 1800s. The drones is made from bog oak. Ye don't see that much no more."

Quite old. And yet Quinn was older by at least a hundred years. He felt Maggie's hand on his arm and took heart. He glanced down at her and smiled, and then turned his attention back to the pipes.

The bag was of red, green, and blue plaid velvet, with three long drones made from a dark, smooth wood protruding from the back, along with the blowpipe. He touched it gingerly, the same thrill he'd once felt as he played the pipes rushing over him as the wood slid beneath his fingertips. Silver ferrules with knot work engraved upon them adored the different sections of the drones, and tassels studded with beads looped between them. It was beautiful.

"I've ne'er played the Great Pipes," Quinn said softly. "Mine are—were—smallpipes."

"I wouldn't say that," Maggie murmured, shooting him a wicked smile.

"Weel noo, take 'em doon and try them oot," the small man encouraged him.

Quinn reached for the pipes and then stopped and lowered his hand. "Another time perhaps," he said.

Maggie laughed. "No, not another time, you stubborn Scot. This is my surprise! I bought them for you!"

Quinn drew in a sharp breath and stared down at her, then shook his head. "Thank ye, but—" Abruptly, he turned and walked out of the shop. Maggie caught up with him halfway down the street.

"Quinn. Quinn, wait!"

He stopped, unable to look at her. She pulled him around to face her, and he felt the hot flush of shame stain his cheeks, along with a solitary tear.

"Quinn," she whispered, her hand going to his face, her

fingers sliding over the moisture and wiping it away. "I'm sorry, love. I thought—"

He captured her hand and kissed her palm, his sorrow under control once more. "I know, Maggie mine. 'Twas so kind of ye. Forgive me."

"I'm sorry," she said. "I was stupid to think—I thought if you—" She looked up at him, biting her lower lip, her blue eyes filled with tears. "I thought it would make you feel more at home," she explained as the tears spilled over. "I didn't know the difference in them, but it was the biggest and the finest and the oldest that he had."

"Maggie," he whispered, "'twas a beautiful thing for ye to do, but—"

"I bought it today, while you were at the library. Maxed out my Visa." She laughed hesitantly. "But I wanted you to see the other pipes, to make sure it was the right one. The look on your face told me that I'd made the right choice, but then—" She broke off and dropped her gaze to the ground. "I'm sorry."

Quinn lifted her chin gently with two fingers, tilting her face up to his. "Lass, do ye know why I was so upset?"

She shook her head again, her eyes downcast.

"Well, I thought of Ian of course, still languishing in his cell, and then of our days together at the MacCrimmons School, and suddenly all these feelings and memories rushed through my mind. But that is not why I shed the first tear of my adult life."

Maggie glanced up at him. "Why, then?"

He gazed into her blue eyes that so matched the sky today. "Because for a brief moment, I had an image of ye and I, sitting by the hearth of our own sweet cottage on a summer's evening, our children playing before us, me playing the pipes. And I—" He broke off and shook his head.

"And you're afraid you won't be able to come back, aren't you?" Maggie said, her voice trembling.

He nodded. "There is always that chance."

Maggie's head drooped, and she stared at the sidewalk with downcast eyes. "You'll come back," she whispered. "It's our destiny to be together." Her head came up and she smiled through shimmering tears. "I mean, you do have the tattoo and all." She linked her arm in his. "C'mon," she said playfully, "let's go get your pipes and tonight you can play them for me. Okay?"

Quinn reached out and pulled her close, resting his chin on the top of her soft red hair as she clung to him. He drew in a deep breath and released it slowly. "Oh-kay, lass," he said softly. "I would be honored."

They spent the evening in front of the cottage's fireplace, Quinn perched upon the stone hearth in front of the fireplace, and Maggie sitting at his feet as he played the pipes for her. She leaned against his leg and closed her eyes. He closed his, too, losing himself in his own faraway past, when he was just a lad with big dreams. He played his favorites for her, "Bonnie Dundee," "The Desperate Battle," "Black Donald's March," "MacLean's Warning," and "MacIntosh's Lament," then slipped into a *piobroch* of his own composition.

When the last lingering sound had faded, he opened his eyes and looked down to see Maggie's face streaked with tears. "Beautiful," she whispered.

"Aye," he said, "but even these tunes, these pipes, canna compare with the beauty of yer face."

Maggie got to her knees and smiled up at him. "Have I ever told you what a charmer you are?"

He frowned thoughtfully. "I dinna think so."

She laughed. "Well, then I'm ashamed. You are not just a charmer, but you are charming. Why is it you never married?"

He stroked her hair back from her face as he gazed down at her. "Because I was waiting for ye to come barreling into my life."

She made a face at him. "I do not barrel. I glide gracefully like a gazelle." Quinn snorted, and she stuck her tongue out at him. "Did you ever meet someone . . . special?"

He thought about it for a moment. There had been lasses in his life, but never anyone special. Certainly no one like Maggie. He ducked his head to hide a smile. "Oh, aye," he said in answer.

Maggie's face fell. "Who?"

"A redheaded vixen who crossed time and space to find me." He tugged on a long lock of her hair. " 'Oh-kay'?"

Her lashes fluttered down and her cheeks flushed prettily. "Okay," she said.

"Now, how about something with a little more joy in it?"

Maggie leaned back on her heels and grinned at him. "That would be lovely."

For the next hour he played her every reel and jig he knew, and then ended with a slow-moving strathspey that had Maggie on her feet and dancing in a less-than-graceful glide around the room. When the music ended, she held out her hand to him.

"Come on, laddie, dance with me."

He stood and shook his head. "Come upstairs and I will dance with ye," he said softly.

She backed away from him and put her hand on her hip, her gaze steady. "You know, that's just about all we do, and though it is amazing, I really think it's time to take this relationship to the next level."

Quinn blinked. "Which is?"

She held out her hand again. "Dancing."

He laughed and shook his head again in weak protest. "I am no dancer, lass."

Maggie tilted her head, her long hair waving over one shoulder. She was so lovely. How could he leave her?

"There's a first time for everything, right?" she said.

With a sigh he put the pipes down carefully and stood, holding out his arms. "Indeed there is. But dinna blame me if I break yer feet."

She put a Rolling Stones CD on the boom box Ellie couldn't live without and turned the volume up high. "I Can't Get No Satisfaction" blared into the room, and Quinn's eyes almost popped out of his head.

"What in the name of all that is music is *that*?" Quinn demanded.

"*That* is rock and roll," she told him, and began to dance her own particular gyrations.

"Maggie, darlin', ye are havin' some kind of fit!" he cried, moving to try and calm her, as another realization struck him. "And where is the music coming from?"

"The CD player," she said, doing a version of the frug.

"What in the name of heaven is a CD player?" he asked frantically.

"Remember my little Nessie gizmo?" she said. "It's like that, except less furry."

Quinn shook his head. "What is a *gizmo*? What is—"

The front door to the cottage opened, and Maggie turned, flushed and happy, to see her sisters and Rachel staring at the two of them.

"What's going on?" Allie asked.

"I'm teaching Quinn how to dance!" Maggie said.

The three women exchanged glances and grinned.

"Well, then, c'mon, baby," Rachel said, grabbing Quinn by the hand, "I'm gonna teach you how to *get down*!"

"Get down where?" Quinn asked, terrified by the sheer exuberance in the woman's face. He wasn't used to twenty-first century women!

"Good grief, Aunt Rachel, next thing you know you'll

be teaching him to jitterbug," Ellie scolded. "You need to start with the basics." She moved to the CD player and deftly switched the music to classical.

Quinn's face changed from bewilderment to rapture. "Ah," he said, "now, *this* is music!"

Maggie laughed, and with the help of Allie, Ellie, and Rachel, Quinn spent the next hour learning to dance the waltz, stumbling from one side of the room to the other before finally getting the flow of it. That was followed by learning dances called the tango, the fox-trot, and some crazy gyration he refused to do, called the watusi. When they tired of dancing, Ellie gave him instructions on how to "microwave" a frozen dinner, which he thought tasted rather flat, but which was amazing. Practical Allie taught him what to do if the cottage caught on fire, and laughed hysterically when she cried out, "Stop! Drop! Roll!" over and over and he obeyed. And Rachel gave him a computer lesson that had him shaking his head in wonder.

Rachel pulled Maggie off to the side at one point and whispered, "Where did you find this guy? In a cave?"

"The people who live up in the mountains of the Highlands are, er, a little sheltered from modern life."

That seemed to make sense to her friend, and Maggie saw her whispering to the twins a few minutes later, no doubt bringing them up to speed on the curious hunk their sister had brought home.

Allie and Ellie managed to get her alone in the kitchen and, giggling, encouraged her to stay in Scotland as long as she wanted.

"This guy's a keeper," Allie said. "Stay as long as you need! We'll come back for the wedding!"

Ellie was not quite as effusive in her praise. "But don't forget about us while you're tripping the light fantastic with Mr. Hunk, okay?"

Then Rachel and the girls discreetly excused themselves, citing "dates" in town, and left the two lovers alone. Quinn and Maggie curled up on the couch together and watched a "movie" called *The Princess Bride,* and though he didn't quite understand all of it, he loved hearing Maggie laugh.

"Such incredible inventions," he said solemnly when it was over and he got up to examine the television. "How in the world is it possible?"

"I have no idea," Maggie said, standing and stretching her arms over her head. "Sorry."

He stood, too, and slid his arms around her waist, bending his head to take her mouth with his.

"That's oh-kay," he said, when they broke apart after quite a long interval. "I don't have to know how everything works." He slid his hands down to her hips and pulled her against his. "I know how this works, though." Her eyes widened, and she pulled away.

"As tempting as that sounds," Maggie said, "I think we need to get back to work." She glanced down at the pile of library books on the floor near the couch.

Quinn's smile faded. "Aye." He turned away from her. "How easily I forget my friend, my duty, my honor." For a moment he felt as though he couldn't breathe.

"No, love," she whispered, moving to put her arms around him. "You haven't forgotten Ian, nor your honor. You're just human, like the rest of us. Besides, I have a feeling that this is the day we will find our answers."

They "researched," as Maggie called it, for hours, when suddenly, Quinn caught his breath. On the page before him was Ian's name—and the details of his death. Hanged on July thirty-first, at the hand of James Graham, Duke of Montrose.

"Ye were right," he whispered, "but 'tis not the answer we were hoping for."

Maggie leaned over and read the page, then rested her head against his shoulder. He could feel her trembling.

"I must go back. 'Tis still a chance I could stop it from happening."

Maggie slipped away from him and stood, pulling him to his feet beside her. He gazed down into her ashen face.

"I am sorry, lass," he said.

"Dance with me," she said, the words barely audible.

Without a word, he took her in his arms and they began to move together, swaying back and forth, waltzing across the room. And as they danced, the reality of leaving her seized Quinn. His fingers tightened around her waist as he suddenly stopped in the middle of the room, unable to move.

"Quinn," Maggie said.

"Maggie, I—"

Then there were no words, there was only that singular moment, and as the pain of their coming parting and the grief of leaving her pierced him like a knife, suddenly Quinn needed her as he never had before. She was there for him, as she always had been.

Cupping her face between his hands, he kissed her, knowing it might be the last time. As their passion deepened, he was tortured by the thought of living without her, and his touch grew more desperate, rougher, but Maggie's response equaled his own. He walked her backward until they were pressed against the wall, the feel of her skin against his, the knowledge that it might never be again, giving fire to his touch.

Maggie pushed him back and he almost groaned aloud, but it was only so she could shimmy out of the tiny scrap of fabric she called underwear. Then she reached out, and unbuttoned his jeans and released the hard length of him into her eager hand. Quinn caught his breath and picked her up. She wrapped her legs around his waist and he slid hot and hard into the sweet center of her body. Her breath was ragged, her eyes half closed, as he pressed her against the wall and pumped himself into her hard and fast, urgent with need, desperate with a despair that had been building inside of him for days.

Quinn possessed her, lifting her with each hard movement that grew faster and stronger until he cried out her name, and she shuddered and whispered his.

"That felt like good-bye," she said, her voice hollow.

He could not deny it. "Aye," he said softly. "It did."

Then he picked her up in his arms and carried her up the stairs to their bed, where he made love to her again. But afterward, when he held Maggie in his arms, she lifted her head from his shoulder and looked at him, her blue eyes dark in the shadow of their room.

Maggie sat up and lifted herself over him, her long auburn hair spilling across his chest. She ran her fingers lightly over the still-raw tattoo on his thickly muscled arm. The tri-spiral gleamed with his blood. A promise to her, written in his own blood.

"I don't want to say good-bye," she whispered.

"Aye," he said again. "And so we will not."

They made love once more, and then talked through the night, telling each other things they had meant to confide. They rushed now to say it all. Maggie explained about her "panic attacks" and how she had learned to control them, told him that her favorite color was teal and that her dream was to travel around the world, discovering ancient artifacts.

In turn, Quinn shared the loneliness he had felt until she came into his life, that his favorite color was blue—the blue of her eyes—and his dream was to be the piper of a clan, and compose his own music.

Then there was silence except for the sound of Maggie's quiet breathing. Quinn kissed her on he forehead and slipped out of bed. He stood watching the beautiful lass sleep for a moment and then turned and disappeared into the darkness.

sixteen

Quinn took another drink of his whiskey and stared at Rob Roy sitting across from him. Rob Roy stared back. The two men sat on benches at one of the rough-hewn tables inside the Clachan Inn. Rob had agreed to meet him there and talk, but now Quinn wished he had chosen another place.

The inn no longer seemed itself after he had visited it in Maggie's time. Everything now seemed rough and unpolished, the people dirty and unkempt, and he recoiled from it, even as he berated himself for his sudden snobbery. He felt strange, as if he didn't quite belong anymore. He had been back in his own time for but a day, and already he missed Maggie so much he could feel the pain down to his marrow. He moved his right hand to rest it upon his left upper arm, pressing down just enough to make his tattoo ache, just enough to remind him that he was going back to Maggie.

"Why have ye asked me here, Quinn? Ye know my answer."

"I am not here to ask for yer help," Quinn said. "Well," he corrected, "not yer help in rescuing Ian."

"Then what?"

"If I am killed trying to save him, or hanged with him," he said, speaking in a low voice, "will ye come and claim our bodies?"

Rob leaned back in his chair for a long moment. "Aye," he said. "I will. Are there any MacIntyres I should summon, in that event?"

Quinn shook his head. "I'm sure there are other MacIntyres to which I am related, but I dinna know them."

Rob nodded. "Aye, I will do what ye ask. But I willna accept the death of my favorite cousin," he said and leaned forward on the table, his weight on one elbow, "nor yers. Decide to live, Quinn MacIntyre, and a way out of this mess will present itself to ye." He shook his head. "I dinna think yer sweet lassie will want to live her life without ye warming her bed."

"Aye," Quinn agreed, "but time grows short." He drew in a ragged breath and stood, holding out his hand. "Give Mary my love," he said.

Rob stood and clasped his hand, half smiling beneath his red beard. "Ye know, I have always suspected that ye had a wee affection for my wife. I'm glad ye have yer own lassie now."

Quinn shook his head and released his hand. "As if Mary would give another man a second glance."

Rob stood there a moment, then leaned closer, lowering his voice. "Live, Quinn MacIntyre, that ye might continue to love yer lass. There must be a way to free Ian other than a straight-on assault."

"That's what Maggie keeps saying," Quinn admitted.

Rob slapped him on the upper arm and Quinn bit back a cry of pain as Rob's hand connected with the raw tattoo. "Then listen to her, lad," the man said. "Mary always says that men dinna give women respect for their minds and ideas, and damn if I think she isn't right. Ask Maggie what she would do, were she planning this escapade. A woman's ways are more subtle than a man's."

"Aye," Quinn said thoughtfully. "I will think upon yer words, Rob."

Rob pushed open the heavy door and looked back at him. "Just dinna get dead if ye can help it, laddie. And bring Ian home safe to us."

"Aye." Quinn said. "I will do my best."

Maggie spent the next two days staring at the ceiling. Rachel and the girls returned, and she pled exhaustion to keep from having to face them. When she could no longer avoid their questions, she told them Quinn had been called away on a family emergency and would be back as soon as possible. She congratulated herself silently for sticking to the truth, and knew Quinn would appreciate the little private joke.

Sensing something was wrong, her sisters and Rachel had hovered around her, until that morning, when Maggie'd practically pushed them out the door just to have a little time alone to think.

She had done quite a bit of moping throughout the morning, and cried a few self-pitying tears, but around lunchtime she began to feel claustrophobic. Rachel and the twins had taken the rental car, but there was no reason she couldn't take a walk. Once her mind was made up, Maggie changed into her green jogging pants and jacket, with a T-shirt underneath, and pulled on her Skechers.

Heading across the living room, she was intent on finding a key to the front door, when all at once, she saw the pile of library books she and Quinn had borrowed. The volumes lay under one of the end tables, forgotten.

Maggie sat down on the floor and smoothed her hand

over the cover of one of the oldest books. It was entitled,
MacIntyre's Lament: A History of the MacIntyre Clan. She
didn't remember checking it out; maybe Quinn had. On
impulse, she picked up the thick book and flipped through
the pages, looking for Quinn's name. Her hands trembled a
little.

She was reading idly, half of her mind thinking about
Quinn, half of it gliding over the names of people who
were his ancestors, when suddenly her eyes stopped.

There it was. His name. Quinn MacIntyre, born April
10, 1685, died August 1, 1711.

With a little gasp, Maggie backtracked to where the
chapter subtitled "MacIntyre's Revenge" began. After reading for several minutes, she leaned against the chair behind
her and closed her eyes.

Quinn had not saved Ian. He'd been captured while trying to rescue his friend. The two men had been executed
two days later.

Maggie stumbled to her feet. It wasn't true. It couldn't
be true. She walked blindly to the front door of the cottage,
still holding the book. She jerked the door open. It was another soft Scottish day, the sky a hazy blue gray, clouds
gathering for yet another rain. It registered but she didn't
see it. All she could see was Quinn dangling from the end
of a rope, dying in the past.

She walked outside. The rental car was gone. Right,
Rachel and the twins had taken it. Maggie stood there,
dazed for a moment, and then spun on her heel and started
walking, striding up the dirt road that led to the secluded
house.

She didn't know where she was going. It didn't matter.
Tears blurred her vision. She stubbed her toe on a loose
rock and dropped the book. Angrily, she kicked the offending stone to one side and picked up the book, then kept
walking.

How could she have let him go back? Maggie stumbled to a stop and doubled over, sobbing uncontrollably until she sank to her knees in the middle of the road. It couldn't be true. It couldn't be. She shouldn't have let him go back. She should have gone back with him. A hundred things she should have done. A million she shouldn't. None of it mattered. Quinn was dead.

Her mind was filled with terrible images. The book hadn't said how Quinn was executed. Suddenly she saw him under the headsman's axe, and next facing a firing squad, and yet another scenario where he was hanging from a gallows, his face blue and bloated.

"No!" she screamed, her fingers twisting in the dirt beneath her, her hair hanging over her face like a widow's veil. "No," she whispered. Maggie got up. She had to keep walking.

She walked as fast as she could, humming the last tune Quinn had played for her on the bagpipes. She didn't remember the name of it. It didn't matter. All that mattered was filling her head with something that would drive out the picture of Quinn dying beneath the Highland sky.

Maggie didn't know how long she trudged across the Highlands, but when she looked up from the ground again, she was only a dozen yards away from the cairn. Usually there were people milling around, but today the mound was deserted. Then she remembered: Alex had gone to Edinburgh for a few days.

Days. The book said Quinn and Ian had died on August the first. Today was July thirtieth. So far, from what she'd been able to figure out, the rhythm of the days in the past and the days in the future seemed to be the same. She had gone back in time on June 27, 2008, and had ended up sometime in June in 1711.

She didn't know the exact date had been when she arrived. But she knew the date she came back, because Jenny had mentioned that morning that it was James's birthday, July twenty-fourth. And she knew that when she returned to 2008, the date was July twenty-fourth, because she had asked Rachel.

So if the dates remained the same . . .

Maggie stopped breathing.

Then right this minute, in the year 1711, Quinn and Ian were still alive.

She climbed to the top of the hill and went inside the cairn, where dry-eyed, she waited for dark.

Quinn sat staring into the fire at the cottage, thinking. He had one day before Ian would be hanged.

Think of a subtle plan, Rob had said. Quinn leaned his head in his hands. He knew only how to fight directly, sword to sword, man to man. He sighed. He was weary, tired of thinking. His mind drifted to his favorite daydream—he and Maggie married, living together in Scotland.

He could see her, holding his son in her arms, gazing down at him with love in her eyes. When he was older, she would tell him stories. Quinn would tell him stories, too, legends, and the history of the MacIntyres and their friends, the MacGregors, just as his father had once told him.

Quinn began to pray.

Maggie was caught in a spinning vortex, the light within so bright that even with her eyes closed, it blinded her. She cried out for release and relief, but there was none. The other times it had not taken this long to reach the other side. Then it happened, what she had feared and dreaded.

No. No!

Her silent scream echoed around her as she felt her spirit, what made her *Maggie Graham*, separate from her body and fly upward. She looked down and saw herself below, encased in a sphere filled with light, as she watched from the vast blackness surrounding the orblike enclosure. And then she began to drift, farther as farther away, as her mind grew languid and fuzzy.

The thought of Quinn and her sisters and Rachel was all that saved her. One fleeting moment of seeing them in her mind, wishing she could say good-bye, spurred Maggie to fight her way back to her body.

She concentrated on returning to her body, on feeling it around her once more, and then suddenly she was flying, rushing downward like a comet across the universe as she reached for the ball of light in the midst of the darkness.

Her speed increased, plunging her faster and faster toward the woman below, and in the brief second before she rejoined her body, she saw her own face and her own dull eyes, just before everything inside of her and outside of her shattered into a billion crystal shards of radiant light.

Maggie regained consciousness slowly, so slowly it seemed that one cell at a time was coming back "online" in the computer called her brain. When she was finally able to open her eyes, she couldn't move.

Panic overwhelmed her for a moment, until she remembered her breathing techniques. Her chest was moving up and down. Air was going in and out of her lungs. She could breathe. She could control her breathing. She closed her eyes and thought only about breathing.

After a while, she became calmer and opened her eyes, only to feel the panic begin again. Above her was the bonny blue sky of Scotland, a few wispy clouds drifting across the broad expanse. She wasn't inside the cairn. Somehow, this time, she had ended up outside! How had that happened?

It's okay, it's okay, Maggie reassured herself silently. *You're alive. You'll be able to move in a minute. Just keep breathing.*

She kept doing her slow breathing, and after a few minutes, she could move her fingers and toes. A few minutes after that, she was able to bend her arms and legs, and finally, after almost an hour, she sat up. She tried to stand, but her legs were like gelatin, and she sank back down, her heart thumping in fear.

She had to get up! She had to get to Quinn! It was the morning of July thirty-first. Tomorrow Quinn and Ian would die, unless she could do something to stop it.

Calm down, Maggie ordered. *Just wait and your strength will return.*

For how long? another voice in her head asked, plaintive and anxious.

"Not long," she said aloud. "I *will* reach Quinn in time. I will!" She threw an anguished look at the sky. "Please, dear God, let me reach him in time!"

Maggie stopped and leaned on the crude staff she'd fashioned for herself from the branch of a dying oak tree. It was too big around and made her fingers ache, but at least it gave her the support she needed to put one foot in front of the other. She could go no farther, at least not without stopping to rest.

It had taken her the whole of one day and part of the next to walk from the cairn to this hill near the cottage. She had cried and cursed her weakened body every step of the way, sometimes having to lift her legs with her hands to force another step forward. She had felt a little better in the last hour or so, and now stood at the top of a knoll, trying to catch her breath.

The sun had already set and twilight was settling over the land. She looked down at the dark waters of Loch Lomond with tears in her eyes. How proud Quinn would be that she had actually found her way here by herself.

There was not one part of her body that didn't ache with pain. She had hobbled over hill and glens without sleep, without stopping, and now her heart pounded painfully as she turned away. It was August first, but the book had not given the time of death. She could still make it. Quinn was still alive. He had to be.

The world spun around for a minute, and Maggie stumbled to a rock and sat down, her head in her hands. Exhausted, she fell asleep and soon was dreaming of Quinn.

They were standing outside a little cottage, two little boys were playing nearby, and she and Quinn were gazing into one another's eyes with love and adoration. Then suddenly the dream twisted. Quinn stepped back from her, his face suddenly cold, almost gray, emotionless. As she watched, he turned into a pillar of dust. The Highland wind came tearing through their little valley and blew him away.

Maggie jerked her head up, gasping, the horror of the dream clinging to her even as she tried to shake it off. She stumbled to her feet, and gripping her staff, started walking once again. She had planned to go to the cottage to rest, to eat something. But it had taken her too long, and this dream was an evil premonition.

She had to press on. The duke's home wasn't that far from the cottage, and now that she was feeling better, she could make better time.

In the dark.

A flood of fear rushed through her mind.

How can I do this? How can I find my way to the manor in the dark? What if I fall down some ravine? What if I'm too late?

"Stop it," she hissed aloud, and forced her backbone to straighten. "You're fine. It's not that dark and the moon will be up soon. You can find the manor. You can make it. Just start walking, damn it!"

Maggie drew in a deep breath, released it slowly, and started walking.

It seemed to take forever, but she finally arrived at the manor house and went to the stables. Bittie would know where Quinn was, and she hurried as fast as she could, her legs and back screaming their outrage.

But when she reached the stables and went inside, she found Bittie sitting on a barrel, his face streaked with tears. Maggie's fear kicked into high gear when she saw the big man reduced to this sorrow. She rushed toward him, her legs trembling as she leaned on her staff.

"Bittie," she said. "What is it? What's happened?"

He turned grief-stricken eyes upon her. "They were caught," he said. "Captured afore they ever left the grounds. Quinn had a plan. 'Twas a good plan, but they caught 'im and the lad."

Maggie's legs gave way, and she sank to the floor at his feet. "No," she whispered.

"Aye." He reached his hand to her as he began to weep again. Maggie took his hand and leaned her head against his knee, staring at the ground, thinking quickly. She would come up with another plan. She would find a way to set them free!

"We'll get them out," Maggie said, squeezing his hand as she pushed herself up from the dirty stable floor. "This isn't over."

Bittie's heavy head came up at that, his bleary eyes filled with horror as he clung to her. "Och, lass, I thought ye knew." His woeful voice sent a chill down her spine. "Quinn is dead." His lower lip trembled. "He and Ian are both dead."

Maggie jerked her hand from his, her throat tight, her breath ragged. "No . . ." she whispered. "It isn't true."

Bittie leaned forward and covered his face with both large hands. "Aye," he said, " 'tis true." And he began to cry again.

Maggie lay in the hayloft where once she had lain in Quinn's arms. She stared up at the window above, now closed and latched. She had held Bittie while he cried, too shocked, too disbelieving to shed her own tears.

But his grief had convinced her. Quinn and Ian were dead. Bittie didn't know how they had died, but there was speculation that their breakfast porridge had been poisoned. All he knew was that they were alive before breaking their fast, and dead after. They had been dead when she stood looking down at Loch Lomond, hope in her heart.

At her request, Bittie had gone to send word to Rob Roy to come for Ian's body. As far as she knew, Quinn had not been in contact with any of the MacIntyres in many years, but Bittie said he would send word to the clan as well.

Maggie knew she should stay hidden. If Pembroke saw her, he would likely put her in the gaol for playing at being a highwayman, but she was numb to those kinds of threats and really didn't care what happened to her now. But as always, her sense of responsibility to her sisters rose up inside of her, and so she put a shawl over her head before trudging wearily to the kitchen to find Jenny.

The two women had fallen into one another's arms, then Jenny had led her sorrowfully to the small chapel, called St. Mary's, on the manor grounds. The bodies had been placed there temporarily. But when she got to the door, Maggie couldn't go in.

Instead, with a choked sob, she turned and ran back to the stables and the hayloft, where she wept until she retched, until there were no tears left to weep. Now she lay in the hayloft, empty, hollow, her mind wandering.

"Maggie," came a whisper from below. With effort, she rolled to her knees and crawled to the edge of the loft to look down into Jenny's eyes.

"I am here," she said.

"And so is Rob Roy MacGregor," Jenny said. "He has come to claim the—the—laddies. I thought you would want to know."

Maggie closed her eyes, her voice echoing hollowly. "Where are they taking them?"

"I dinna know," she said. "To Craigrostan, perhaps."

"I must go with them," Maggie said. She stood and brushed the hay from the skirt and blouse Jenny had provided her. Once down the ladder, Maggie started to move past the little maid, but to her surprise, the girl stopped her, one hand on her arm.

"Please, Maggie, dinna risk yerself. Quinn wouldna want ye to do so. Please." Her voice was insistent, and Maggie put her arm around the girl and gave her a hug.

"Thank you, darling Jenny. I promise I'll be careful." She started to walk past her and then turned back. "Do you know what happened? What went wrong?"

Jenny shook her head, her blue eyes sorrowful. "Nay. James was not on duty last night, but had been assigned to guarding one of His Grace's guests on her return trip to Glasgow. All I know is that Quinn tried to break Ian out of the dungeon, and was captured."

Maggie nodded. "If you—if you hear anything more, will you come to me?"

Jenny put her arms around her and held her close. "Aye, darlin' Maggie," she said. "That I will. Now, will you guard yourself from harm?"

She shook her head. "I must be there, Jenny. No matter what."

"Aye, but could ye not disguise yerself somehow?" The girl's round eyes filled with tears. "I couldna stand it if something happened to ye, too."

Maggie was too weary to argue. "A disguise? What do you suggest?"

As if she'd been waiting for the go-ahead, Jenny moved quickly to a pile of clothing on top of a barrel. "I brought one of Cook's old skirts and a blouse. I was thinkin', perhaps we could stuff it with rags and make ye look larger. If ye kept a shawl over yer head, I think t'would make a good disguise."

Maggie's shoulders slumped. She didn't want to sneak around. She wanted to rush up to Pembroke and beat her fists upon him until she had no more strength. But Jenny was right: If Pembroke spotted her, there would be hell to pay, and she'd never see her sisters again.

"All right," she agreed, listless. "Will you help me?"

"Aye," Jenny whispered.

"I have come to claim the body of my cousin, Ian, and his friend, Quinn."

Rob Roy MacGregor made the proclamation from the back of the golden brown horse he rode. Maggie hid at the back of the crowd of servants gathered in the duke's courtyard to watch the meeting between the laird and the man who was reported to have stolen over one thousand pounds from him.

Rob Roy was decked out in what was surely his best plaid, as well as a leather jacket and tilted black bonnet on his head, garnished with three feathers as befit a chieftain. Word had it that Montrose was threatening to have him arrested for daring to come forward to claim the bodies of the two outlaws. Maggie would have been worried if she hadn't known the history of the soon-to-be notorious Rob Roy.

Behind Rob Roy sat another of his clan on the driver's seat of a wagon. Another hundred or so men surrounded him and the wagon, on horses, or on foot. Their faces were grim.

Phillip Pembroke and the Duke of Montrose glared up at Rob Roy, their figures rigid with anger. Pembroke, tall and thin, standing beside the shorter, dumpier Montrose, reminded Maggie of Laurel and Hardy, but she wasn't laughing.

With a shawl over her head, and a thoroughly padded bottom and front, Maggie wasn't worried about being recognized by anyone, as long as she kept her head down. But when eight of Montrose's men began walking toward the crowd, each group of four carrying a still figure wrapped in white cloth between them, Maggie almost gave herself away.

She had expected the men to be brought out in wooden coffins, and too late, remembered that the practice didn't come to the Highlands until much later. Seeing the actual bodies of the man she loved and his best friend encased in shrouds sent a shudder of grief through Maggie that she could barely control. She gripped her hands together in front of her, her fingernails biting into her flesh until they drew blood. The crowd parted and let the impromptu pallbearers walk past, but Rob Roy stopped the men, moving his horse to block their way.

"And so," Rob said as he gazed down at the bodies, "ye dinna even have the decency to give the lads a trial, nor a public execution, but murdered them without a second thought."

"These ruffians were highwaymen!" Montrose said tersely. "They acted against the law and against the Crown! Killing was too good for them."

"Dinna forget the words of the Good Book, James Graham, 'Ye reap what ye sow.'"

"Guards!" Pembroke motioned to the unit of men standing nearby. "Arrest this man!" He glared at Rob Roy. "You'll not threaten the Duke of Montrose while I live and breathe."

Montrose raise his hand. "Nay, Phillip," he said, glancing up at Rob Roy. "Ye have what ye came for MacGregor. I suggest that ye leave now, before I remember a certain debt that is owed."

Rob Roy's face turned almost as red as his hair. "Ye will be repaid for that which was stolen from both of us," he stated, his shoulders squared.

"So ye say. Now take yer leave, while ye still may."

Pembroke folded his arms over his chest and stepped forward. "By your leave, Your Grace," he said to Montrose, "but I would like to escort this riffraff from your estate.

"Thank you, Phillip," Montrose said, "see to it."

"We will be honoring our dead this day," Rob Roy said. "I trust your 'escort' willna be present there at our most holy of ceremonies."

Pembroke stepped forward again. "What? You will not wait the traditional three days' time? Why the rush to dispose of your 'honored dead'?"

Rob Roy turned his gaze slowly from Montrose to the smirking man. "Dinna ever suppose that ye know what are our ways," he said. "Ye will never know, neither our ways, nor any other. Ye have no country, and from what I hear, no family that will claim ye save for the duke, and that because of obligation."

It was Pembroke's turn to flush scarlet. "When His Grace puts a price upon your thieving head, I will take great joy in severing it from your neck."

Rob Roy nodded, acknowledging the challenge. "And I shall cast a stone at yer grave someday." As Rob and his men moved out, Maggie slipped away from the mob, and as soon as she was clear, ran back to the stable. She would find a horse and ride to Loch Lomond, to bid her love good-bye.

s e v e n t e e n

By the time Maggie reached the loch, the bodies of the two men had been placed in two separate boats half in the water, half on the shore. Behind them Loch Lomond was dark and foreboding, with a stormy sky above promising rain and rocky sailing upon the black waves.

Maggie had discarded her disguise in the stables and dressed in the jogging pants and T-shirt she'd worn from her own time. Over that she put the skirt and blouse Jenny had lent her, and her own green jacket. Once she told Quinn good-bye, she would return to the cairn.

But it still didn't seem real. Even now, as she stared at the stone-cold faces of Quinn and Ian, it didn't seem real. The winding cloths had been taken off the faces of the men, and from a distance, the two looked like porcelain statues, pale and lifeless. She fought back a sob, and suddenly, Maggie knew that she had to tell Quinn good-bye, no matter what the cost.

She pushed through the crowd and stumbled out beside the boats, falling to her knees beside the one where Quinn lay. He was beautiful, even in death. She lovingly gazed at his face, memorizing each and every feature—his strong jaw, his chin with the slight cleft, his aquiline nose, his full lips, his dark, arched brows over closed eyes, his lashes making dark crescents against his alabaster skin.

It seemed that any moment he would open his eyes and she would see the emerald sparkle that she knew so well. Tears flooded down her cheeks as she brushed one long wavy lock of hair back from his face, remembering all the times he had done the same for her.

Openly crying now, she leaned down and kissed his cold lips. The crowd around the banks of Loch Lomond began to murmur. She didn't care. Nothing mattered. Quinn was gone, and with him, her world.

"Oh, Quinn," she whispered, and collapsed to her knees once again, doubled over as she sobbed her heart out.

In another moment, Bittie was there, lifting Maggie from beside the boat as she continued to sob uncontrollably. Through her tears she saw Rob Roy climb into Ian's boat, as a man in a long robe climbed into Quinn's.

"Where are they taking them?" she whispered to Bittie, trying to get control over her tears.

"To an isle in the middle of the loch, where they once played together as boys," he answered. He seemed much calmer now. "Rob is acting as their next of kin, and the man is a priest."

"They'll have a ceremony there, I suppose," she said dully.

Bittie frowned down at her. "Aye. All is arranged, lass. I'm sorry about before, in the stable. I thought ye knew."

"It's all right," she said, leaning against him for comfort, "I understand."

The man in Quinn's boat lifted his hands and began to pray. The people around Maggie bowed their heads and her heart cried out to God, too. But the only word she could form inside of her was *Why?* It was the same question she had asked when her parents were killed. She had not found an answer then, and she couldn't imagine receiving one now, but she prayed anyway. The pastor or priest—she wasn't sure which—finished praying and sat down in the wooden boat.

Bittie's beefy arms held Maggie tightly beside him, as another Scot in each boat pushed the vessel away from the shore and dipped a long paddle into the dark water. Maggie watched, her heart breaking.

Then, from behind the crowd came the sound of the pipes. Her tears began to flow again as she recognized the tune; it was one of Quinn's, called "MacIntyre's Sorrow," and that was when it hit her. She would never see his face again, never kiss him, never touch him, never have his children, never grow old beside him.

Her legs gave way and only Bittie kept her erect as she began to keen, crying out her pain, sending it across the loch, her sorrow sending Quinn on his way. Several other women joined her, sobbing their grief, when suddenly, one by one, the sounds ceased.

"Whist," Bittie said. "Look."

The crowd began to shift, and Maggie looked up, her cries fading as she saw that the loch had gone suddenly still, though storm clouds still raged above, and the haunting notes of the pipes echoed across the water, now spread before them like a sheet of black glass.

Maggie closed her eyes, letting the last notes of Quinn's music wash over her soul, vowing to never forget, to never stop loving the man who had given her so much. She would spend the rest of her days remembering and loving Quinn MacIntyre.

The two little boats sailed across the huge loch until they could no longer be seen. She turned to Bittie, her voice quavering, but her resolution firm.

"Good-bye," she said, as the crowd around them began to disperse and talk softly. "Thank you for all you've done for me, and for Quinn." She reached up and pulled the big man down to her so that she could whisper in his ear. "You were a good friend to both of us," she said, and gave him a kiss on the cheek. He blinked back tears.

"Och, lass, I loved him like a brother." He gazed down at her sadly. "We'll miss him, and Ian, too. Do ye know what ye will do now?"

She blinked, and for a moment it wasn't Bittie's question, but perhaps some Higher Power sending her guidance. Did she know what she would do? She looked out across the dark water, the smooth surface now dissolving into chaos as the storm struck, and the waves rolled beneath an angry sky.

"Yes," she said softly, "I suppose that I do."

Bittie took the horse she had ridden back to the stables at Maggie's request. After he had grown small in the distance, she walked away from the loch and headed in the general direction of the cairn.

As she walked, she cried out her anger and grief and fear and loneliness to the hills and the glens, cursed and screamed as she tramped across them, stopping at the burns to drink and rest from time to time, remembering each bittersweet moment she'd spent in the Highlands with Quinn.

The skirt slowed her down and eventually she discarded it, leaving her clad only in her jogging pants and jacket, and the blouse Jenny had lent her. As she walked, she braided her long, tangled hair. By the time the sun began to set and the familiar misty twilight swept over the land, Maggie had arrived at the top of the hill where the cairn sat. She stared at the mysterious mound where her adventures had all started. Where now all of her dreams would end.

Wearily, she walked to the other side of the structure, to the opening she had created the first night she appeared in the past. She fell to her knees and crawled inside, then stood. She wrapped her arms around her waist, the sorrow inside of her rising up again to swallow her whole. But she had no tears left to cry, only an aching emptiness she feared would never go away.

"Och, poor lass," said a familiar voice.

Maggie spun around. Even in the dim light of the cairn, she could see who had climbed through the opening behind her. The man wore velvet and satin and a long, curling blond wig.

"Pembroke," she whispered, real terror flooding over her.

"Yes, my dear," the duke's henchman said, his voice smug, his dark eyes dangerous. "How pleased I am that you recognized me in your current state of despair over the deaths of the two outlaws."

She swallowed hard. "How did you—?"

"You didn't think that I would attend the funeral?" he said, interrupting her trembling question. "That would have been so rude. I was there, at the back of the crowd, and afterward, I followed you. It was quite illuminating to watch your grief." He arched one pale brow. "Tell me, did you bed both of the highwaymen, or only the one who came to your rescue?"

He moved toward her, and Maggie backed away to the center of the cairn. She was completely alone and at his mercy. Quinn would have never let her set out for the cairn alone, but Quinn was gone, and she was on her own.

"An interesting place," Pembroke said, his heavy-lidded gaze sweeping over the round room. "Why is it, I wonder, that you came here instead of staying with your friends?" He fussed with the lace at one sleeve and then glanced up at her. "Could it be you already have a new lover and planned to meet him here?"

"I wanted to be by myself," Maggie said, taking several more steps back until she was standing in the center of the spiral that had brought her through time.

Pembroke frowned and looked down at the floor. "Fascinating," he said, pointing his toe and brushing it against the raised ridge of the spiral. He began to walk on the edge of the spiral, putting one foot closely in front of the other.

Maggie's heart began to pound furiously. What if he traveled through time? What kind of damage could a man like this do once he discovered such a powerful weapon? Her fear distracted her, and suddenly Pembroke was beside her, his face too close as he grabbed her, his fingers biting into her arms as he jerked her against him.

"You knew I would come after you, didn't you, dear Maggie? You knew I would make you pay for what you did to me and I think, perhaps, that you are a girl who likes punishment, eh?"

The cologne he wore was cloying, and the smell made her feel nauseated and weak. She shook her head, wordless.

"But what is this you are wearing?" He stepped back again, though keeping a grip on her, and let his gaze rake lazily over her body. "Breeches on a lass?" He shook his head and *tsked* softly. "I'm afraid this will never do."

He turned her around by the shoulders, and Maggie flushed as he patted her bottom and gave it a squeeze. "Though I do like the way the material molds itself to your derriere. Perhaps I will allow it in the privacy of my rooms; however, I generally like my women to wear clothing that allows easy access, if you know what I mean."

Maggie whirled around, some of her usual spunk returning. "I am *not* one of your women, and I never will be."

Pembroke cocked one brow at her again, his lips pursed for a moment. "Ah, but you are, dear Maggie. It is either that, or you will be hanged for conspiracy."

She lifted her chin. "I would prefer hanging to being mauled by a pervert like you."

His hand moved so swiftly Maggie didn't see the slap coming. The pain slammed into her mouth and laced up into her cheekbone as she cried out and jerked away from him, turning to run, only to feel her neck snap backward as he grabbed her by the long braid trailing down her back. She stumbled and fell, then lifted her head to find the man looming over her, chuckling softly.

Maggie tried to stand, but Pembroke shoved her back to her knees. Slowly he unbound her braid, gently parting the twisted locks and framing her face with them as he forced her to look up at him.

"You bastard," she said, wiping the blood from her lip with the back of her hand.

"Now, that's better," he said, ignoring her words. "I think I will forbid you to ever braid your hair. It is so lovely unbound." His eyes narrowed as he grasped her face with one hand, his fingers digging into her skin, while the other moved to his belt buckle. "Since you are already on your knees, perhaps it is time to teach you exactly which of us is in command."

Maggie's throat tightened, and she tried to summon her courage. Rachel would head butt the guy's genitals. She was too afraid. From behind her back there came a noise, and suddenly she sensed they were not alone.

"Aye," a deep voice said. "I think it is, indeed, time."

Maggie gasped. Her heart began to pound as hope surged through her body.

"Quinn?" she whispered. It couldn't be—Quinn was dead.

"Let go of her, Pembroke," said the disembodied voice. "Now."

Maggie looked up at her captor and froze as she saw Pembroke's face distort with rage. Moving swiftly, he pulled a dirk from a hidden sheath at his waist, and then grabbed Maggie by the hair, swinging her around, placing her between him and the stranger, his blade to her throat.

"I think I would reconsider that order, if I were you," Pembroke said.

Maggie cried out as he curled his fingers more securely into her hair and jerked her head back, exposing her throat even more, making it impossible for her to see the unknown man. She was afraid to trust her own ears. Pembroke answered her beating heart's question with his next words.

"So, MacIntyre, you are looking remarkably well, for a corpse."

"Aye," Quinn said, "and ye are looking remarkably alive for one who is a dead man walking."

Maggie closed her eyes as the knowledge that it was Quinn's voice, true and strong, filled her with joy. He was alive. *He was alive!*

Then she heard the sound of a sword being pulled from its sheath, metal against metal, and fear replaced joy. She knew Quinn would give his life to save hers. "Let her go," Quinn commanded.

Pembroke pressed the tip of the blade he held into her neck, making her gasp. "Put down your sword and surrender, MacIntyre, or should I say, Piper?" He laughed shortly. "Put it down or she dies."

Quinn's voice was smooth, steady. "And what do ye suppose will happen then to ye? After she dies?"

Pembroke's grip on her hair eased a bit, and Maggie lowered her head enough to see her protector. Relief flooded over her like the water in a burn, cascading down a hillside, as she actually saw him.

Quinn stood there, broad and tall, his plaid flung across his chest, his sword in his hand, his dark brows colliding over forest green eyes reflecting a calm, controlled rage. Her Quinn. Her love.

"Back away, MacIntyre, or she *will* die," Pembroke said.

"And then ye will die. But t'will not be a quick death." Quinn's thunderous gaze sharpened and became quietly lethal. The cold certainty in his next words sent a shudder through Maggie's soul. "I will cut ye to pieces, bit by bit," he promised, "and leave ye to drown in yer own blood."

Maggie felt the knife at her throat ease off the slightest bit. "My men are on their way here," Pembroke said. She could feel his heartbeat quicken as he pressed against her back. "I told them to give me an hour's head start and then to follow."

"And why is it I dinna believe ye?" Quinn asked, taking a step closer to the two. "Perhaps because I know that ye prefer to have no witnesses to yer particular brand of perverseness? Just be grateful that I arrived when I did, before ye had a chance to harm her." He glanced down at her and his entire face shifted into gentleness. "Hello, Maggie mine. Are ye all right?"

"Yes," Maggie whispered, gazing back at him with all the love in her heart. "I'm all right."

"What the devil are ye doing here?" he said fondly.

She smiled. "It's a long story."

Quinn raised his eyebrows. "I canna wait to hear it." He turned back to Pembroke. "Come now," he said, "let this be between the two of us. Only a coward hides behind a woman."

"Will you give me leave to draw my sword?" the man asked.

"Aye. If ye let the lass come to me first."

Maggie felt Pembroke's hand move from her hair, and she glanced up at him, not trusting for a minute that he would do what he said. His gaze was locked on Quinn, and as he pulled her to her feet, she saw the familiar slyness sparkle in Pembroke's eyes.

"Quinn!" she warned, but too late. Pembroke threw the dirk in his hand toward Quinn, even as he shoved Maggie to the ground.

Maggie screamed just as Quinn ducked, and the blade clattered harmlessly against the stone wall behind him, and then to the floor of the cairn. She tried to stand, but her exhaustion made her slow. Before she could move, Pembroke had her again, his arm around her waist, his sword held diagonally across her body, the sharp blade at her throat.

"Ye honorless son of a bitch," Quinn said. "I said to let her go first!"

"And I said that we would see who is in command here." Pembroke laughed. "Apparently, *I* am. Come, strike at me if you dare. Or let me leave in one piece with your lady fair. Surely you would rather she be alive and grace my bed, than be skewered on my blade."

Quinn's face was as dark as a Highland storm. "Ye will never take Maggie with ye."

"I beg to differ," Pembroke said, his voice lilting with pleasure. "To reach me, you must go through her and now I am armed and ready to defend myself."

Quinn cursed the man roundly, and Pembroke laughed again, backing away from the Scot. He moved in a circle, forcing Quinn to parallel his moves as the man inched his way toward the crumbled opening.

Panic swept over Maggie. Suddenly she couldn't breathe. Pembroke was going to carry her with him. Quinn was alive, but she was going to be taken from him again, and she knew he would die trying to stop the evil man who held her. She couldn't breathe.

"Maggie!" Quinn's voice brought her back from her terror, and she raised her eyes to his. There was a fierceness there she had never seen before. "Maggie," he said, more softly, "he willna take ye. Breathe, lass."

She obeyed, taking a deep breath, letting it slide slowly from her lungs. She repeated the process several times while Pembroke dragged her first one direction and then the other. Finally she had her panic under control once again, but she was still trembling.

"So what is it to be, MacIntyre? Will you risk her life?"

But Quinn's gaze was on Maggie. "Maggie," he said, "do ye remember what to do in case of a fire?"

Maggie's eyes widened. "Aye," she said. "Stop." She dug her heels in and brought a startled Pembroke to a stop. "Drop." She dropped like a stone, letting the suddenness of her dead weight break his hold upon her. "And roll!" Flinging herself over and over across the hard stone floor, she was ten feet away from Pembroke before he could register what had happened.

Now Quinn advanced upon him, his sword slicing through the air as Maggie scrambled out of the way. Pembroke raised his own blade in time to keep from being cut in half. The captain of the guard was a good swordsman, and as Maggie watched, huddled on the floor, she prayed silently for the man she loved.

The two men fought across the cairn and back, lunging, feinting, parrying, stabbing, retreating, dancing across the ancient spirals beneath the ancient dust. Pembroke was faster, but Quinn was stronger, making them evenly matched. Around and around the room they battled, sword against sword, until both were growing tired. Then Quinn stumbled over a part of the spiral sticking up from the floor and dropped his sword.

Pembroke saw his chance. He lunged for Quinn's chest, and Quinn reacted by throwing his right hand out in front of him. The sword pierced his hand, and Maggie screamed. Quinn fell to the floor and rolled, just as Pembroke's sword came crashing down, missing him by inches. Quinn grabbed his own sword as he rolled past it and was on his feet in seconds, the weapon in his left hand.

Maggie had to bite her lip to keep from crying out and demanding that they stop. She didn't want to distract him. Thankfully she didn't see great quantities of blood, so no major artery had been severed, but Quinn was right-handed—how in the world could he defeat Pembroke now?

Laughing, sure now of his victory, Pembroke took the offense, driving Quinn back, forcing him to keep moving around and around the circle. "What if I make you a proposition, MacIntyre?" he asked, as he slammed his blade against Quinn's, pushing him toward the wall. Maggie could tell that Quinn's left hand was getting weaker, as he struggled to hold his own.

"There is no proposition ye could make that I would yield to," Quinn said.

"But you haven't heard it yet!" Pembroke cried, circling slowly. "Here it is—you surrender, and I promise that I will only lay with your wench on Mondays and Wednesdays!"

Maggie shifted her eyes to Quinn and saw that although his face was grim, he was not out of control. Pembroke's jibe had not had its intended result—leading Quinn to attack in rage and leave himself open to mistake.

"And I have a proposition for ye," Quinn said as he matched the man's movements, his gaze wary. "Ye throw down yer sword, and I willna cut off yer balls and feed them to ye."

Pembroke's eyes narrowed.

"But of course, my friend, if you are in a hurry to die, I will happily oblige you."

The clash of the blades rang out again, and Maggie hugged the stone wall behind her, watching fearfully.

Pembroke was wearing Quinn down and the captain knew it, his vicious smile growing broader as the other man's sword grew obviously heavier in his hand.

The cairn had grown warm with the midday sun, and the two men were sweating profusely as they squared off again and again, Quinn doing his best to defend himself. Then, in a burst of energy, Pembroke drove him back with his flashing blade, trapping Quinn against the ogham stone, his sword crossed over his throat in an effort to keep Pembroke's at bay.

"You have no strength left," Pembroke sneered, his face inches from Quinn's. "Give up, MacIntyre, and I will spare your life." He glanced over his shoulder. "In return for fair Maggie."

"You bastard!" Maggie cried, looking around for a weapon. There was nothing but Pembroke's dirk, and she took a step toward it.

"Maggie!" Quinn shouted. "Stay out of this!" There was warning in his voice, and if it had been anyone but Quinn, she'd have ignored him. But she knew that sound. He had a plan.

"Well, what do you say, you Scottish bag of refuse?" Pembroke said, gleeful in his victory as he leaned harder on his sword, his blade pressing Quinn's almost into his throat.

Quinn's face was red, and he spoke with real effort. "I say"—he took a breath—"that there is something ye dinna know."

"And what is that?"

Without warning, Quinn used his sword as leverage and shoved Pembroke backward. The move gave the outlaw just enough room and enough time to toss his blade into his right hand and lunge forward, piercing the other man straight through the chest.

Pembroke sputtered and gasped, blood bubbling from his lips as he took a step backward and his sword clattered to the stone floor. In one smooth move, Quinn pulled his blade from the man's body, and the captain of the guards fell to his knees, and then flat on his face, dead.

Quinn looked down at the man and finished his explanation. "I am not left-handed."

Maggie stared at Quinn in astonishment, then she was at his side. His right hand was still bleeding, but apparently he'd been favoring the wound as a ploy to make Pembroke think it was worse than it was. Maggie was still reeling from the blatant violence, and the measure of justice that had been given.

Quinn glanced up at her and she tried to hide the horror in her eyes. His own gaze softened.

"Did ye know that he raped Jenny?" Quinn asked her.

"I didn't know for sure," she said, hate rising up suddenly inside of her.

"Jenny never told James," Quinn told her, "but he found out. That's why he was willing to help us."

Jenny. Sweet, shy little Jenny. No wonder she jumped at every shadow.

"He would have killed you and raped me," Maggie said. "I'm glad you killed him."

Quinn moved to take her in his arms, and she leaned against him.

"I thought you were dead," she whispered, finally speaking the words she'd wanted to say since he'd first appeared in the cairn. "I thought I'd never see you again."

"Och, darlin' Maggie." He led her over to the opening near the base of the cairn. "Let's go out from this place of death for a moment."

Maggie crawled out and he followed, then pulled her to her feet and held her again. The unseasonably warm

Highland evening wrapped itself around them as in the distance, the first faint curve of the moon could be seen rising above Ben Lomond.

"I am so sorry," he whispered. "I dinna have a clue that ye would come follow me."

She slid her arms around his waist and rested her head on his chest. "I read about your death, and Ian's, in a history book," she told him. "I knew that whatever plan you had cooked up, it wasn't going to work. I had to come back and save you."

Quinn gazed down into her face, smoothing her hair back gently, sweetly.

"Ah, but it worked perfectly. Ye just didn't know what the plan was to be. Ye see, I made a grand show of trying to break Ian out of the dungeon and was captured, just as I'd planned. I had a pouch of herbs a healer gave me. Once eaten, within fifteen minutes, the person appears to be dead. Ian and I both ate the herbs the morning after I was arrested, and suddenly Montrose is being accused of poisoning us."

Maggie shivered a little. "Bittie told me you were dead, and he was so distraught—"

"Aye, poor Bittie," Quinn said. "I dared not tell a soul my true plan, except for Ian."

"Ian." She pulled back from him, suddenly cold. "Did he— Is he—?"

"Ian is fine. We split up after we left our 'graves,' arranging to meet here to say our good-byes." He shook his head. "I had no idea you'd be here with the devil on your heels."

She wasn't over the terrible trauma of thinking she had lost him, but having him standing right in front of her was going a long way toward healing that wound.

"How in the world did you ever come up with this amazing plan, that, by the way, was actually very dangerous? The herbs that could put you into that condition are nothing to be messing around with!"

"Aye, so the healer tried to tell me. She was a good friend of my mother's and was firmly against it until I convinced her that there was no other way."

"What made you think of such a thing?" she asked.

He hugged her closer. "'Twas from an old story my mother used to tell me. A MacIntyre woman was held captive and her children forced to live with her far from their father. Over the next ten years, one at a time, she faked each child's death, and then sent their 'bodies' home over the mountain for burial with their clan." He grinned. "Genius, eh?"

Maggie cleared her throat. "Ahem. I'd like to point out that a woman came up with that plan."

"Och, lass," he said, "I'm learnin' that a woman's plans are always the best kind. I'm so happy to have ye in my arms once more."

"Well, there's just one thing I have to say about the whole thing," she said softly.

"Aye? And what is that?"

Maggie stepped back and slugged him in the arm. "Don't you *ever* do something like that again!"

Quinn scowled, one hand to his arm. "Damn, woman, my tattoo is not yet healed!"

"Well, it serves you right—do you know what I went through? I thought you were *dead*!" she cried, and then threw her arms around his neck and bawled.

"Quinn! Maggie!"

Maggie jerked her head around. Coming up the hillside to the cairn was someone tall and blond. "Ian!" She flew out of Quinn's arms and met the man halfway to throw her arms around his neck. He stopped, startled, and then hugged her in return. "I thought you were dead, too!" she cried. "Oh, I'm so happy!"

He smiled down at her, his arm around her shoulders. "Well, I dinna expect such an enthusiastic greeting." She rocked against him for a minute as he cocked his head at Quinn. "Would ye like to gae us a few minutes of privacy, lad? I think ye've been replaced."

Quinn folded his arms over his chest, shaking his head. "I've already defended her honor once tonight."

Ian's face darkened. "Who? What happened?"

"Pembroke," Maggie told him.

"Did he hurt ye?"

"No." She shook her head. "A big, bold highwayman cut him down before he could."

Ian's shoulders relaxed, and he glanced at Quinn. "Well done, brother. That is good news indeed, but I'm afraid I have some bad news as well."

"What?" Maggie asked, her heart sinking.

"There is a patrol just a few miles from here. Apparently, Pembroke followed Maggie here and sent his adjutant back to the manor with word of where the guards should come. He suspected all was not on the up-and-up with our deaths, it seems."

Maggie shot Quinn a sharp look. Now was the moment she'd been dreading, and been hoping for, depending on what Quinn chose to do.

Quinn frowned and pulled Maggie gently from Ian's casual embrace. "Ye must leave, Ian. If ye disappear, there is no way they can prove or disprove yer death, nor link ye to Pembroke's."

Ian blinked. "Where will ye be?"

He looked down at Maggie and smiled. "Maggie and I are running away, to a place where there is peace and a chance to start over again." He raised his eyes to his friend. "Go to Edinburgh," he said, "change yer name and sail out on the first ship ye can find. Go to France or the colonies."

Maggie saw the lost look that came across Ian's face.

"Leave?" He shook his head. "Quinn, I dinna want to leave. This is my home."

"Ye must, lad. At least for a time."

Ian nodded, downcast. "Aye, ye are right, Quinn." He reached out to clap him on one shoulder and Quinn did the same. "I will miss ye sorely, brother."

"Aye," Quinn said, "I'll miss ye as well."

"Guys, guys," Maggie said, moving between the two. "Wait just a minute." She turned toward Quinn. "Remember how you said women always have the best ideas?"

He frowned. "Aye."

She put her hands on her hips and, gazing out across the Highlands as the moon rose and the shadows stretched across the valley, she smiled.

"Well, I have a doozy."

epilogue

"Maggie, have you seen my necklace?" Allie said, as she rushed into the small room off the sanctuary of the little kirk in Drymen.

"Over there, on the desk," Maggie told her.

"Maggie, have you seen my *skean dhu*?" Ellie said, as she rushed in right behind Allie.

"It's in my backpack, out of harm's way," she told her sister.

"Maggie—"

"Maggie—"

"Girls, girls!" Rachel came frowning through the room, her hands on her hips. "Your sister is getting married today, remember? Kindly let her have ten minutes to get dressed before the ceremony starts!"

The twins grumbled, but soon scurried away, leaving Maggie in peace, with only Rachel for company.

"Thanks, Rach," Maggie said. She stood in front of a full-length mirror, turning to and fro, admiring her wedding gown. Ellie had found it at a Renaissance shop in Edinburgh and brought it home for Maggie's approval, just last week.

After Quinn popped the question again and they set the date for just a month away, October ninth, Maggie had despaired of ever finding the right dress in time. But when she saw the colonial-style wedding gown made from creamy Indian silk dupioni, with a bodice corset layered with silk, an underskirt, and romantic full sleeves with a long "frill" falling from the elbow, both made from custom-embroidered net lace, she knew it was The One.

Just like she'd known that Quinn was The One, in spite of the interesting "challenges" of their relationship.

She laid her hand over the "stomacher" of bridal satin, trimmed with white braid and accented with handmade silk roses, all in a creamy white and laced up the back, and sighed in contentment. The dress fit her perfectly, and she felt like a princess. She smiled at her reflection. Her long, auburn hair hung to her waist in curling waves, and her tiara was a garland of white forget-me-nots, with a veil of embroidered lace falling from the flowers to the floor.

The bridesmaid outfits were traditional Scottish dresses, and Maggie had picked them out herself, giving Allie the deep blue skirt, with a lavender, blue, and cream plaid bodice; Ellie the purple skirt, with purple, blue, and cream plaid bodice; and finally, Rachel in the forest green skirt, with green, blue, and cream plaid bodice.

Each of the girls would be wearing blouses made from the same net lace in the same blouse style as Maggie's, and each wore a blue forget-me-not garland in her hair.

She was in heaven. Not only was she marrying the man of her dreams, but she now had the job of her dreams. Alex MacGregor, inspired by his success in discovering the triskele in the "Drymen Cairn" as it was now called, had turned over a new leaf and abandoned his "archaeological digs for beginners" con and instead had actually applied for and received a grant to further explore and excavate the cairn.

And he had asked Maggie to be his *paid* assistant. Quinn had surprised her by asking Alex to be one of his groomsmen, and he'd offered to bring along his friend Davey, so that all three of the bridesmaids would have escorts.

"Maggie! Do you have your something old?" Rachel demanded, orchestrating the wedding like a drill sergeant.

"My mother's pearls," she said, turning and showing her the necklace.

"Check. Something new?"

"The tri-spiral ring you had made for me—which, by the way, I love!"

"Check! You're welcome. Something borrowed?"

"Er, Ellie's black garter?"

"Don't understand that one, but check! And finally, something blue?"

Maggie turned and lifted a nosegay of blue forget-me-nots from a plastic box. Creamy white ribbons fell from the base, along with more custom-embroidered lace.

"A present from the groom," Maggie said proudly.

"And check!"

Rachel sighed in satisfaction and stood beside her best friend, her arm around Maggie's shoulders as they gazed into the mirror together. "Okay. I just want to say one thing."

Maggie bit her lower lip. From the serious look on Rachel's face it must be important. "Oh-kay," she said.

"I call dibs on Ian."

Maggie laughed and hugged her friend. Her idea to bring Ian home with them from the past would remain her and Quinn's secret. He was still adjusting to the strange, new world in which he found himself, but as he said, it was better than rotting in the duke's dungeon.

"Sorry, kiddo," Maggie said, "but Ellie has already called him, and Allie is livid. Oh, and Ellie's furious that he's escorting you down the aisle today instead of her!"

Rachel grinned. "Hey, is it my fault that I'm the maid of honor, and he's the best man?"

"This is a dream," Maggie said softly. "I'm afraid that I'm just going to wake up and none of it will be real."

Rachel turned her friend to face her and put her hands on her shoulders. "Of all the people I've ever known, Maggie, you deserve this the most. You are the kindest, most generous person in the world, and I am so honored to have you as my friend."

Tears slipped down Maggie's cheek and she laughed. "Now, see what you've done!" she cried, but then, unmindful of her makeup or gown, she clasped her friend tightly. "Thanks, Rach. I love you."

Rachel was leaving the next morning to go back to the States and Maggie was going to miss her terribly. The twins had decided to stick around awhile and get an apartment together in Edinburgh. Maggie suspected that the arrival of Ian had something to do with that, and perhaps Alex as well.

"Maggie!" Allie and Ellie rushed into the room, their dresses flying, their faces glowing.

"It's time!" Allie said.

"Come on," Ellie cried. "You don't want to be late to your own wedding!"

"Uh, before we go into the sanctuary . . ." Maggie turned to the three women and gave them her very best "stern teacher's look." "Do you three remember your promises?"

They all rolled their eyes and spoke in unison. "Ye-es," they said.

"No jokes on my wedding day. Right?"

"Would we do that to you, Maggie?" Allie asked, all innocence.

"Right?" Maggie said again, more emphatically.

"Right," Rachel said.

"Fine," Allie agreed, "but we will definitely owe you one."

"Hey," Maggie said, gazing around at the three, "I love you all very much. Thank you for making this such a special day with no jokes. Really, it means a lot."

The three exchanged glances.

"I told you," Ellie said.

"It's not really a joke," Allie began.

"It's really more for her own good, if you think about it," Rachel explained.

Maggie folded her arms over her dupioni silk and glared. "Okay, nobody leaves this room until you confess."

"Well," Rachel went on, "we don't quite trust you, so—ready girls?"

Allie grabbed one arm. Ellie grabbed the other. Rachel slapped something around Maggie's wrist and she stared down, horrified, at the ugly black bracelet.

"What in the world is this?"

"GPS unit," Allie said. "Big sis, we are never going to lose you again."

"Here," Ellie said, opening a plastic florist's box and taking out a wrist corsage made of forget-me-nots. She put it on top of the ugly wristband and almost completely hid it. "See, we think of everything."

"You guys are insane," Maggie said, glaring down at her wrist. She sighed and looked up. "But I couldn't live without you."

The door opened and Alex stuck his head inside. "Hey, are ye getting married today, lass, or what? Quinn thinks ye ran out the back door. Come on!"

Hastily the girls lined up, Allie, Ellie, Rachel, Maggie.

"Tell them we're ready, Alex," Maggie said.

He nodded and disappeared, and a few minutes later,

the sound of bagpipes echoed through the hallways of the tiny kirk. The tune was one of Quinn's. He'd written it for her. Maggie's throat tightened as the three women headed out of the room. They paused, lining up at the curved doorway leading to the kirk, and she began to tremble.

Marriage was a big deal to Maggie. Her parents had been very happy together and she wanted to be happy, too. Not only was Quinn from another country, he was from another *time*. Not to mention the fact that he was much, much older than she. She smiled feebly at the thought.

What if he didn't like the twenty-first century? Of course, he'd seemed thrilled to be there and had enrolled in music theory classes at the local university and had joined a pipe band.

But what if he changed his mind?

She looked up and saw that it was her turn to walk down the aisle. With her heart in her throat, she took the first step forward, hoping the beautiful pipe music would take away any fears, any qualms. She tried to smile as she approached her fiancé.

Quinn stood straight and tall, as she walked down the aisle toward him. Well, he *looked* like he was happy. So far, so good.

He wore the pattern of the ancient hunting tartan of Clan MacIntyre across his chest and in his kilt. The cornflower blue and Kelly green background with the thin bands of red and white looked classy, but Maggie couldn't help but miss his green and cream plaid.

He did look gorgeous, his dark hair curling over the collar of the romantic, full-sleeved, open-necked cream shirt Maggie found for him at a faire. He hadn't liked the sissy socks and shoes that she'd talked him into wearing, but when he learned his groomsmen were wearing them, too, he had politely given in.

Maggie's mouth was going dry as she walked toward

this man, this stranger, to whom she was about to pledge her entire life. Marriage could be a trap or a beautiful union, and she wanted more than anything to have that union.

She finally reached the altar and Quinn took her hand. She was trembling and afraid to look at him. Then he bent down, just slightly.

"Ah, Maggie mine," Quinn whispered, "ye are beautiful."

And just like that, Maggie wasn't afraid at all. This was her love, her friend, her partner in laughter and in sorrow, and as she looked into his eyes, she realized that no other couple in the entire world had ever had, or ever would have, the experience what they had lived through together. No other man and woman would ever battle time and space and evil and death to find each other once again. No other husband and wife would ever reach across three centuries to join their lives together in love and joy and happiness.

So, of course . . . they had it made.

And as Quinn and Maggie stood before their friends and their families and kissed, and the pastor of the small church pronounced them husband and wife . . .

On the other side of Drymen, in the heart of an ancient cairn, three spiral carvings, forged together by Time itself, began to glow.